One Last First Date

A romantic comedy of love, friendship and cake

Cozy Cottage Café Series

- Book 1 -

Kate O'Keeffe

Wild Lime
Books

ISBN-13: 978-1536896121
ISBN-10: 1536896128

Published by Wild Lime Books

CHAPTER 1

"SO, WE ALL AGREE? We're really doing this?" Marissa's upturned face was illuminated by the crackling fire as the waves continued their dark, rhythmic pounding against the shore.

We stood in a tight little group, empty wine glasses discarded carelessly on a picnic blanket next to the glowing fire. I looked from one of my friends to the other. They were both smiling, their faces full of hope and excitement, their right hands placed on top of one another's, awaiting mine.

I bit my lip as goosebumps rose on my bare legs in the late summer evening breeze. "After more than ten years of dating, we need to take things into our own hands." I placed my hand on top of theirs. A surge of anticipation hit me, and my face broke into a grin. "Let's do this."

"Yes!" Paige cried, almost piercing my eardrum.

"Good," Marissa added more calmly, nodding. "Let's begin, then." She cleared her throat. "We, the three present on this beach tonight, agree that—"

She was cut short by Paige. "Umm, Marissa?"

"What is it?" Marissa asked.

"It's just . . . shouldn't you name us?"

"Why?"

"To make it, you know, more official," Paige replied.

We were still standing in the circle, our hands piled up on top of one another. My arm began to hurt.

Marissa rolled her eyes. "Okay, Paige. I'll start again." There was a sizeable note of irritation in her voice. Marissa cleared her throat once more, closing her eyes momentarily to collect her thoughts—and, perhaps, to try to remember our middle names.

"We, Marissa Jane Jones, Cassandra . . ."

"Clementine," I whispered after a beat.

She shot me a surprised look. "Really? Pretty."

I rolled my eyes. "Long story."

She nodded. "Cassandra Clementine Dunhill, and Paige Prudence Miller, agree that—"

"Why does my name have to be last?" Paige interrupted again, sounding indignant, as she dropped her hand from ours.

I let out a frustrated breath. "Does it matter whose name comes first, Paige? It's getting cold here."

"Of course it matters, Cassie," she insisted. "It won't be real otherwise. Plus, Marissa always puts herself first. We need to be more . . . egalitarian."

"Egalitarian?" Marissa questioned. "This isn't some sort of committee, Paige. We're just three friends on the beach, who have, quite possibly, had a little too much to drink and have decided to make a pact."

There was a low rumble of thunder in the distance, diverting our attention. All three of us broke into nervous laughter as the wind picked up, whipping our hair around our faces. I glanced around the deserted beach. All we needed now was a cauldron on the fire and we'd look like a coven of witches, brewing up a spell.

Paige shrugged, looking wounded.

"I guess this was Paige's idea," I offered, ever the peacemaker.

Marissa's hands shot up into the air in surrender. "Okay. Do you want to do it?"

Paige's face beamed. "Yes, I do." She smoothed her full skirt down and stuck her hand out in front of her.

Marissa and I added ours once more.

Paige looked from Marissa to me and back again. She tossed her dark hair in a dramatic fashion, and then began. "We, the three maidens of the beach—"

Marissa sniggered. Paige glared at her. Unperturbed, she continued, "The three maidens of the beach, Paige Prudence Miller, Cassie Clementine Dunhill, and Marissa Jane Jones—"

Marissa scoffed.

"—agree that the next date each of us goes on will be with the man we marry."

A Girl Scout knot looped in my belly.

"We agree to this pact in the presence of the Goddess of the Beach," Paige continued.

My eyes darted around, half expecting to see a goddess floating nearby. Hmm, definitely too much chardonnay for me tonight.

Marissa scoffed again. "I don't remember agreeing to any goddess crap," she protested.

"Just go with it, will you?" Paige replied, arching her eyebrows. "I know what I'm doing; this isn't my first beach pact."

I looked at Paige in surprise. "It's not?"

Paige shook her head. "No."

I let out a breath. Goddess or no goddess, I didn't care; it was the pact that mattered to me—and meeting the man of my dreams. "I agree to the pact."

"I agree to the pact, too," Marissa said at length.

Paige held her chin high, a strange look on her face—perhaps triumph? Or solemnity? Or a combination of both. "Then, it is set."

There was a sudden flash of lightning followed immediately by a loud crash of thunder. Marissa and I leaped a good four feet back from one another. Marissa fell on her butt, narrowly avoiding the fire. I stumbled but managed to right myself.

"What the heck was *that*?" Marissa exclaimed, pushing herself off the ground and brushing the sand off her jeans.

"Whatever it was, it scared the living daylights out of me." I let out a short, sharp laugh, my heart pounding in my chest.

Paige remained standing stock still, a look of pure exhilaration on her pretty face as the wind whipped her hair and made her skirt billow around her. She looked like something out of *Game of Thrones*. "That, my friends, was the sealing of the pact. There's no going back now."

The sealing of the pact? I looked at her, wide-eyed, half expecting her to regale us with some lame ghost story, a flashlight illuminating her face in a prepubescent attempt to freak us out.

"Actually, I think it was that storm we're expecting," Marissa replied in her pragmatic way. She leaned down and scooped the picnic blanket and the empty bottle and glasses up. "We might need to take cover, girls."

I looked up and scanned the dark night sky, shivering as the evening turned cold. A large blob of rain landed on my face. I blinked. Within a heartbeat, the heavens opened and the rain came pouring down on us. I pulled my hoodie up and made a dash for shelter, followed closely by a loudly protesting Marissa.

"No way am I getting wet," she exclaimed, pulling her own hood up as protection from the elements.

"Wait! We haven't finished!" Paige called out to us both, her voice thin through the growing storm. "Come on, you two. We have to do this right."

I paused to squint back at her. She hadn't moved from her spot by the dying fire. I glanced up at the house, the windows glowing with light. I let out a sigh. Warmth and dry clothes were so, so close. "Marissa! Let's finish this off, then get back to the house, okay?" I called out.

"Have you seen what happens to my hair in the rain?" she called back.

"I'll sort it out for you, I promise." I clambered up the beach and grabbed her arm, pulling her back with me. She muttered something about hair straighteners and ice cream under her breath.

Once back by the smoking fire, Paige extended her now wet arm toward us once more.

"Make it quick," Marissa warned.

We resumed our positions.

Another flash of lightning illuminated the beach as the waves crashed with force against the shore. When the thunder hit, my heart leaped into my mouth. This was like something out of a movie!

Paige continued in her *Hammer House of Horrors* voice, louder this time to be heard over the lashing wind and rain. "From this day forth, we, the maidens of the beach, have just One Last First Date." She paused between each word, piercing us with her intense gaze.

"One last first date?" I questioned, panic inching its way up from my toes. In my bid to find Mr. Right, I'd been on so many dates I'd totally lost count. Having only one more really put the pressure on. It was going to have to be with the perfect guy. I swallowed.

"That's right," Paige replied, looking at me intently. "One Last

First Date. We've got one shot at this, ladies."

"Agreed," Marissa said quickly, possibly more to get out of the rain and save her hair from the dreaded frizz than for any real desire to agree to Paige's terms.

I chewed the inside of my mouth and glanced at both of my friends. One last first date meant whoever I next dated would end up being my husband. Either that or I'd become celibate, adopt seventeen cats, take to wearing ill-fitting mismatched clothes, and possibly smell a little funky to boot.

I chose dating.

"Cassie, come on!" Marissa urged, the rain still blobbing heavily down on us.

"Agreed," I added as a surge of nerves, excitement—and hope—rose in my chest.

One Last First Date it was.

CHAPTER 2

- 3 Months Later -

"CASSIE!"

I looked up at my boss, mortified I'd been caught so obviously daydreaming, not only in front of him but the entire sales team. A bit of quick thinking was required. Stat!

"Sorry, Richard, my mind was on"—I glanced down at the file on the table in front of me—"the Nettco account." I gave him my best professional-serious-sales-representative look, hoping he'd buy it.

Richard peered at me across the table through narrowed eyes. "Is there an issue with the customer, Cassie?"

"Ah, yes. And no," I bumbled. *What?!* "What I mean is in some ways yes, and in other ways . . . no." I smiled at him. Perhaps my smile was so dazzling he would ignore my frankly ridiculous answer? My right eye began to twitch.

Will Jordan, the company's most successful sales rep, and possibly the most annoying man on the face of the earth, sniggered under his breath beside me. I shot him a don't-mess-with-me stare, something I was forced to do with annoying regularity around him.

Richard slid his fingers down his notes until he found what he was looking for. "Ah, here we go. Nettco Electricity. Expected revenue of three hundred thousand per annum. You've said here the likelihood of success is ninety-nine percent." He looked up again. "That's confident in anyone's books. If there's a problem, we need to know about it, Cassie."

I swallowed as my cheeks heated up. "It's nothing I can't handle, Richard."

Can't we just move on?

"Good, good. This is shaping up to be a tough quarter, and when you estimate success at almost one hundred percent, you set a certain expectation. Will?"

"Yes, Richard?" Will asked, smiling like the smarmy suck-up he was.

"Can you go through the deal with Cassie, see if you can add any value?"

Will's grin was broad. "Absolutely, Richard. You can count on me."

I closed my eyes. That was all I needed. Will Suck-Up Jordan helping me fix a fake problem with one of my accounts.

Turning to me, he added, "It will be my pleasure to help you with this problem, Cassie."

My eyes almost popped out of their sockets, I rolled them so much. I pursed my lips as I looked at Will's smug face. "Thank you so much," I managed through gritted teeth. *Wonderful.* I had to spend more time with Will Jordan. And all because I had been caught daydreaming about what will most likely be the biggest date of my entire life tonight.

Talk about the punishment not fitting the crime.

Truth be told, I was a bit of a star at work. I'd been at AGD for four years and had worked my way up through the ranks to the heady heights of Senior Account Director through hard slog. Although I didn't quite have Will's sterling success rate, I didn't trail too far behind. Richard telling Will to help me on an account in front of everyone felt like a slap in the face with a wet fish—not that I knew what that felt like, but I bet it would be pretty unpleasant. And smelly. Definitely smelly.

"That's settled then," Richard said, collecting his files. "Thanks, everyone. Now get out there and bring in those sales! The clock is ticking on the financial year."

As the team filed out of the stuffy meeting room back to their respective desks, I felt a hand on my arm.

"I bet I know what you were really thinking about," Marissa said under her breath, grinning at me. "And it had absolutely nothing to do with Nettco Electricity."

A smile spread across my face as a group of construction workers fired up in my belly. "I can hardly believe I'm going out with him tonight."

Marissa smiled back at me. "Cassie, I'm so happy for you. I have a really good feeling about this guy."

"Me, too. I think he's the one."

She raised her eyebrows. "Well, after all the research and vetting you've done, he'd better be."

I had met Parker Hamilton, my One Last First Date, almost five weeks ago. He was a good friend of Ryan, Marissa's older brother, and he had to be as close to flawless as any guy could be. With his sandy blond hair, sea-green eyes, and square jaw, he was good-looking enough to make many a woman swoon. Plus, he was smart, he was sweet, and he was a doctor. You heard me: a *doctor*. All in all, he was easily Mr. Great-On-Paper—and I had high hopes he'd be Mr. Great-Everywhere-Else, too.

I mean, I was taking this whole One Last First Date thing very seriously. He *had* to be the right man for me. No question.

Since we'd met at Marissa's apartment, I had found out absolutely everything I could about him. Ryan must have thought I was some kind of super-stalker, I asked him so many questions: from Parker's shoe size to his family and everything that fell between. Which was a lot of stuff.

I got a little borderline obsessive over it all, I have to admit. Perhaps to the point of mental imbalance? Who can say? What I *can* say is Parker Hamilton passed with flying colors. And he needed to; tonight was The Big One. There were no second chances.

Parker and I had been texting, emailing, Facebooking, Tweeting . . . you get the general picture. But no actual date. Yet. He'd been asking me out since the day we met, and I had come up with excuse after excuse as to why I couldn't go. My best work to date had been that my dog had had puppies, my dog's puppies were sick, my dog's puppies were better but now needed 'round the clock walking to help them regain their strength.

The fact I didn't have a dog, let alone one with health-challenged offspring, was totally beside the point.

And, for me, this was so much more than the pact we had made on the beach back in summer. Since I was eleven years old, I'd had The Plan: get my career where I wanted it, married by twenty-eight, followed by baby number one (a boy called Christopher) by age thirty, baby number two (a girl called Charlotte, Lottie for short) by age thirty-two. That way, I'd be fifty when the youngest left school and would have my beautiful grandchildren (names to be determined) by my mid-sixties when I was still able to enjoy them and not laid up in some old people's home on a respirator or something.

Problem being, at twenty-seven, I was at risk of falling behind schedule. And for an organized girl with a plan like me, that could spell potential disaster.

There was a *lot* riding on tonight.

We walked through the meeting room door, out into the corridor.

"One Last First Date," Marissa said, as though echoing my thoughts.

I sucked in a breath of air. "I know. This is it, right?"

She grinned. "Sure is. You're the first of us three to *actually* do this. Nervous?"

I shrugged. "A little." *A lot!*

"You'll be fine. He's been more closely vetted by you than even the CIA could manage. If he had any skeletons in his closet, you'd have them jangling on a string by now."

Paige slunk up to us. "Are you talking about what I think you're talking about?" Her voice was quiet, conspiratorial, as she leaned in.

"Sure are," Marissa confirmed. "Cassie got busted in our meeting for daydreaming about him."

"I don't blame you." Paige crossed her arms, shaking her head. "Tonight is a really big deal. Huge. Bigger than huge."

Those construction workers got out the jackhammers. "Not helping the nerves, Paige."

She waved her hand at me. "Oh, you'll be fine. This is meant to be. I just know it. What are you wearing?"

"Well, it's dinner, so I thought that blue cocktail dress I wore to Marissa's birthday bash last month. You know, the one with the full skirt?"

Paige clapped her hands together with glee. "Oh, gorgeous!"

"Great choice," Marissa confirmed, always more sedate. "It sets the right tone: 'this is a date, I'm serious about you.' You need to look sexy but not cheap, classy but not boring. Striking the right balance is imperative."

I bit my lip. Can one dress do all *that*?

Oblivious to my nerves, Marissa continued, "It's important you give him the right signals from the get-go. No friend zoning, no easy lay. Serious, long-term relationship for the rest of your lives."

Just as I'm about to defend myself as never having been "easy" in my life, thank you very much, smart-aleck Will Jordan poked his uninvited nose into our little group.

"Is this a political meeting?" he questioned, taking in our trio, talking quietly amongst ourselves. "Are you going to become revolutionaries and overthrow the current regime?"

"Oh, ha ha!" I replied, my voice dripping with sarcasm. "We're just . . . talking."

"That's a shame. I quite like the idea of being a revolutionary," he sniffed, running his fingers through his wavy dark hair.

I scoffed. "I bet you fancy yourself as a Che Guevara type or something."

Will looked off into the distance, a whimsical look on his face. "Yeah. I like that idea."

I shook my head, rolling my eyes at my friends. Marissa smirked back at me as Paige blushed every shade of red known to humanity, which was what she did every time Will was around. Although, why she liked him was totally beyond me. Sure, he was good-looking in that obvious handsome kind of way, and half of the women at AGD thought he was the cat's pajamas. But he was too confident, too much of a ladies' man for my liking.

"So, if you're not plotting to overturn AGD's management, are you talking about this hot date Cassie's going on tonight?" Will asked as though he was one of the girls.

I glared first at Marissa, and then at Paige. They were the only two who knew about my date tonight with Parker, so it had to be one of them who'd blabbed to Will. I noticed Paige began to fidget, avoiding eye contact with me. I raised my eyebrows at her in accusation.

Denial was the best approach. "No, Will. As a matter of fact, we were talking about work, if you have to know." I turned to my friends. "Thank you for your input, Marissa. Paige, I'll see you later." *When I roast you,* I wanted to add.

Paige smiled weakly at me as my friends peeled off, leaving me alone in the corridor with Will.

"Now, if you'll excuse me, I have a job to get on with," I said brusquely.

"Well, that makes a change today. Not sure you were quite 'in the room,' as they say, just now." He had a cheeky grin on his face.

I wanted to slap it right off. "Very funny."

"I thought we could talk about that account you're having trouble with. Nettco Electricity, right?"

Dammit! "Ah, yes. But it's fine, really. Thanks anyway." I began to walk away.

"I've got a couple of minutes." He walked over toward the empty conference room door and swung it open. "Take a seat. I'll grab my laptop, and then I'm all yours."

Great. That's all I needed, the company's best sales rep helping me solve a fake problem on my account. *How do you get yourself into these scrapes, Cassie Dunhill?*

I made myself comfortable in the conference room, doing some quick thinking. There may not have actually been a problem with Nettco, but it was true I hadn't signed the deal with them yet. They kept asking for revision upon revision for the telecommunications solutions I'd presented to them, which kept delaying things. Although I would be the last person at the company to admit it, maybe I could do with some help.

He returned with his laptop and sat down next to me, a little closer than I preferred. I pushed my seat away a couple of inches. Not quite far enough, but it would do.

He raised his eyebrows at me, a look of amusement on his face. "Comfortable?"

"Yes, thank you." I didn't smile. I knew I was about to get a lecture from Mr. Top Salesman, and I wasn't looking forward to it.

"So, tell me all about the issue." He leaned back in his chair, watching me with interest.

I took him through what I had done to date, trying to ensure I sounded professional and in control of the situation. Which, of course, I was.

"Have you considered 'The Sheldon'?" he asked once I'd finished.

I laughed. "No. What's a Sheldon?"

"Not *a* Sheldon, '*The* Sheldon.' It's a solution I came up with for one of my customers with similar needs to Nettco. It combined the connectivity they needed with the data, voice, and web presence they wanted. Here." He opened his laptop and typed something in. Turning it around, he showed me a screen with all the key components of "The Sheldon." He talked me through each element, the pricing, and how it all fitted together.

I didn't like to admit it, but it looked good.

"Why did you call it that? I mean, it's not exactly a technology name, is it?"

He shrugged. "I'm kind of a *Big Bang* fan. I've got 'The Leonard' and 'The Raj,' too, plus, I'm working on 'The Howard' with one of my customers right now."

"Nerd." I loved *The Big Bang Theory*, but I wasn't going to tell Will Jordan that.

He laughed. "Sure, if you say so. Name-calling aside, do you think it could work for your customer?"

I looked through the solution elements and realized it could. In fact, "The Sheldon" may have just been the perfect fit for Nettco.

"I can't make any promises, but I'll present it to them at our next meeting."

"Great!" His grin stretched from ear to ear.

Although it physically hurt me, I muttered, "Thanks."

"Don't mention it. Glad I could help, Dunny."

I narrowed my eyes at him. I hated that nickname with a passion. Dunny, short for Dunhill, my last name. It could be considered cute if it wasn't for the fact "dunny" is Australian slang for toilet, a fact I was absolutely certain Will Jordan was aware of.

"Tell me something. Why do guys feel the need to hand out nicknames to everyone? Girls don't do it. I'm going to lunch today with Marissa and Paige. And guess what? I call them Marissa and Paige. It's really quite straight forward."

He chuckled. "Yeah, and pretty boring."

"It's not boring. It's the way it should be. Men go out together and call each other Bucko and Mac and . . . Spotty Dick."

"Spotty Dick?" He chuckled. "Isn't that an English dessert? Definitely something no guy would want, that's for sure."

I brushed his comment away with my hand. "You know what I mean. Silly, stupid names."

"They're not stupid." He shrugged. "It's a guy thing, I guess."

"I'm not a guy, in case you haven't noticed. Believe me, I'd much rather be called Cassie or even Cassandra rather than 'Dunny.'"

He raised his eyebrows at me. "Cassandra, huh? I bet you're only called that when you're really naughty."

He was so immature. "Just call me Cassie."

"Sure, Dunny. I mean, *Cassie*." He grinned. Not satisfied with insulting me by naming me after a toilet, he added, "I bet this new guy you're going on a date with has a nickname."

I crossed my arms. "I bet he doesn't."

"Care to make it interesting?"

"All right. Five bucks says I'm right."

"Ten."

I glared at him. "Twenty."

He extended his hand, and we shook on it. "How will I know if you're telling me the truth? I mean, he could have a nickname and you could pretend he doesn't.'"

I smirked. "You'll just have to trust me."

He looked at me for a long moment. "Actually, I know exactly when you're lying."

"No, you don't."

"Oh, yeah. It's your eye. It twitches. Around about here." He pointed to a spot under my right eye. "It's cute."

My hand went straight to my face. I pulled it away quickly, embarrassed. "No, it doesn't." Even my tone was lame, unconvincing.

His phone rang. He glanced at the screen. "Excuse me, *Cassie*. I have to take this."

"Sure." I stood up, ready to leave.

"Hey, babe. Where are you? Oh, you're in Milan?" He put his hand over the receiver. "It's my girlfriend, Samantha. She's a model. I thought she was in Tokyo."

I nodded at him. How very not interesting.

"No, this is a great time. How are you, babe?"

I pushed my way through the conference door and closed it firmly behind me. The last thing I wanted to hear was Will Jordan getting all smoochie on the phone with his international supermodel girlfriend.

I had a job to do. And a One Last First Date to prepare for.

CHAPTER 3

THIS WAS IT. After all my research, my vetting, my planning—
frankly, my obsessing—I was finally going on a date with Parker
Hamilton. And not just any old date, this was my One Last First
Date.

Forever.

We agreed to meet at a bar overlooking Auckland's spectacular
harbor for a pre-dinner drink. And I needed it. I was more nervous
than a turkey at Christmas as I perched uncomfortably on a
barstool in the friend-approved blue dress and heels, my long
auburn hair in a loose ponytail.

I ordered my favorite alcoholic beverage—a gin and tonic—and
surveyed the bar. Being a Friday evening, the place was almost
full, most of the patrons still dressed in their corporate day job
clothes. A guy about my age, standing with a group of other men
close by, caught my eye and smiled at me. I shot him a quick smile
I hoped said thank-you-but-no-thank-you and averted my eyes.

My drink delivered, I paid the barmaid and took a sip. I glanced
over at the table in the far corner. Marissa and Paige were doing a
very poor job of appearing as though they weren't watching my
every move.

Although I was initially as happy about them being here as a cat
in a bath, I eventually conceded, on the basis they would stay
completely out of the way. Being the first of our little trio to go on
their One Last First Date, we all knew tonight was nothing short of
crucial.

My friends smiled and waved at me, their faces beaming with encouragement. I gave them a couple of nerve-racked nods before turning my attention to my posture. Back straight, chest out, butt out, tummy in, legs crossed.

There was a lot to remember.

I glanced at my reflection in the mirror behind the bar. I looked about as natural as a mannequin in a shop window—and felt about as comfortable, too.

"Hi, Cassie?"

I looked across the mirror. My heart skipped a beat when I saw Parker standing next to me. Tall and sexy, he was looking oh-so handsome in a crisply ironed sky-blue shirt, a pair of khaki pants, and an uncertain smile.

Both dressed in blue, we looked like we belonged together.

Butterflies batting their wings in my belly, I turned to him and half stood from my barstool, wedged up against the bar. We hugged awkwardly, and I breathed in his freshly showered scent. He took the seat I had saved with my purse next to me.

"You look beautiful," he commented, the corners of his eyes crinkling as he smiled.

I returned the smile, warmed inside, those butterflies doing a Highland fling. *He's it. He's my future husband.* "You do, too."

He raised his eyebrows, smiling.

I let out a nervous laugh. "I mean, you look handsome."

"Thanks." His sea-green eyes twinkled. "I see you've got a drink." He gestured to my glass. "Is that a gin and tonic?"

I nodded.

"Great choice." He got the barmaid's attention and ordered one for himself.

I beamed. Already so much in common. In a flash, I could see us sitting down together in our gracious living room after a long day at work, with the French doors open to the lawn, the curtains moving gently in the light breeze. We could be enjoying a gin and tonic, talking about our days while our children played, darting in and out to show us their drawings and tell us how much they loved us.

But, perhaps, I was getting a little ahead of myself.

As Parker sat down next to me, I was suddenly at a loss for words. I was finally on this much-anticipated date, and I knew so much about him from my research. I couldn't think of a single thing to talk about.

Thankfully, he said, "It's great we're finally doing this."

"Yes, isn't it?" I took a sip of my drink.

Gawd! What do I say now?

My mind shot to my list. Marissa, Paige, and I had put together a bunch of topics for us to discuss if this situation should arise. At the risk of looking like I had some amateur tattoos, I had written down some bullet points on my wrist before I left my house tonight.

I surreptitiously rolled my hand over and glanced down. My eyes landed on the last bullet point. *Doctor.*

"So, Parker. You're a doctor. Tell me what that's like."

He chuckled. "You want to know about being a doctor?"

"Absolutely. I'm fascinated by it. Tell me everything." I smiled at him, prepared to be riveted to his every word. My future husband: the brilliant doctor.

He furrowed his brow. "Okay. Being a GP is . . . great. Sure, the hours are long, and the work can be challenging, but I love it. As cheesy as it may sound, I believe it's my calling, I guess. I had this one patient today who . . ."

As he talked, I watched his face light up. He was sitting upright on his barstool, gesturing as he spoke. My heart swelled. He was a good man. He cared about others. He'd care about me, about our children. Not just emotionally, medically too. Fixing all those boo-boos, knowing what to do in a medical crisis, talking with the doctors in the hospital when our son, Christopher, broke his arm falling out of that large oak on our back lawn . . .

"What are you grinning at?" he asked, punctuating my daydream.

"Oh, just listening to you talk," I managed, pushing Christopher's damaged limb from my mind. "You really love what you do, don't you, Parker?"

"Yup. Why would you spend your time doing a job you hate? Life's too short for that."

"You're so right. My job is great, too. Not that selling communications solutions is anywhere near as important as being a doctor."

He shrugged. "Everything is important in different ways."

"That's true." I gazed at him. He was a philosopher, too?

I raised my glass, and Parker followed suit. "To doing what you love in life." We clinked. I took a sip, although I was down to the dregs. Parker noticed and offered me another drink.

"Shouldn't we get to the restaurant?"

He glanced at his watch. "I didn't realize what time it was. You're right. We should get going." He stood up from his barstool, paused, and turned to me. "You're so easy to talk to, Cassie."

Bees buzzed around my tummy, making it tingle. "You, too," I added breathlessly.

Suppressing a grin—*this was going so well!*—I leaned down to collect my purse from the hook under the bar. As I stood and turned to leave, the skirt of my dress must have caught on the barstool because, the next thing I knew, I was dragging the stool across the floor as I tried to walk.

Argh!

I stopped, glanced at Parker beside me, hoping he hadn't noticed. But of course he had. Who would fail to notice a piece of furniture stuck to someone's clothes?

"Are you all right, Cassie?"

I channeled my inner Control Queen. "Yes. Thank you." I shot him the breeziest smile I could muster and turned my attention to my dress's recent attachment.

I tugged at it; it stayed put. I tugged again, nothing. It was firmly wedged in the stool's wooden join. Tension crept across my forehead. How did this even *happen*? A barstool attached to my dress simply wasn't part of the look for my One Last First Date.

I had images of myself dragging this stool around with me for the rest of the date, even bundling it into my car at the end to head home.

I leaned down and peered at my dress. In the low-lit bar, it was hard to see exactly how the dress was attached. I grabbed hold of the fabric and twisted it, hoping to loosen it off.

"Do you need a hand?" Parker asked.

I looked up and shot him a terse smile. "No, I've got this. Thank you, though."

He shrugged, watching me tug. "It looks pretty stuck."

I tugged and tugged. It still wasn't budging. I took a deep breath, trying to quell the now frantically buzzing bees in my belly.

I needed to give this all I'd got before the evening was ruined. I grabbed a firm hold on the fabric and pulled with all my might. In an instant, it snapped free, my hand—still holding my dress—hurtling upwards.

I blinked, unable to prevent contact, as my fist smacked straight into my face, causing my head to snap back. "Ow!" I screamed, clutching my nose, still holding the skirt of my dress. My eyes began to water with the throbbing pain.

"Cassie! Are you okay?" Parker asked, his voice filled with concern.

"Yes, I'm fine," I lied.

Why oh why oh why did this have to happen on my One Last First Date?

My dress still in my hand, I glanced down. No underwear flash from the front. Good. Slowly, expecting the humiliating inevitable, I turned my head to look behind me. Oh, god. I scrunched my eyes shut and dropped my skirt immediately.

In my wisdom, I had made the decision to wear something I was wearing the day I met Parker. After all, who was I to mess with Lady Luck? I needed all the help I could get to make this the best One Last First Date known to humanity. No pressure there.

I was not a frilly, complicated underwear kind of girl. I liked practical, plain white cotton. Occasionally, I'd go crazy and buy a different color—I had pink, salmon, and even lavender in my not-so extensive collection—but really, I was a plain 'n practical panties kinda gal.

But this pair? They were a joke present from Paige for my last birthday. Plain white, yes. So far so good. However, emblazoned across the back were the words *Bite Me!* in bold red letters with a blue outline. Seriously? I mean, *come on!*

I consoled myself with the fact Parker was standing in front of me. There was no way he could have seen what was written across my butt. And then I remembered the mirror behind the bar. Oh, god.

"Cassie! Lean back, hold your nose here. We need to stem the blood flow."

Blood flow?

Underwear logos were forgotten immediately. In a daze, I did as Parker instructed, sitting back down heavily on the offending barstool.

I heard Parker ask the waitress for some ice in an efficient, doctorly tone. As I sat, head back, I wished I had a remote control so I could rewind the events of the last few seconds—was that all it'd been?—and get a do-over. Jeez, how I would love a do-over.

We hadn't even got to dinner yet! This was so *not* the impression I wanted to make on my future husband.

Parker, proving to be every inch the caring doctor of my fantasies, gently placed a bag of ice wrapped in a towel on my nose. I winced, and he handed me a wad of tissues, which I immediately placed above my lips.

"The ice will help stem the flow as well as lessen any swelling."

Swelling? Great.

"Thanks," I muttered from my awkward position, only able to catch a glimpse of Parker out of the corner of my eye. "I'm so sorry about this."

"Don't be. It could have happened to anybody." He smiled at me. "Well, maybe not anybody."

I let out a weak laugh. It hurt.

"Try and stay still if you can, Cassie. I'll need to check to see if it's broken."

Oh, this was getting better and better.

Parker pulled the ice pack away from my nose. "Hold still, this may hurt." He gently tweaked it, moving it from side to side. I must have looked beyond ridiculous. In all my fantasies of how tonight would go, not a single one involved my future husband gently tweaking my bloodied and painful nose as I leaned against a bar, surrounded by onlookers.

"Miss Dunhill? I think you're going to live. Your nose is not broken," Parker declared at the end of his examination.

To my eternal humiliation, tears stung my eyes. I blinked them away quickly. Whacking myself in the face and flashing the world's tackiest underwear at the man I wanted to marry was more than enough humiliation for one night. I wasn't adding crying like a little girl to the list.

I forced a bright and breezy tone. "Well, that's a relief!" I sat upright on the stool and noticed Parker watching me, concern etched across his handsome face. I shot him a sheepish smile.

"Looks like the bleeding has stopped, which is good."

"Yeah, it feels okay now." I tucked the bloodstained tissues into my purse. Keen to get this date back on track, I added, "We'd better get to the restaurant."

"As long as you're sure? I can cancel the booking if you'd prefer to go home."

Was he kidding? Never before in the history of romance has a date been so anticipated as this. There was no way I was going home right now.

"Don't be silly. It's nothing. I'm fine." I stood up, smoothing my skirt down to ensure there wouldn't be a stool-attached-to-dress repeat performance. Once in a lifetime was more than enough.

His face broke into a smile. "Great."

I glanced over at my friends. They looked anxious. "I might go to the ladies' first, though, to check on the damage."

He nodded. "Of course. I'll wait here."

I reached the bathroom and peered in the mirror. My nose was red and swollen, my makeup smudged beneath my eyes. I looked like a panda who'd lost a fight. As I grabbed some toilet paper to make some repairs, the bathroom door banged open. Marissa and Paige came flying in.

"Oh, my god. Are you okay?" Paige asked, bringing me in for a hug.

"That had to have hurt," Marissa added, shaking her head.

Pulling away, I replied, "I'm fine, really. Just embarrassed. Parker was a total gentleman."

"Oh, yes. We saw that. He was amazing. That's one good thing to come out of this . . . mess," Marissa replied tactfully.

Embarrassed, I brought my hand up over my eyes, accidentally banged my nose, and winced. "Ow!" I let out a heavy sigh. "This is so not what I had in mind for tonight."

Paige rubbed my arm. "I know."

"You know what? Men love to be in control, right? They love to feel like they're being all manly and crap. You gave him the opportunity to do just that," Marissa stated.

Hope rose. "You think?"

"Absolutely!" Paige confirmed. "Marissa's right. You've made him feel special, needed. He's got to love that."

Huh. They may have a point.

"Now, fix your face up and get yourself out there. You've got a date to go on." Marissa's tone was brisk.

Resolved, I swept away my smudged makeup, powdered my nose as gently as humanly possible, ran a comb through my hair, and freshened up my lipstick.

Marissa held the door open for me. "Go get 'em, tiger."

A moment later, I was by Parker's side once more.

"Ready?" he asked.

"Yes." I nodded, smiling. He took my hand in his and led me through the throngs toward the door. It felt nice. I glanced quickly back at my friends. They both gave me the thumbs-up, grinning.

Parker and I walked the short distance to the restaurant. He held my hand the whole way. Weirdly, conversation flowed much better since I'd banged my own fist into my face. Who knew? Perhaps the blood loss improved my conversation skills.

Once seated, we ordered our meals, and Parker asked me about my family. I told him about how my parents had been married for thirty-one years, how I don't see them as much as I would like, and how I saw my annoying little sister, Bella, *more* than I would like. He smiled and told me about his family. I began to feel so comfortable with him, like I'd known him all my life—not just researched him and cyber-stalked him for the past five weeks.

We discussed music taste. His was very refined: classical music, jazz, a smattering of classic rock. Mine was more at the Katy Perry and Taylor Swift end of the scale. I decided there and then it wasn't a problem: we could introduce each other to our music, share it with each other. We could go to concerts and concertos—or whatever those things are called. And I could develop an appreciation for classical music and jazz, no problem. In fact, I secretly suspected I would love classical music and jazz, only I hadn't heard much of it.

I grinned to myself. Oh, yes. My One Last First Date was going really, really well.

"Parker? What do your friends call you?" I asked once our meals had been delivered.

"Umm . . . Parker." He looked at me uncertainly, like I was demented for asking him such a stupid, obvious question. "Why do you ask?"

"No reason." I couldn't help but smile. Cassie: one, Know-It-

All Will Jordan: zero.

"Your crab looks good. He's watching me with his little beady eyes," I said, picking up my silverware to tuck into my own meal.

Parker chuckled, picked his crab up in his hand, and wobbled it from side to side. "Hi, Cassie. I'm Colin Crab. How do you do?" His voice was high-pitched and silly.

I giggled. Parker looked so cute being a goofball. "I can't really pick my pasta up to respond, Colin Crab."

"Oh, that's okay, Cassie. You're so pretty."

I blushed. I looked down at my plate and piled some pasta onto my fork to hide it.

"Bite me!"

I snapped my head up, startled. Did Parker really just say "bite me"? I looked at him, wide-eyed as mortification seeped up my body from my curling toes. "What did you just say?" I asked, breathless.

Parker wobbled the crab from side to side once more. "Bite me! Bite me!" he repeated in his silly voice.

Did he see my underwear reflected in the mirror? He didn't seem to have at the time, but then he did go straight into competent doctor mode. And if he did see it, why would he want to mock me?

Parker returned the crab to his plate. "By the look on your face, I took that a little too far. Sorry."

"No, no. It's fine." I returned my attention to my pasta. "This is good," I lied, not having taken a single bite. "How's yours?"

"I'll tell you in a second." He broke into the crab and took a large mouthful of meat. He grinned at me. "It's delicious."

I nodded at him. Whether he did see my "bite me" panties or not, I needed to move past it and get this date back on track.

I reverted to my bullet pointed wrist, chose a topic, and asked him a question. To my eternal relief, before too long we were laughing and sharing and having a great time once more.

At the end of the evening, after a delicious dinner, Parker walked me to my car, hand in hand, down along the water front.

We reached my little hatchback, parked in a side street. "This is me."

We stopped and stood by my car. "I've had a really great time tonight," Parker said.

"Me, too." My heart pounded as the bees in my tummy took

flight. "You know, other than injuring myself, that is." I let out a nervous laugh as my nose gave a throb, reminding me of my humiliation.

He smiled at me, taking a step closer. Was he going to kiss me? *Please, kiss me!* In my head, this was how the date ended. A perfect first kiss. A perfect *last* first kiss at the end of the not-quite-so-perfect One Last First Date.

"Can I see you again?" he asked, looking in my eyes.

"Oh, yes." My voice was breathless. "I mean, that would be nice."

"Great." He bit his lip.

Was he nervous?

"I'll . . . ah . . . be going then." He didn't take his eyes from mine.

"Okay."

"Unless—?"

I raised my eyebrows at him. "Unless what?"

Without further warning, he took me around the waist and pulled me in for a kiss. His nose banged against mine. I let out a wince as my eyes began to water.

"Sorry," he muttered. "I forgot. Are you all right?"

I nodded. "Yes." I was quite clearly not.

He smiled at me. "It hurts, doesn't it?"

I nodded again. "Kinda. But I don't want it to." I knew I sounded like a sulky child.

"You'll need to ice that again when you get home." He paused. "Well, I suppose I'd better get going. Early start tomorrow."

I looked at him in shock. Was that it? Was he leaving? There was no way I was letting my One Last First Date end without a one last first kiss.

I took hold of his hand and gazed up at him. Being considerably shorter than his six feet, it was a long way. But he seemed to know what I wanted. He leaned down, and I closed my eyes, my lips prepared for a long, sweet, *careful* kiss.

And it was just that. A wonderful first kiss. A first kiss to end all first kisses.

"I've wanted to do that since I saw you sitting at that bar," Parker said.

"Me too."

He kissed me again. "Well, good night, Cassie."

"Good night, Parker. And thanks for . . . everything."

I watched as he walked down the street. Once he was out of sight and I was safely sitting in my car, I grabbed hold of the steering wheel and let out an excited squeal. *He likes me! He likes me! He wants to see me again!*

I knew this was it. I knew he was the one for me. We were on our way.

Everything was coming together as planned.

CHAPTER 4

I FLOATED INTO THE I office the following morning in my wonderful, Parker-filled dream world.

Mr. and Mrs. Parker Hamilton. *No, too old-fashioned.* Mrs. Cassandra Hamilton. *Hmm, I like the sound of that.* Mrs. Cassandra Dunhill-Hamilton. *Ooh, fancy.*

"You look happy."

It was that annoying Will, smirking at me from behind his desk. Well, he won't bother me today. I had officially moved up to Cloud Nine, and I fully expected to buy a spot up there and stay. Permanently.

"Good morning, Will," I replied in what I hoped was a superior, school ma'am tone as I walked past him toward my desk.

To my irritation, he jumped up and followed me. "So, how was the big date with . . . what's his name? Prince Charming?"

I tried to stop myself blushing at the thought of Parker dressed as Prince Charming. *Swoon.* He would look a-mazing.

I reached my cubicle and placed my laptop bag on my desk. "Actually, Will, I have some work to do. So, if you wouldn't mind?"

He sat himself down on my desk, blocking my progress.

"Excuse me!" I protested. I gestured with my hands in the internationally recognized sign of get-your-sorry-butt-off-my-desk-this-minute.

He peered at my face. "Whoa! What happened to you?"

"What? Nothing." I darted my hand self-consciously to my

nose. I had to put my makeup on this morning with extreme care. It was still swollen, but, thankfully, only sore to the touch. Small progress, but at least it no longer throbbed like a bass guitar at a rock concert the way it had last night.

"It doesn't look like nothing," he replied, sizing up my face. "In fact, I would say it looks like *something*." He frowned. "What happened?"

"It was an accident. Last night. It's fine, really."

He raised his eyebrows. "Last night? On the big date?"

I nodded, willing this conversation to be over. Now.

A cloud passed over his features. "He didn't hurt you, this guy?"

"No, no. Nothing like that. He's a total gentleman. I kind of . . . hit my nose by accident getting my dress unstuck."

Will leaned back on my desk and roared with laughter. "Now, that I'd like to have seen."

I colored. Why had I bothered telling him? "Anyway, I've got some work to do."

To my immense frustration, he stayed firmly put, smirking at me. "So?"

I let out an exasperated breath. "So, what?"

"Aren't you going to tell me about your big date? Or did this," he waved his hand at my nose, "mess it up for you?"

I crossed my arms and pursed my lips. He was not going to get up and leave until I gave him *something*. I went for generic. "It was lovely, thank you. Parker and I had a very nice time together."

He raised his eyebrows at me. "And?"

I shrugged. "And nothing."

He scrunched his nose. "You struck out, huh?"

"No!"

"Ha! So, you got lucky! Cassandra Dunhill, I didn't know you had it in you."

Annoyed I had fallen into his trap, I pushed my auburn hair behind my ear, willing my deepening blush to somehow magically disappear. It didn't.

"It wasn't like that. We . . . He . . . It was all very chaste."

He sucked in air. "Oh, that's not good."

"Well, not *chaste* exactly. We kissed—" *Why am I telling him this?*

"Did you, now?" His eyebrows did a Mexican wave.

I ignored him and instead shook my head. "Anyway, why is my love life of any interest to you?"

He picked a paperweight up off my desk, turning it in his hand. "It's not. I'm just making conversation, that's all. Dunny, what the heck is this?"

"It's a curled-up fern."

"It looks like a dog turd."

I stretched my hand out. "Nice."

He handed the paperweight back to me, and I returned it to its rightful position on my desk. He was right; it did look like a dog turd. *Damn him!* "Oh, before I forget. You owe me twenty bucks. Parker doesn't have a nickname." I shot him a defiant grin, stretching my hand out once more, this time for the money.

Will raised his eyebrows at me. "Is that so?" He stood up and reached into his pocket, pulling out his wallet. "You know, I would be pretty suspicious of any guy who doesn't have a nickname."

"You would." I pushed my hand closer to him. "Pay up."

He handed me a fresh, crisp twenty-dollar bill.

"Thank you." I slipped it into my wallet.

"Hey, have you had the chance to present 'The Sheldon' to Nettco?" he asked, changing the subject. Much to my annoyance, he remained perched on my desk. When was this guy going to leave?

"Actually, that's what I need to work on today. So, if you don't mind . . .?" I gestured for him to leave.

"When's your next meeting with them?"

"This afternoon."

He pulled his phone out of his pocket and peered at his screen. "I can make that."

I guffawed. "You want to come to my meeting?"

He stood up. "Sure. Some of us have already made our targets for the quarter, you know."

I gave him a steely glare. "So you said."

"Right then, it's a date." He smiled at me.

"No, Will. It's a *meeting*." I shooed him out of my cubicle. "And I suppose you can come if you want to," I added begrudgingly.

He grinned at me, placing his hand over his heart. "Thanks for the warm invitation. It means a lot."

I ignored his jibe. "It's at two o'clock over at the Nettco head office. We'll need to leave here at one thirty."

He typed into his phone, then looked back up at me with a cheeky grin plastered across his face. "I'll look forward to our non-date, then."

I rolled my eyes. "Sure, whatever."

We heard a sound like a muffled animal whine nearby. We both watched as Shelby, Richard's assistant, hurried past, holding her hand over her mouth, her eyes red. The door to the ladies banged behind her as she bustled through.

"You women. So emotional," Will commented, looking back at me, his eyes teasing.

"Your compassion knows no bounds, Will Jordan. I wonder what's wrong with her."

"Who knows?" He shrugged, clearly not caring. "See you later, Dunny." He turned to leave.

I searched my brain, trying to come up with an equally insulting nickname for him. "Yeah, well, see you later . . . 'Poop Boy'."

"Poop Boy"? How old am I? Seven?

He stopped, turned, and looked at me. He raised his eyebrows and pressed his lips together to suppress a grin. "'Poop Boy'?"

I cringed. It might not be my best work, but I was committed now. I squared my shoulders. "You call me Dunny, that makes you 'Poop Boy'."

His face broke into a wide grin. "Fair call." He wandered off, chuckling, muttering "Poop Boy" to himself.

With Will gone—*finally*—I settled into work. Well, work and fantasizing about my future as Mrs. Cassandra Dunhill-Hamilton, that is. I called Nettco Electricity to inform them Will "Poop Boy" Jordan would be accompanying me to our meeting today and that we had a solution we thought should fit their needs. Then, I settled into work.

After about half an hour, I decided to go and find Paige and Marissa to give them the down low on the rest of my date last night. I knew they'd be dying to hear all about it, and it was strange they hadn't come to see me already today. They must be caught up in meetings or something.

I poked my head over the wall of my cubicle and scanned the

room. I noticed the office was quiet, without the usual conversation and Richard calling out to one or other of us. Strange. I spotted Marissa and Paige with a salesperson from my team over by Richard's office. They appeared to be talking in hushed tones. Paige noticed me and waved me over.

"What's going on?" I asked when I joined them.

"Haven't you heard?" the other sales rep, Sally Saunders, asked.

"Heard what?" I asked, confused. I glanced at their serious faces. "By the looks of you all, someone died."

"Kind of," Sally said grimly. "Hey, what happened to your nose?"

Heat rose in my cheeks. "Nothing. Just a bump. So, what's going on?"

"Richard's been fired," Marissa stated, her tone low and tense.

"What? When?" My mind spun. Richard? Richard, my boss, has been *fired*?

"It happened last night, apparently. We're all in shock." Paige's bottom lip trembled.

I regarded her for a moment. Paige was not even in the sales team, she worked in Marketing. Why would she know about this before me? I looked around the group. Everyone seemed completely shaken up.

"Why was he fired?" I asked when no one offered any further information.

"I think it's because of his affair with Shelby," Paige offered.

I blinked at her. Richard and Shelby, his sweet, plump assistant, were having an affair? Well, I guessed that explained her tearful rush to the ladies' earlier. But an *affair*? I peered through the window into Richard's office, noticing the pictures gone from the walls, his desk bare. I swallowed.

"No, as I said, there has to be another reason. You don't lose a job over an affair," Sally replied, thoroughly French in her attitude.

"Depends who it's with," Marissa scoffed.

"Oh, his poor wife," Paige commented, shaking her head. "And poor Shelby. She must be so upset."

"What's going to happen now, do you think?" Sally asked.

Marissa shrugged. "I guess they'll have to find a replacement."

All eyes turned to me. As one of two Senior Account Directors in the team, I would be a logical choice to take Richard's recently-vacated job.

I put my hand to my chest. "Me?" Would I want it? Could I even do it? Richard always said I had leadership potential. Perhaps now was my big chance to step up to the plate?

"Do you think you'd want it, Cassie?" Marissa asked. "It's a lot of responsibility."

"I . . . ah . . . I've never thought about it," I replied truthfully.

"I would if I were you." Marissa looked off into the distance, her eyes glazing over. "Nice office, great pay, everyone having to do what you tell them." She let out a sigh. "Total heaven."

I giggled. All three shot me an angry look.

"Sorry," I muttered. "Inappropriate."

"Well, it'll either be you or Will." Sally crossed her arms, nodding. "One of you two would be the logical choice."

Before I had the chance to process Sally's comment, I heard someone behind me say, "Hello, ladies. Catching up on some gossip, are we?"

We all turned to see Laura Carmichael, Richard's boss—well, *former* boss now—standing beside us.

"Sorry, Laura. We're all just a bit shocked," I replied.

She nodded, looking bleak. "That's totally understandable. There's a meeting in the conference room at nine thirty. I'll see you all there."

A couple of minutes and much speculation later and we're all packed into the conference room like a maxi tin of sardines. Laura was standing at the front of the room, and I noticed Will lurking near her. Marissa, Paige, Sally, and I managed to get seats at the back. We sat down, all of us anxious to know what was going to happen next.

Everyone was murmuring. It was hot and stuffy and someone near me was in dire need of a shower or deodorant. Preferably both. I scrunched my nose. It hurt.

"Thanks for coming, everyone," Laura said. The chatter dropped to silence.

"As many of you already know, we had to let Richard Ackerman go yesterday." She paused.

No one said a word; everyone already knew *that*. Even me.

"I'm not at liberty to say why we had to do this. There's a legal situation pending, and we would appreciate you keeping as much of this within these walls as possible."

There was a general murmur as people took in this information. "A legal situation" didn't sound good. And it sounded a lot more than a clichéd affair with his secretary.

Marissa turned to me. "What do you think that means?"

"He was up to no good, that's what."

Laura continued, "Richard is not at liberty to discuss any of this with current employees, so we would discourage you from contacting him directly."

I glanced across the room and spotted Shelby, her face pink and puffy, as she tried in vain to appear normal. Poor girl—and stupid girl. Getting involved with a married man is *never* a good idea.

"In the meantime, we're not going to leave Richard's team without a leader." Laura smiled. "We're lucky to have had someone step forward to act as Interim Manager while we find a more permanent replacement."

There was more murmuring. I looked at Marissa, and mouthed, "Who?" She shook her head, shrugging.

"Will Jordan has offered to step up. Will?"

My jaw dropped open. I watched, wide-eyed as "Poop Boy" himself stepped toward Laura and shook her hand. He had his I-mean-business look on his face, exuding confidence and leadership, looking every bit the person for the job. *Damn him.*

My rather enjoyable residence on Cloud Nine appeared to be at an end.

"I'm honored you chose me, Laura, and thankful I took that call during my game of pool last night." He turned to face us. "It'll be business as usual as we head into the last month of the quarter. I know I have some big shoes to fill—and not just because Richard had feet a Hobbit would be proud of."

There was general laughter. Next to me, Paige giggled. I nudged her and shot her a look.

"At times like these, I firmly believe we need to pull together and face . . ."

I rolled my eyes and stopped listening to him babble on. My mind raced. Will not only knew Richard had left when we talked this morning, he also knew he was going to be Interim Manager. Why hadn't he mentioned it? Was it because he knew I would have wanted the job, too?

Will droned on. I flipped my phone over and checked my call history. One missed call from Laura Carmichael yesterday evening at eight seventeen. That would have been about the time Parker was waggling his crab at me—and yes, I knew that sounded a lot worse than it actually was.

I surreptitiously dialed my voicemail and listened to my calls. The first message was from Laura, asking me to call her, her voice crisp and efficient. I bit my lip. I wondered whether she had called Will first or me?

I looked back at him, droning on about teamwork, blah de blah blah blah. I narrowed my eyes at him. If I hadn't been on such a crucial date last night, it could have been me standing up there right now.

"I want to meet with you all individually to find out where you're at this quarter. I'll schedule something in your calendars," Will continued.

So that must be why he insisted on coming to my Nettco meeting this afternoon. He was coming as my boss, not my colleague. The slime ball.

"Right now, I'd like to end by saying, although it's under difficult circumstances for us all, I'm eager to do the best job I can for you."

To my surprise, the room erupted into spontaneous applause. People stood up and approached Will, shaking his hand and congratulating him. You'd have thought he'd just won an Oscar or a Nobel Prize, not stolen a job rightfully mine.

Paige bobbed up next to me.

"What are you doing?" I asked, glaring at her.

"I'm going to congratulate Will." She was innocence itself.

"If you have to, I guess." I knew I sounded hurt.

She paused. Marissa and she shared a look.

Marissa stood up and put her hand out. "Come on, you." I took it, and she pulled me up. "Let's go to the Cozy Cottage for a debrief. The cake is on me this morning."

Before you could say "sugar addiction," Paige, Marissa, and I were sitting at our regular table in the window of one of our favorite places in the world, the Cozy Cottage Café, our cups of coffee and slices of cake ordered. My choice was always the mouth-watering-ly good flourless raspberry chocolate cake,

Marissa's was the orange and almond syrup cake, and Paige's choice was the carrot cake with cream cheese icing.

Even though it wasn't the closest café to our office, the Cozy Cottage was our absolute regular hangout of choice. It was the sort of place you felt instantly at home when you walked through the door. It was a charming oasis in the heart of the concrete jungle: relaxing, inviting, like being at home.

All three of us loved this place. It could lift you up if you were feeling blue; it could make the happiness sparkle. It was also most definitely a guy-free zone. That's not to say there weren't any men in the café, just none of us ever brought one here. It was our place. Special to us three.

Auckland doesn't get very cold, even in winter, but we do have some chilly mornings, and today was one of those days. The moment we walked through the door, we were hit by the tempting aroma of coffee, hot chocolate, and gingerbread. Just what I needed today.

Marissa was holding court. "He's only Interim Manager, Cassie. Who knows? He might mess it up royally, and then you can swan in and snaffle the job from under his big, fat nose."

"Will Jordan does not have a big, fat nose," Paige sniffed.

"It's an expression, Paige," Marissa responded.

I bit my lip. "Maybe. But I can't kick the feeling it should have been me. I've been at the company the longest, and I'm the only other Senior Account Director. What's more, Laura called *me* last night, probably before she called 'Poop Boy'."

"'Poop Boy'?" Marissa smiled, her eyes wide.

I brushed her off. There were more important fish to fry right now. "Look, it doesn't matter. The point is, when Laura called me I was on my date with Parker, so I'd turned my phone off." This whole work drama had completely eclipsed last night. I was beyond irritated.

Paige's face lit up. "Oh, I almost forgot! How did the rest of the date go?"

Despite my irritation at the day's events, my face broke into a smile as my belly did a little flip-flop at the thought of Parker. "Good. Really good."

Paige clapped her hands together. "I knew it!"

"By the smile on your face I would say it was not just good but great," Marissa added.

"Yeah, okay, it was great," I conceded.

"Tell us everything."

The café owner, Bailey, delivered our coffee and sweet treats, her habitual smile on her face.

"Thanks, Bailey," we all said in unison.

"You're more than welcome, ladies. You know you're my favorite customers."

"We know," I replied. Being Bailey's favorites simply added to the charm of the place.

"Cassie's been on her first date with that new guy," Paige told Bailey. "She's about to tell us all about it."

"Oh, my gosh. Really?" Bailey squeaked. "This is big. Huge."

Bailey knew all about our One Last First Date pact.

"It is," Marissa confirmed.

Bailey wiped her hands on her red polka dot apron and looked around the room. "It's too busy right now to stop, but you have to fill me in on all the juicy details. Promise?"

"Promise." I smiled up at her. Bailey had bought the café with a business partner about a year ago, and under her expert guidance, it had become the homey, welcoming place it was today. She was lovely, about our age, give or take, single, and I secretly suspected, wished she'd been in on the pact with us.

"Have fun, chickadees." Bailey headed back to the counter.

"Now. Don't leave out any details," Marissa instructed, plunging her fork into the yummy, syrupy cake. She slipped some into her mouth. "God, this is good."

Paige and I glanced at one another and laughed as we watched her.

"What?" she asked, cake stuck to her teeth.

"You look like you're having an orgasm," I replied. "A really, really good one."

She licked the cake from her lips. "Tell me when you last had an orgasm that wasn't really, really good."

"Fair point." I shrugged. "Anyway, my date was fantastic. He was sweet and funny, and he's so intelligent. We had the best time."

"He was so nice looking after you the way he did with that ice pack and things," Paige said, a dreamy look in her eyes.

My hand went to my face, lightly touching my nose. "He was, wasn't he? You know, I now look at what happened as an opportunity for us to get closer last night."

Marissa took a break from her cake orgasm. "Not a humiliating disaster, then?"

"No!" I protested. I took a bite of my own cake. "Oh, yes. So good. After that whole punching myself in the face incident, we had the best dinner."

"And?" Paige asked leadingly, an eager look on her pretty face.

I paused for dramatic effect as they both looked at me impatiently. "And he's a good kisser."

"Ha! I knew it!" Marissa said. "Ryan said he would be."

I regarded her with alarm. "How would your brother know Parker would be a good kisser?"

She shrugged. "I don't know. A weird man-friend thing, I guess. I didn't ask."

"It's love, isn't it?' Paige asked. "It is, I can tell. Or at least it will be. The pact has begun to weave its magic. You'll be married before the year's out, mark my words."

Married. My tummy warmed at the thought.

"Maybe. Or maybe it's just that Cassie researched this guy, stalked him even. If they do get married, it'll be as a result of rational analysis and compatibility, not some beach pact thing."

"Rational analysis and compatibility? There is no romance in your soul, Marissa Jones. Eat your cake." Paige turned to me. "Well, Cassie, I for one am ecstatic for you. When are you seeing him again?"

"We haven't made any specific plans as such, but he did ask if he could see me again at the end of the date. Of course, I said yes."

As if by some cosmic coincidence—and Paige would swear it was the Goddess of the Beach doing her *thang*—my phone rang. I glanced at it as it vibrated on the table next to my latte.

"It's him."

"Pick it up, pick it up!" Paige insisted, her eyes shining.

I flicked my hair and cleared my throat before I pressed "answer." I put on my best sexy Scarlett Johansson voice. "Hello, Parker."

"Hi, is that Cassie?" He sounded uncertain.

"Yes, it is, Parker. Hello, there," I replied.

"Do you have a cold coming on? Your voice sounds a little . . . odd."

I cleared my throat. "I'm perfectly fine, thanks."

"Well, that's a relief. It's almost flu season, you know, and you can't be too careful."

I smiled. Parker cared about me already. "I'm fine, really."

"I wanted to call and let you know I had a really great time last night."

I blushed, my eyes darting between my friends faces, both of whom were watching me closely. "Me, too." I turned away from them, trying to gain at least a small modicum of privacy.

"How's your nose?"

"Fine, fine. Nothing to worry about."

"Great. Cassie, I . . . I know I'm meant to wait for at least three days before calling you . . ."

"You are?"

"Yes. That's one of the guy dating rules. Three days or they'll think you're keen."

"Huh. I never knew that. What are the others?"

"What's he saying?" Paige stage-whispered.

I put my index finger to my mouth. "Shhh."

He chuckled. "I could tell you, but I'd have to give you a frontal lobotomy. Sorry, doctor joke there."

I laughed. I could totally get on board with medical jokes from my doctor husband.

"The thing is, I didn't want to wait three days."

I blushed again as I gripped my phone closer to my ear. "Me neither."

"So, do you want to go out again?"

"I'd love to. How about tomorrow night?"

"Tomorrow night sounds great. Shall I pick you up from your place?"

We arranged the details. All the while, Marissa and Paige watched my every move, grinning knowingly.

"Say what you like, Marissa. The pact is working," Paige said as I turned back to face them.

Eventually, after much Parker discussion, we headed back to

the office. I couldn't help but float right back up to Cloud Nine, knowing I had a one last *second* date with the man I was made for.

CHAPTER 5

WHY DID WILL JORDAN have to look like Ross Poldark's better-looking brother? I mean, Poldark had to be the most swoon-worthy guy on television right now, and Will Jordan had nearly ruined my enjoyment of watching him strut his stuff in his tight breeches, with his dark, brooding looks and romantic, wind-swept hair. I narrowed my eyes at him. If his nose were larger, his eyes smaller, and perhaps he lost some of that thick, dark hair of his, things would be so much better.

Well, not for him, *obviously*. But for me. Definitely for me.

"It looks as though you're on track to a strong end to the quarter." Will looked up from my account status report and smiled at me. "Great work, Dunny."

I ignored the degrading nickname. "Thanks." I gave him my least sincere smile—the one that didn't reach my eyes. I glanced at my watch. "Is that all? Only, I have a couple of things to get done before we go to Nettco." It still grated I had to take Will to my meeting. Especially now that he was my boss, temporary or not.

"Sure, of course. Do you need anything else from me for that meeting?"

"I've got it in hand."

There was a knock at the door. I spied Paige through the glass. I stood up and opened the door. Paige smiled at me, her color already rising at the prospect of being enclosed within these four walls with the object of her desire.

Some people have no taste.

"Hi, I hope I'm on time?" she said breathlessly to Will.

I could warm my chilly hands on her face, she was blushing so profusely. I placed my hand on the doorknob. "He's all yours, Paige."

"Come on in, Millsey," Will said.

I shot him a look. Why did she get "Millsey" when I got named after a latrine?

"And thanks, Dunny. I'll see you at one thirty."

I winced as I closed the door behind me, glad to be away from my new boss. Ha! As if that could ever happen. Not if I had anything to do with it, anyway.

I dropped my files on my desk, picked up a box with a pretty ribbon and an envelope entitled "Private and Confidential," and headed to the stairwell. I bounded up the stairs, two at a time, in my strappy heels—no easy feat, if you would pardon the pun.

I reached the door to the executive floor. I smoothed my hair, smacked my lips, and took a deep breath. I pushed the door open and stepped onto the plush dark gray carpet. I looked around at the sleek interior: the tasteful art on the walls, the soft, inviting leather chairs, the large glass windows with their view of Auckland's sparkling blue harbor. As far as the corporate world was concerned, this place was so luxurious I could almost hear the chorus of angels sing.

I sighed. Oh, yes, this was where it was at. This is where I was destined to be. Now, to work on making that happen.

Holding the box and envelope, I approached Brian, Laura's executive assistant and trained Rottweiler. Seriously, all he needed was the studded collar and a bit more drool and he wouldn't look out of place at the pound. I stifled a giggle at the thought as I stood, waiting for him to finish what he was working on. I waited. And waited.

Eventually, he looked up from his computer at me. "Cassie. How nice." His voice oozed sarcasm. "How can I help?"

"Hi, Brian! How are you?" I said with as much enthusiasm as I could muster. "You look fantastic in that . . ." I glanced over his outfit. He was wearing a white collared shirt, a gray waistcoat, and a blue and white striped bowtie. He looked like he was about to jump up onto his desk and sing barbershop with a group of similarly dressed men. ". . . ah, snazzy ensemble."

Snazzy?

He gave me the least genuine smile I'd seen in weeks, narrowing his eyes. "Thank you."

"I brought you something." Pushing the envelope under my arm, I opened the box and presented him with an apple turnover, stuffed to the brim with stewed apples, cinnamon, whipped cream, and, quite possibly, a thousand calories.

Brian's eyes bulged in his chubby face. "Are you trying to bribe me, Cassie Dunhill?"

"Not at all!" I protested, my eyes wide. I placed the open box in front of him and picked up a pen on his desk. I began to play with it. "Is Laura in, Brian?"

He held out his open hand. I placed the pen into it like a chastised child.

"Do you have an appointment?" he asked, knowing full well I didn't.

"No, I was just hoping to catch her for a little chat. You know, while you eat that delicious apple treat you've got there."

He pursed his lips, still looking at me through narrowed eyes.

It was time. I needed to go big or go home. I took a couple of steps toward Laura's closed office door. "Shall I just go on in?"

Quicker than you could say "juicy bone," Brian the Rottweiler bounced out of his chair faster than I would ever have expected a man of his impressive girth could and beat me to the door. "I'll check. You . . . shoo."

Shoo? What am I, a stray cat?

I took a step back and waited as Brian and Laura spoke in hushed tones, the door ajar.

A moment later, Brian swung it open. "Laura can see you now."

"Thanks, Brian. You're a real sweetie."

He did his best to suppress a smile as I walked past him. Who knew? Brian the Rottie was really a soft, fluffy Spoodle at heart.

Laura looked up from her desk momentarily. "Cassie. Come on in, have a seat." She continued to work.

I did as instructed, enjoying the feel of the soft leather chair as I sat, waiting for her to finish.

Closing her laptop, she looked at me. "What have you done? You look . . . different."

I was getting tired of this. "I banged my nose. It's fine."

"Good, good. Now, I think I know why you're here. We needed to act fast last night, and Will was ready and able."

I shrugged, hoping I look relaxed, despite my raging internal anger. "It's fine, Laura," I lied. "I understand you did what you had to do, what was best for the business. I apologize for not having been available last night when you called."

She brushed my apology away with her hand. "Don't mention it. We have a solution, and I'm hoping it will be business as usual down there."

I nodded. "Of course. Business as usual," I said through gritted teeth, thinking of "Poop Boy" strutting around, the power totally gone to his head.

"I do very much hope you'll apply for the permanent role, however. We plan on advertising it shortly."

Hope rose in me like a hot air balloon. "Oh, I plan on it."

She smiled. "Good."

"In fact . . ." I reached across her desk and handed her the envelope. "Here's my CV."

She took it, raising her eyebrows at me. "You're organized, I see."

"I really want this job, Laura."

Her phone rang, interrupting us. She picked it up and looked at the screen. "I have to take this. Talk soon?"

"Sure," I replied. I got up to leave. "And Laura? Thanks."

* * *

At one thirty on the dot, I knocked on Richard's door, resenting the fact it was now Will "Poop Boy" Jordan's door and not mine, no matter how nice Laura had been about it. I had barely removed my knuckles when the door swung open.

Will stood in front of me, suit jacket and tie on, laptop bag in hand. "Ready to go?"

I shot him an irritated look. "That's why I'm here."

"Great." He patted his right thigh, then his left. I shot him a confused look. Is this some sort of superstitious dance he performs before a big meeting?

"Keys," he explained.

"You won't need those. I'll drive." I dangled the keys to my car in front of him.

"No, really. You relax while I drive."

"I'm happy to, honestly."

"No. I insist."

I sighed, giving in. This was becoming ridiculous. "Sure."

It was going to be a long afternoon.

Once in his car—a late model European that made mine look like the overlooked bridesmaid at a wedding—he talked continuously about the Nettco deal. He was full of advice and examples of successes he'd had with his accounts. Eventually, I'd had enough.

"Yes, yes. We all know you're our rock star. You don't need to keep banging on about it so much."

He looked at me sideways. "Is that why you think I'm telling you about my accounts? To brag?"

"Why else?" It seemed pretty freaking obvious to me.

He looked at me for such a long moment, I was forced to yell, "Watch the road, Will!"

He seemed to snap out of it, returning his eyes to the road—where they needed to be. We both fell silent. It wasn't one of those easy silences you can have with friends. No. This silence was more akin to nails being dragged down a blackboard.

I think we were both relieved when we finally pulled up outside the Nettco Electricity head office.

Will parked the car—still silent—and we walked the short distance to the building entrance. As I was about to walk through the automatic doors, he placed his hand on my arm. I stopped and looked at him, expecting a last-minute pep talk about how amazing he was. Or something equally nauseating.

Instead, he paused and said, "I'm actually a pretty good guy, you know."

I shifted my weight. Why did he care what I thought of him? "Sure. Of course. No one said you weren't."

"Well, actually, you did. Back there, in the car. You accused me of bragging."

I rolled my eyes. "I didn't accuse you of anything."

"You did. I was only trying to give you some examples of my solutions. I wasn't trying to boast."

I put my hands up in the air in surrender. "Okay. You weren't bragging, and you're a great guy."

He looked at me for a moment before his face broke into a cheeky grin. "I'm glad we cleared that up, Dunny."

I smiled back at him despite myself. "Do *not* call me that in this meeting."

"Is Cassandra better? Oh, I forgot, that's only when you're really, really naughty." He did that irritating Mexican wave thing with his eyebrows again.

My lips formed a thin line. "'Cassie' will do just fine, thank you. Now, shall we go in and close this deal?"

Forty-five minutes later, we'd shown John, Michelle, and Ferdinand how well "The Sheldon" would fit their business model with a presentation to be proud of. Knowing them as I did, I could tell they were impressed. I hoped it was enough to get them across the metaphorical line and sign the all-important deal.

To my unutterable surprise, Will didn't dominate the meeting and didn't even claim "The Sheldon" as his own design. He did, however, ensure no one forgot he was my boss, mentioning it needlessly throughout the discussion: "Your user interface would look like this, and I'm Cassie's boss," and "As Cassie's boss, you'll see how competitively priced this nodule is," and, my personal favorite, "Can you tell Cassie's boss where the bathroom is?"

Okay, I exaggerate, but you get the idea. It was *so* unnecessary.

John, Nettco's Head of Information Technology, was especially exuberant in his handshaking at the end of the meeting. "This is exactly what we need, Cassie. Thank you."

I smiled at him. I could almost see that deal being signed on the dotted line. "I'm so pleased, John."

"You should have brought The Old Willster here months ago! Saved us all this to-ing and fro-ing."

The Old Willster? What was this, a boy's club?

"Ah, yes," I replied through gritted teeth. I took a furtive glance at Will, aka The Old Willster, aka "Poop Boy". Of course, he was beaming from ear to ear, thinking he'd just closed the deal and that my months of work meant zip.

Will shook John's hand. "I'm just glad we have a solution to fit your needs, John . . . or should I say 'Chicken'?"

John looked sharply at Will. My eyes darted between Will's

smiling face and John's, like I was watching a tennis match. What on this sweet earth possessed Will to call my important customer "Chicken," just as it looked like we'd finally reached a deal? Was he certifiably *insane*?

To my eternal relief, John burst into laughter, slapping Will on the back. "You know Spongey and Toad, do you?"

"Shoot pool with them every Wednesday night. They're a great group of guys. Hey, you should join us some time. Word on the street is Chicken's got a pretty good game."

I glanced at Michelle. I bet *she* didn't have a stupid, immature nickname like "Spongey" or "Chicken" and play pool with "Toad" on a Wednesday. She rolled her eyes at me in an act of female solidarity, and I smiled back at her, shaking my head. No, she was a grown-up, known as "Michelle." As she should be.

After the pool conversation finally dried up, I agreed to present John a formal offer by the end of the week and we left—after more male bonding, back-slapping, name-calling, and general grunting and chest beating. I tell you, all we needed was a fire and we'd have a bona fide caveman convention on our hands.

Will was still smiling to himself as we drove back to the office.

"Why don't you draft the contract with Legal and I'll have a look over it?" Will suggested as he drove out of Nettco's parking lot.

I bristled. "I'm quite capable of putting the contract together myself. I've been doing this for much longer than you, you know."

"I know. And you're great at it."

I looked at him out of the corner of my eye. Will was complimenting me now? What was he playing at? "Err, thanks."

After a beat, he added, "I need to approve it, you know, as your boss."

Suddenly uncomfortable, I shifted in my seat. The boss thing again. "Oh. Right."

"How's Friday morning for you? Does that give you enough time?"

I tried to sound relaxed, unfazed. "Sure. No problem."

In the interest of driving harmony, I decided to change the subject. "So, what actually is your nickname? The one Chicken and Toad and other assorted animals use?"

He grinned. "Guess."

I crossed my arms. "I'm not going to do that. It could be anything."

"What if I give you a hint?"

I shook my head. "You know what? I don't really care. You're 'Poop Boy' as far as I'm concerned."

He chuckled. "You're not very good at nicknames, are you?"

"No. And I don't care to be either."

CHAPTER 6

"CASSIE, YOU LOOK WONDERFUL. I like your hair like that," Parker said, standing at my front door. He was dressed in a pair of khakis and a polo shirt, down to the very last detail like the kind of guy you want to take home to your parents.

"You, too," I replied wistfully. Suddenly shy, I smoothed down my pale green, slim-fitting dress and clenched my toes in my silver heels. Since my favorite date dress got itself snagged on a barstool with disastrous consequences on its last outing, this dress has moved up the ranks to officially become Number One Date Dress.

Parker leaned in and kissed me on the cheek.

"Thanks." I beamed at him—my future husband.

He smiled back at me, arching an eyebrow. "Thanks for kissing you?"

"Err, yes?"

He laughed. "Well, you're welcome then. How's the nose? It looks better I see." He took my face in his hand and moved my head from one side to the other, like he was a doctor. Which, of course, he was.

It did not feel romantic.

"It's a lot better, thanks," I replied, my face still a little squished by his hold.

"That's great." He let go. "Shall we?"

I shrugged my jacket on and collected my purse from the table by the door. "Absolutely. I'm looking forward to this."

He took my arm in his like we were in an old-time musical and were about to sing a happy number together as we sashayed down the street.

"We're going to walk, if that's okay with you. It's nice out tonight, and the club is only about ten minutes away."

I glanced down at my shoes. I was wearing the ones Marissa called my "killer" shoes, not because they looked good—although they most certainly did—but because they hurt my feet more than any other shoe known to humanity. They were high, adding a much-needed handful of inches to my diminutive height, strappy, and sparkly. In short, total shoe nirvana. Or at least in the looks stakes. In the comfort stakes? Not so much.

"Sure!" I replied brightly. "That sounds great. Just great."

As we walked through the city streets—one of us in ever-increasing pain—we chatted about our respective days. I told him about my success with Nettco and about how I'd applied for the Regional Manager's job. I left out the bit about Will "Poop Boy" Jordan acting as Interim Manager. I didn't want to think about him while I was on my second date with my future husband.

With every step, my poor, battered feet screamed at me. And with every step I repeated in my head, *Nearly there, Band-Aids in purse.*

We stopped outside a boutique with pretty summer dresses in the window. My feet screamed at me some more.

I forced a smile.

"Here we are," Parker said.

I looked up and down the street. "Where, exactly?"

"At the club. It's down here." He led me to a dark door next to the boutique. The sign above the door read "Sammy's," lit up by a spotlight. I hobbled along beside him, hoping Parker wouldn't notice.

He opened the door and a cacophony of sound, which I had to assume was jazz, blasted out, up the stairs, and onto the street.

I swallowed.

Parker shot me a concerned look. "Are you all right, Cassie?"

"Yes. Absolutely. I'm just so . . . excited."

"I bet you are. I remember the first time I went to a jazz club. It. Blew. My. Mind."

Listening to the discordant noise from down the stairs, I could well imagine that.

We walked down the stairs into the boutique's basement. I surveyed the room. The whole place was dark, and other than the bar and where the band was playing, the only light came from the small lamps on the tables covered with red and white checked tablecloths.

The band stopped murdering their instruments, and the crowd erupted into applause. I darted a look at Parker. He was also applauding, so I joined in.

A man in a black shirt and pants approached us. "Parker! Great to see you, man." He pulled Parker into a hug, one of those manly types in which they punch one another's backs. It looked to me like it hurt. Women would never do that to one another. Men are weird.

"You too, Ray. I'd like you to meet Cassie. Cassie, this is Ray, we go way back."

I offered him my hand, hoping I would avoid the back punching, body slam masquerading as a hug. "Hi."

Thankfully, he took my hand and shook it. "Hey, Cassie. Great to meet you."

"Cassie's a virgin," Parker said to Ray, raising his eyebrows.

I snapped my head toward Parker, my color rising.

Alert! Alert! He thinks I'm a virgin?

"Well, I'm not exactly . . ." Words failed me. I tried again. "I am twenty-seven and a half and most women have . . . you know . . ." *This was not working.* I looked between Ray and Parker. I bit my lip and tried again. "It's not like there have been *that* many guys, you know?" I tugged on Parker's arm, pulling him down to me. "Is that important to you? That I'm a . . . a virgin?"

He threw his head back in laughter. "Cassie. I meant you're a *jazz* virgin." He reached for my hand and gave it a reassuring squeeze.

"Oh." Mortification crept up my body. *No no no no no! How embarrassing.*

I glanced at Ray, blushing profusely, glad the room was dark. He regarded me with lightly veiled amusement.

"Cassie's never been to a jazz club," Parker continued by way of explanation. "You've never even listened to it, right?"

"No." I tried my best to recover. "Well, I have heard Michael Bublé on the radio. My mom likes him. He's pretty good."

Parker and Ray both laughed heartily, their hands on their bellies.

Okay, clearly not the right thing to say.

My mortification crept higher. If Parker wasn't my future husband and my shoes hadn't committed a serious crime against my feet, I might have considered running home to hide under my bed. With a tub of ice cream. And chocolate. A lot of chocolate.

Parker gave my hand another squeeze, and I shot him a thankful look. I may be a jazz-illiterate non-virgin with a serious blushing problem, but he still seemed to like me.

"Let's get you two seated. The band will be back soon for their second set," Ray said, his face shining.

I followed Ray to a table for two directly in front of the stage, shots of searing pain in my feet with every step I took. I thanked him with as much dignity as I could muster and sat down in the chair Parker pulled out for me—such a gentleman—my embarrassment mercifully beginning to subside.

"Would you like a drink?" Parker asked once he was seated.

"Sure, thanks. I'll have a glass of Chardonnay, please." *Make that a bottle.*

Parker gave our drinks order to a waitress, and we began to peruse the dinner menu.

"The pizza here is really good."

"Oh, I love pizza. I could eat it all day. My dream would be to move to Italy and eat pizza and gelato from sunrise to sunset."

Why am I saying this? I sound like some kind of food addict.

Parker chuckled. "That sounds like quite the dream. Shall I order pizza for two?"

"Sounds great."

I have got to get on top of these nerves.

"So, tell me all about—" I began, only to be interrupted by the band sauntering back on stage.

"Oh, look. They're back," Parker said as he sat back in his seat, smiling at me.

I shot him my most excited smile. "Awesome!" Surely, they were just tuning their instruments before and now they were going to play actual music. I got myself comfortable in my chair, happy to be experiencing this with Parker.

"Hey," the lead singer said into his microphone to hoots, claps, and cheers from the audience.

I looked him over. I didn't know quite what I'd expected a jazz singer to look like. Probably old, wearing a black turtleneck, with a sax slung around his neck. This guy looked like my high school chemistry teacher, right down to the brown cardigan and Velcro shoes.

"Here's a little number we like to call 'Saturday Sanity,'" Singer Guy continued to more excitement from the tables around us.

Parker leaned closer to me. "This is an original piece."

"Oh. How wonderful."

The band began to play. Unlike the noise we'd heard when we arrived, this "piece" actually had a melody. Singer Guy sang his first few notes, and I sat up in my chair in surprise. He had a lovely voice, a little like Harry from One Direction, only on a guy who looked like your dad. Which was a shame, really.

After another couple of sips of wine, I started to relax and enjoy the music. Singer Guy wasn't going to give Michael Bublé a run for his money anytime soon, but the music was nice enough, and it didn't try to violently assault my eardrums like the earlier stuff.

I stole a look at Parker. He was swaying to the music and bobbing his head, a half smile on his handsome face, clearly reveling in the music. He looked so darn adorable it made me warm inside. He turned to me and smiled. I smiled back. So what if I don't know anything about jazz? I could learn. And Parker liked me.

I relaxed into the music, confident in our burgeoning relationship. As I shifted in my seat, I moved my feet and had to stop myself from wincing. My feet were actually throbbing. Well, there's one thing to be said for this evening: I seemed to have the answer to that age-old question, "What is the cost of beauty?" It turns out it's four blisters, feet that feel like they're on fire, and a touch of blood, squelching between the toes. Not pretty, but there you have it.

As the music carried on—and Parker continued to move his head in that cute way—I began to fantasize about taking my shoes off and soaking my poor feet in iced water. But I knew if I slipped those killer heels off, I'd be a dead woman. There would be no way on this sweet earth I'd ever get them back on again.

I sighed.

"Good, huh?" Parker said, his face bright.

"Oh, yes. So good," I confirmed, reaching across the table and giving his hand a little squeeze. "Thank you for bringing me here."

"My pleasure." He beamed at me.

It was at that point the music changed from having a melody to totally losing the plot. For reasons known only to Singer Guy and his cronies, without warning, he stopped singing actual words and let out a barrage of weird sounds, his eyes closed as he clutched onto the microphone.

And it went on. And on. *And on.*

I glanced around the room as I began to wonder whether anyone else had noticed Singer Guy had totally lost his marbles. I looked at Parker. He was still doing that adorable head bobbing thing, as were most of the members of the audience.

Needing to understand why Singer Guy had abandoned the use of actual words and no one seemed to mind, I leaned over to Parker. "What's he doing?" I stage-whispered over the music in his ear.

"That's scat," he replied.

I leaned back in my chair. "Oh, of course." I pretended I understood what he was talking about. But, at least no one else was wondering about Singer Guy's sanity.

The music finished—not a moment too soon—and we applauded along with the rest of the audience. Our pizza was delivered, and we tucked in as Singer Guy launched into another "piece."

Eventually, after a lot more head bobbing and incoherent babbling—and that was just the band—they left the stage to much applause and calls. Our pizza long gone, Parker ordered us a second round of drinks.

"So, what did you think?" He had an eager look on his face.

"It was really, really great." *Damn you, eye twitch!*

"I'm so pleased you think so. I thought they were amazing."

I nodded along. "Yes, so amazing. And you're right, his voice did have a very feline quality to it. He did it well."

"A what?" he asked, looking confused.

"Singer Guy . . . I mean, the lead singer. When he did the cat, I was confused, but then when you explained it to me, I totally got it.

He sounded a bit like a cat in a bad mood to me. Especially in that last song . . . ah, piece."

His face crinkled in a smile. "It's called 'scat,' not cat."

My old friend mortification came flying back. "Oh."

Parker reached across the table and took my hand in his. "You know what, Cassie? I think I like your take on jazz so much better. I'm going to think of it as 'cat' from now on."

I looked up at him through my lashes. "You must think I'm pretty dumb."

"Not at all." He scooted his chair around the table so we were sitting side by side, our arms touching. "In fact, I think you're adorable. And you don't know much about jazz. Yet."

He slid his arm around my seat and pulled me into him, brushing his lips against mine. I closed my eyes and reveled in our kiss, allowing my embarrassment to seep out of me, down through the floorboards.

"Adorably dumb?" I questioned, only half teasing him.

"Adorably adorable," he confirmed with another kiss. "Now, can I walk you home?"

Forgetting my debilitated feet, a smile crept across my face. "That would be nice."

Parker paid for our drinks and dinner like the gentleman he was, and we headed back up the stairs to the street. I tried my level best not to wince with each step. I know I failed because Parker asked me what was wrong.

"It's just these shoes, that's all. They're not great for walking in."

He chuckled. "That's kind of a fundamental flaw, don't you think? We may not ask a lot of our footwear, but to be able to walk in them seems to me to be a pretty basic requirement."

I rolled my eyes playfully. "You're not a woman."

"Take them off. It's warm out."

The idea of being free from these devices of extreme torture was very appealing. I leaned down and undid the clasps, slipping the shoes off with a relieved sigh. I stood back up next to him, feeling like a small child next to his six-foot-three height.

He took one of my shoes in his hand. "They are pretty hot, though, despite the blood."

I laughed, embarrassed once more. There was certainly a theme to this evening.

"Are you okay to walk? I could carry you."

Not wanting to appear any more ridiculous than I'd already been, I declined the offer and we walked hand in hand through the moonlit streets of Auckland together. It was picture-perfect romance.

"I'm so pleased you enjoyed the music. Jazz means a lot to me, sharing it with you feels somehow . . . important."

My heart squeezed. I floated on air the rest of the way, reaching my place all too soon. "Thank you for a lovely evening. I had a great time." I stood on my tippy toes and wrapped my hands around his neck and kissed him good night.

"Would you like to get together at the weekend?"

I grinned at him. "Absolutely. I'll call you."

"Great. Night, Cassie."

I slipped my key into the door and turned to say good night, only to be swept up by him in a fresh kiss, leaving me breathless.

"Sorry, I had to do that." It was his turn to look embarrassed.

"That's okay. It was really nice. You can do it anytime."

"Anytime? How about Saturday night, then? Dinner?"

I nodded at him, smiling. "Dinner would be lovely."

"And kissing. Lots more kissing."

I watched him walk down the street. Once he was out of sight, I pushed my door open and floated inside, trying to decide whether white or ivory would best suit my complexion when I walked down that aisle to Parker, my future doctor husband.

.

CHAPTER 7

MARISSA AND PAIGE WERE both looking at me over our coffee and snacks as we sat at our usual table at the Cozy Cottage Café.

"All that aside, was it amazing?" Paige asked, a dreamy look in her eye.

"Yes." I sighed. I'd just told them about my "scat" bumble and the whole virgin thing. I wasn't feeling great about my date performance, despite the fact he'd asked me on another one. "I don't know. I keep messing up around him. First the skirt slash punching myself in the nose debacle, then this virgin slash cat fiasco. He's going to think I'm some sort of uneducated, self-harming klutz if I'm not careful."

Paige's face lit up. "I've got it. Perhaps you need to get him to do some of the things *you* love?"

"I'm hardly going to get him to come on a scrapbooking weekend, am I? A bunch of ladies with middle-aged spread and bunions sitting around, pasting things together. It's hardly rock and roll, is it?"

"Hey!" Paige protested. "I love scrapbooking."

"I know. And me, too. Just, it doesn't seem like the kind of thing a guy would be into."

"Derek likes it," Paige objected.

"Derek is sixty-three, never been married, lives with his ninety-year-old mother, wears brown cardigans with leather elbow patches all year round, and smells kind of funky."

"Ha!" Marissa almost choked on her orange and almond syrup cake.

"Good point. So maybe not scrapbooking." Paige stirred her coffee.

"I know. What about Pilates class? You've been going for years. I bet you could show him how amazing you are at it. He might see you in a new light," Marissa suggested.

I drummed my fingers on the table, deep in thought. It wasn't a bad idea. Paige was right, I was pretty darn good at Pilates—a Pilates Princess, even. No, that sounded terrible. The point was, I was good at it. It had been my go-to stress buster for years, and it had given me a six-pack you could almost see in certain lights. Well, on a good day. A very, very good day.

A smile spread across my face. "Marissa? You're a genius."

Paige shrugged. "We're just doing the Goddess of the Beach's bidding."

Marissa rolled her eyes, shooting Paige a "whatever" look. "Tell us again about the kissing."

"You guys," I protested, although I was secretly thrilled. "It's embarrassing."

"I bet it was so romantic." Paige sighed, her eyes dreamy.

"Me, too. Come on, Cassie," Marissa chimed in. "Us boring singles are living vicariously through you. You *have* to tell us."

"Okay." I spread my fingers out on the table, a smile teasing the edges of my mouth. "We had our good night kiss and he was about to leave, and then he . . . I don't know, seemed to have a burning need to kiss me again." I shrugged. "So, he did."

"And?" Paige lead as she held her cup halfway up to her mouth, as though frozen in midair.

"And it was . . . nice."

"Nice?" Marissa questioned as she leaned back in her chair, looking disappointed. "Nice doesn't quite do it for me. This is the guy you're planning to marry, Cassie. If I were you, I'd want the kissing to be way more than just 'nice.'"

Paige looked miffed. "What do you mean, he's the guy she 'plans' on marrying? She's going to marry him. One Last First Date, remember? We don't get any second chances with this."

"Sure, of course. Only Cassie's the first one of us to take the plunge and actually date someone, so . . ." Marissa paused.

"So, what?" I asked.

"So, I guess the pressure's on."

"Awesome," I replied, my voice dripping with sarcasm.

"Does it feel right to you?" Paige asked.

I thought for a moment. Parker was a complete gentleman. He was kind and sweet, and the way he bobbed his head up and down to jazz was so endearing. What's more, he was a doctor, about my age so probably wanting to settle down, and seemed to like me. A lot. He was definitely Mr. Good-On-Paper, that was for sure, and being with him felt . . . good. No, great.

"Yes, it does." I smiled as the excitement of what I was saying rose inside me.

Paige clapped her hands together, bouncing up and down in her seat. "That's so wonderful, Cassie. Isn't it, Marissa?"

"Yes," Marissa responded, her mouth full of orange and almond syrup cake, so it came out more like "meb."

"Cassie's getting married! Cassie's getting married!" Paige squealed.

I looked around the room, embarrassed. I noticed people at the surrounding tables smiled at me. An elderly woman leaned over and congratulated me on my upcoming nuptials. Self-conscious, I thanked her and hid my left hand under the table and glared at Paige.

Luckily, level-headed Marissa came to my rescue. "Let's not get ahead of ourselves here, Paige. She's only gone on a couple of dates with the guy."

"I know. It's just so exciting the pact is working," Paige replied, undeterred in her enthusiasm.

Marissa let out a sigh. "Well, for Cassie, maybe. Neither of us have any inkling who we're going to go on our Last First Date with, do we Paige? You're it."

I took a sip of my coffee and looked at Paige. She had turned as red as a ripe tomato. "Paige?" I questioned.

She fanned her face in a vain attempt to cool it off. Her blush deepened. "Is it me or is it hot in here?"

Marissa arced her eyebrows. "I think it's just you."

The fanning continued. "Well, I must be having a hot flash or something. That's it. It must be the menopause."

"Paige, you're twenty-seven."

"Okay, so not the menopause. Maybe I'm ill?"

"I know what it is. You like someone, don't you?" Marissa prodded.

By way of response, Paige's blush turned positively nuclear. "Well, I kind of . . . umm . . ." She looked frantically from me to Marissa and back again. "No, no I don't."

I put my hand on Paige's. "You can tell us, honey. If you've met someone, you know we'll be incredibly happy for you."

"And help you vet the living daylights out of the guy," Marissa added.

"Absolutely."

Marissa and I sat as patiently as two friends who've just heard this potentially life-changing news can as Paige studied her hands. "I'm . . . I'm not quite ready to say anything yet."

"Why?" I asked gently. "Is it because you don't know him very well, or are you not sure how you feel about him?"

"No, I know him pretty well, and I've liked him for a while now." Paige bit her lip.

A man's face popped instantly into my head. I narrowed my eyes at her. "It's not 'Poop Boy', is it?"

Marissa laughed. "'Poop Boy'? You crack me up."

Without taking my eyes from Paige, I replied, "Yes. Will Jordan."

I noticed Paige clasp her cup tightly. *Bingo.* I put my hand on her arm. "It is, isn't it?"

Paige nodded. Marissa and I shared a look. We both knew about Paige's crush on Will—hell, it was so well known it could be a recurring item in the company newsletter—but we'd never thought she'd act on it. Or that she would consider Will for her One Last First Date.

"Are you thinking of asking him out?" I asked, trying to sound casual.

Her eyes darted between us. "I . . . I don't know."

Marissa shot me a concerned look. "He has that supermodel girlfriend, doesn't he?"

"Yes, but that won't last forever."

"How do you know?" I asked.

"She's never here. She's always off on some modeling job in a glamorous city. I mean, have either of you actually *met* her?"

We shook our heads.

"Well, no," Marissa replied truthfully. She put her hand on Paige's arm. "This is big. I mean, if you ask him out and he says yes, this is your One Last First Date."

Paige swallowed. "I know." She loaded her fork up with carrot cake with cream cheese icing and took a bite. And then another. She looked lost in thought.

I raised my eyebrows. "He'll need to dump Supermodel Chick before you go anywhere near him. And then there's the fact we don't know how he feels about you. Plus, he's a bit of a jerk, always boasting about himself and things. Frankly, what you see in him is beyond me."

Paige arced an eyebrow. "Finished with all the reasons why he can't be my One Last First Date?"

"Sorry," I muttered, realizing I'd taken things too far. "He's very good-looking. You know, in that obvious, 'look-at-me' kind of manly way." I hoped my offering would placate her.

Marissa laughed. "Us women hate those obviously good-looking guys, don't we?"

Paige managed a smile. "Yeah, we prefer their good looks to be well hidden."

"Look. All those things aside, if you like him and you've really thought this through, then ask him out. Right, Cassie?" Marissa looked at me.

I shrugged. "Sure. Of course." I scooped some of my flourless raspberry chocolate cake into my mouth. Poor Paige, this can only end in tears—for her. "If he breaks up with the model."

Paige beamed. "Thanks, guys."

* * *

Back in the office, I sat at my desk, preparing for my next meeting with Nettco when my phone rang. It was Rottweiler slash Spoodle Brian, Laura's apple-turnover-loving executive assistant.

"Laura would like to know if you could meet with her on the twelfth at ten."

A rush of butterflies flapped around in my belly. "Yes, of course." I tried to sound business-like and professional. With the excitement of what a meeting with Laura meant, I suspect I sounded more like I'd just taken a large breath of helium.

"It's to interview for the position of Regional Manager, Sales," Brian continued needlessly.

"Sure. Great. Thanks, Brian." *Gulp.*

He hung up, and I sat for a moment, staring at the screen. This was really happening. I was about to interview for Regional Manager. Perhaps even *get* the job. I took a deep breath, steadying my nerves.

My phone rang again, making me jump out of my seat.

"There's something for you at reception," Debbie, our receptionist, said.

"That's weird. I'm not expecting anything."

"You'll want this," Debbie replied elusively.

Intrigued, I walked through the office and out into reception. Will was leaning against the desk, chatting to Debbie. I ignored him. "Hi, Debbie. What have you got for me?"

She greeted me with a smile. "It looks like you have an admirer." She leaned down to get whatever she had for me from behind her oversized desk. I tapped my fingers as I waited, staring at the picture behind the desk.

"Having a good day?" Will enquired.

"Yes, thank you." I shot him a terse smile. He might be my temporary boss, but I didn't have to like the guy.

Debbie resurfaced with a large gift basket, covered in cellophane, a pink bow tied at the top.

"What is *that*?" Will asked, quirking his eyebrows and smirking.

I took the basket eagerly and surveyed its contents. Sitting in the basket, holding a saxophone, a red heart-shaped balloon, and a bunch of flowers, was a smiling fluffy ginger cat stuffed toy with pretty green-blue eyes and long whiskers. My heart melted at the sight.

"So? Put us out of our suspense. Who's it from?" Debbie asked eagerly.

"I bet I know," Will responded.

I placed the cat on the desk, located the card, and opened it. A smile spread across my face as my heart contracted. *For my Cassie. No longer a jazz "cat" virgin xx*

I let out a contented sigh as I held the card to my chest,

relishing Parker's words. My Cassie. *My* Cassie.

Debbie was watching me. "Oh, it looks like someone's got it bad. Right, Will?"

Will shook his head. "Date number two must have gone well."

I shrugged. "Maybe." I couldn't help but grin. *Maybe* my foot. Despite my embarrassing jazz *faux pas*—which, judging by the gift I'd just received, Parker found endearing—I was now "Parker's Cassie." Things couldn't possibly be any better.

Debbie turned the gift basket around. Looking it over, she asked, "Why a cat? I mean, don't most guys give teddy bears?"

I blushed. "No, that would be too generic. Something happened on our last date, that's all." I admired the cat, holding the saxophone. "This is perfect."

Will gave me a sideways glance. "Something happened involving a cat?"

"Kind of." There was no way I was going to let Will Jordan know how I had mixed up "scat" with "cat" at the club. Parker may have liked it, but I had my dignity to consider.

Not letting up, he said, "That sounds like a story. Doesn't it, Deb?"

She nodded, her eyes sparkling. "It sure does."

They both looked at me with expectation.

Not wanting to go anywhere near what had actually happened, I collected my basket in my arms. "And not one I'm going to be sharing. Thank you, Debbie."

I turned on my heel to leave, but that pesky Will followed me. "Come on, Dunny. Spill the beans."

I bristled at the nickname. "It's personal." I picked up the pace.

He kept up with ease. "You can tell me. We're friends, aren't we?"

I stopped and turned to face him. He nearly ran into me, stopping in his tracks just in time.

"Look, Will. It's between Parker and me, okay?" *Now shut up!*

He shrugged. "Sure." His voice changed. "Are you serious about this guy?"

I stiffened. Why was Will Jordan asking me such a thing? Like my love life was any concern of his. "As a matter of fact, yes."

He fingered the gift in my hands. "You might want to reconsider. I mean, any guy who gives you a stuffed toy has to be—" He trailed off.

I looked at him in expectation, my anger peaked. "What? A nice guy? Sweet, kind, thoughtful?"

"I was going to say about twelve years old."

I pursed my lips. "Sure. Whatever. You can deride him all you like, but he's wonderful." *And you're not.*

I turned and walked toward my desk.

"Hey, Dunny?"

My face tightened. I let out a puff of air before turning to face him. The haven of my desk was only five feet away, damn him! I pasted on a smile. "What is it, *Will?*" I should have called him "Poop Boy".

"How's the Nettco contract coming?"

"It's looking good, thank you. I'm hoping to present it to them within the week."

"That's great. Let me know if you need any more help."

I took a long inhalation of breath. He was going to ride this I'm-the-one-to-get-Nettco-across-the-line wave for all it was worth. "Will do."

He nodded at me. "Good. Well, I'll let you settle your cat into its new home. Did he get you a litter box for it?" He laughed at his own joke.

"'Bye." I sat down at my desk and opened my laptop to show I meant business.

Thankfully, he got the cue and sauntered back off toward his office. I pretended to type something until I saw him disappear behind his door. Once he was safely tucked away, I pulled the card out to read what Parker had written again. *My Cassie.* I ran my fingers over the handwriting. Was it his or the florist's? It was neat, so probably not his—you know, the whole illegible doctor's scrawl.

Within about two point three seconds, Marissa was at my desk. She patted the cat's head. "From Parker, I assume?"

I grinned. "Yes. Look at what he wrote." I handed her the card and studied her pretty face, waiting for her reaction.

"Aww!" She grinned at me. "Oh, Cassie. He's the best. Making your mistake into something so cute?"

I nodded, my heart giving a squeeze. "I know. I'm so lucky."

She shook her head. "You're going to marry this guy."

I bit my lip. My tummy did a flip-flop. "I am, aren't I?"
And in that moment, I just knew I was.

.

CHAPTER 8

I SAT IN MY car a few days later, clutching a contract firmly in my hand. I let out an excited squeal. They had signed! After all this time, after all the legal to-ing and fro-ing, I had managed to get Nettco to sign on the dotted line, giving us their business for the next three wonderful years. I stomped my feet on the floor as my heart pumped in my chest. *Yes!*

With this account won, I had now officially met my annual sales target. No, scratch that: I'd *exceeded* my annual sales target! I let out a deep long breath as the adrenaline rushed around my body. I couldn't help but grin from ear to ear. I was in serious bonus territory now and had positioned myself very nicely indeed for my interview with Laura for the Regional Manager's position.

I liked Cloud Nine. I was Parker's Cassie, I'd signed the deal, and I'd made my targets. This had been a good week, a very, very good week.

I picked up my phone and pressed Parker's number. It went straight to voicemail. I hung up. I might be his Cassie, but this sort of news deserved more than to be told in a voicemail. I turned the car over and pulled out of the Nettco Head Office car park, happier than a kid at Christmas.

Once back in the office, I burst into Will's office and slapped the contract down on his desk in front of him. He looked up at me, startled. *Good.*

He furrowed his brow. "What did that poor paper ever do to you, Dunny?"

"Nettco signed with us. For three years." I beamed at him, triumphant. Even Will Jordan's stupid nickname for me couldn't put a dent in my euphoria today.

His face broke into a grin, his eyes dancing. "Really?"

I could barely contain my excitement. "Yes, *really*! They've agreed to all the terms and want us to roll 'The Sheldon' out as soon as possible."

"That's amazing!" He bolted out of his chair and around his desk. With his long legs, he was at my side in two seconds flat. He reached out to me. For a moment, I thought he was going to collect me up in a hug. Instead, he stopped short and patted me on the arm awkwardly. "Congratulations. I knew you could do it."

I narrowed my eyes at him. What, no "You couldn't have done it without me"? Was Will Jordan's famous arrogance slipping? I couldn't help but beam at him. "Thanks."

He brushed past me toward his door.

I watched him, puzzled. "Where are you going?"

"We need to ring the bell."

Most sales organizations like to recognize a new big deal when it's signed. For AGD that recognition came in the form of a large brass bell on the wall outside the Regional Manager's office. Will grabbed a hold of the rope and gave the bell a loud ring, grabbing everyone's attention.

When all eyes in the room were on him, Will announced in a loud voice, "Dunny . . . I mean, *Cassie*, just signed the Nettco Electricity deal!"

Everyone clapped, some even cheered. I grinned at the sea of faces, even giving them a little bow. I thoroughly enjoyed the moment.

Marissa came over to me and gave me a hug. "Awesome work, Cassie."

I breathed in her perfume. "Thanks." I grinned at her, my pride surging. I didn't think I'd ever be able to stop smiling today.

After pats on the back and congratulations from my fellow salespeople, I sat back down at my desk. I picked up my phone and pressed Parker's number again. This time, he picked up after a handful of rings.

"Hi, you."

A smile spread across my face at the sound of his voice. "Hi."

"How's your day going?"

"Well." I paused for dramatic effect. "I just signed—"

"Hold on a sec, will you, Cassie?"

I could make out a voice as he muffled the phone. I waited patiently. I knew he was a doctor. I knew he was busy. My news could wait.

"Sorry, Cassie. Look, I have to go. Call you later?"

Despite my rational brain telling me it wasn't personal, I deflated like a punctured balloon. "Sure. That would be nice." I hung up and sat stock still at my desk. I would get the chance to tell him later when he called back. And he would be thrilled for me. After all, I was *his* Cassie.

"Dunny." I was so lost in thought I didn't notice Will until he arrived at my desk. "We need to celebrate this win." He turned to face the team. "Drinks are on me!"

The sales team erupted in cheers.

"Five o'clock at O'Dowd's." He looked back at me. "See you then," he added with one of his cheeky winks

"Sure," I replied, my balloon inflating once more. "And . . . err, thanks."

Five o'clock rolled around, and the sales team arrived *en masse* at O'Dowd's, the lively local Irish bar a stone's throw away from the office. Even though technically Paige isn't part of the team, it wouldn't feel right not to have her there, so Paige, Marissa, and I stood with the assembled masses in the bar as Will made sure we all had a drink in hand.

"Attention, everyone!" Will raised his bottle of beer as heads turned his way. "I'd like to make a toast. To closing a big deal and showing us all how it's done. Cassie Dunhill, known as Dunny to her closest friends." There was a ripple of laughter among the team. "To Dunny!"

"To Dunny!" everyone echoed, raising their glasses and grinning in my direction.

I smiled and nodded back at them, all the while devising how I was going to murder Will Jordan for sharing that repulsive name with the team. "Thanks, everyone. You're awesome!" I ensured my tone was bright and positive. "It's always great to get a big win. And thanks to . . . err, Will for his help with it, too." I knew I had to thank him, even if it riled me to do so. "Cheers back atcha!"

I raised my glass of white wine to toast them all. My short-but-sweet speech over, the crowd returned to their conversations and I turned to Paige and Marissa. "I've got some other news."

My phone vibrated in my suit jacket pocket. "Hold on." I pulled it out and noticed it was Parker calling.

"You can't do that to us!" Marissa complained.

"It's Parker. Be right back." I rushed out of the bar to the relative quiet of the city street outside.

"Where are you? It sounds rowdy."

"I'm outside a bar. We're celebrating my big win."

"What did you win?"

"A big deal. I signed a contract with a customer today. It's kind of a big deal." I swelled with pride.

"That's amazing. Well done."

"Thanks." My future husband, Mr. Supportive-Of-My-Career. I remembered what Paige had said about having Parker on my stomping ground, to show him I was more than a jazz virgin and girl who got barstools caught on my dress. "Hey, do you want to go to a Pilates class with me?"

"Pilates? Is that where you lie down on the ground and do lots of breathing?"

I laughed. His ignorance was both endearing and encouraging: I could totally shine in front of him at a class. "Sort of. It's a bit harder than just that. I go quite often. There's a class on Saturday morning at my studio in Herne Bay. We could go to it, and then grab some brunch afterward?"

"I'd love to but I have golf that day."

My heart sank. I remembered he'd told me he played golf every Saturday morning and that he was a little obsessed with beating his friends. "Oh. No matter."

"Actually, do you know what? I can skip golf this week. I can lie down and breathe in Herne Bay. Let's do Pilates."

My happiness threatened to brim over. "It's a date."

Back in the bar, I found Marissa and Paige in the same spot.

"So?" Paige asked, her face expectant.

"So, we're going to my Pilates class on Saturday."

"Perfect," Paige proclaimed.

"And what was your other big news?" Marissa asked. "You really left us hanging there."

I shrugged. "My future husband was calling." There should be no need to explain further.

Marissa smiled, shaking her head.

Paige stomped her foot. "Tell us!"

With a surge of excitement, I shared the news of my pending interview for Regional Sales Manager with them. I'd played it close to my chest up until now, not wanting to jinx it in any way. But, with the way things were going in both my love life and work life, the Regional Manager's job seemed totally within my reach.

"Oh, my gosh, Cassie! Everything is falling into place," Paige said, nodding her head, her eyes huge.

"Oh, no. Don't you start with that goddess stuff again," Marissa warned.

"It's just what Cassie does now is so important for us," Paige protested, shaking her head. "The fact that things are going so well with Parker, she won the account, and now she's got this interview *has* to mean something."

"Yeah, it does: she's a lucky cow." Marissa nudged me, and we both laughed.

"And it'll be our turn next," Paige added, a look of quiet confidence on her face. I noticed as she glanced over at Will. He was propping up the bar with a couple of my beat-your-chest, he-man team members, laughing at something one of them had grunted. Probably "Me make fire; you get woman."

She blushed when he looked over at us and raised his eyebrows.

"Hey, didn't you say Will helped you win this deal?" Marissa asked. She drained her glass.

I looked back over at him. He was drinking a beer and laughing at something one of The Cavemen had said. "Yeah, he did."

"Why didn't he boast about that, then, do you think?" Marissa asked.

I wrinkled my brow. Why indeed?

* * *

I set my alarm early on Saturday morning, and it pulled me out of a deep, dreamless sleep with a terrible shock. I hit the "snooze" button and rolled over, determined to catch another few minutes of precious sleep when my eyes pinged open: I had my Pilates date with Parker this morning!

Despite the chill of the morning air—and the fact it was dark and miserable outside—I threw my blankets off and bounded out of bed, heading straight to the bathroom. I had set my alarm extra early today to allow enough time to look super Pilates cute for Parker. And that took time, people! Sadly, I was not one of those women who rolled out of bed looking well rested and beautiful. Oh, no. My hair was usually flattened on one side of my face and all bird's nest-y on the other, my eyes puffy, and for reasons known only to some mysterious force, my nose actually looked bigger. Still, it was nothing a shower, hair straighteners, and a touch of makeup couldn't fix.

Sometime later, I was dressed in my cutest top and yoga pants, my socks with special grips so I didn't slip over and embarrass myself in front of Parker again, and sneakers. My hair was freshly straightened, my makeup perfect. I glanced in the mirror as I collected my keys from the kitchen counter. *Yes.* I looked just right.

We'd arranged to meet at the Pilates studio a few minutes before the class. As I pulled up, I saw Parker, dressed in track pants, sneakers, and a sweatshirt, reading something on his phone outside the entrance. I jumped out of the car and walked over to him, my mat rolled up under my arm.

"Good morning, handsome," I chirped.

He looked up from his phone, and his face broke into a wide grin. "Hey, Cassie." He took me by the hands and pulled me in for a kiss.

"Ready for this?"

He shrugged. "How hard can it be?"

I grinned. "You'll see."

Once inside the studio, I greeted a few of the regulars and Parker and I found a spot toward the back of the room where I rolled out my mat.

Parker looked at it down on the floor, concerned. "I didn't bring one of those."

"No worries. I'll get you one." I wandered to the front of the class and picked him up one of the studio mats. I placed it next to mine.

Parker crooked his finger. I took a step closer to him.

"You look really cute in your Pilates gear," he whispered in my ear with a smile.

I blushed. "Thanks."

"So, what do we do?"

"See the woman near the front? That's Monica. She's the instructor. She'll get the music going, and then start the class."

"Music?"

"Not jazz." I laughed. "More regular stuff. You know, the sort of thing you'd hear on the radio."

Someone approached us. "Hi, Cassie. Who's your friend?" It was Nancy, one of a gaggle of super fit, middle-aged, stay-at-home mothers.

"Hi, Nancy. This is Parker. He's my . . . ah . . ." *Do I say boyfriend? Man of my dreams? Future husband?* My tummy did a flip. *Definitely can't say the last two.*

In the end, I didn't need to put a label on him—Parker did it for me. "Hi, Nancy." Parker extended his hand. "I'm Cassie's boyfriend." He gave me a sideways glance and grinned at me.

Heat radiated through my chest. I smiled so much my face could have cracked in two. I was Parker's girlfriend. Parker's girlfriend! We were Parker and Cassie. Cassie and Parker. I wondered what our celebrity couple name should be. Passie? *Ah, no.* Carker? *Yeah, I'll need to work on that.*

"Oh!" Nancy's eyes got huge. "This is news. Cassie?"

With great reluctance, I tore my eyes from Parker's. "Umm, yes. Parker's my boyfriend." Like a magnet, my eyes were drawn immediately back to Parker's now glowing face. He reached across and took my hand in his. It was warm and reassuring, adding to my bliss.

Nancy clapped her hands together. "Well, don't you two look a picture."

"What's this?" One of the other gaggle's interest had been piqued. Nicole, a larger woman with thighs of steel who could outdo us all with her impressive lower abdominals, joined our group.

"This is Parker, Cassie's new *boyfriend*," Nancy declared.

I knew I was blushing. I didn't care.

Nicole raised her bushy eyebrows, not-so-subtly sizing Parker up. "Well, you're quite the strapping young man, aren't you?"

"Err, yes. I guess," Parker replied with a laugh.

I squeezed his hand.

Nicole grabbed him by the upper arm. "Not bad. Do you work out?"

"Yes, I do. I go to the gym three times a week, run, and play golf."

"Well, golf isn't going to do that for you, honey," Nicole scoffed. "What do you do for a living?"

And so began what we would later refer to as The Great Interrogation of Parker. He held up well, answering their questions with aplomb, never once letting go of my hand. When Janice and Claire got in on the action, Parker began to look a little overwhelmed. And who could blame him? Four menopausal women poking and prodding him like he was a piece of prime cut steak, quizzing him mercilessly about me, about his life, about anything they wanted to know, really. At least no one had asked what his intentions were toward me, although they came pretty close.

I was relieved for both of us when Monica addressed the class. "Hello, all. Welcome, welcome. Let's all start with a few warm-up exercises, shall we? Get those bodies moving on this cold Saturday morning?"

We went through a series of movements as Parker and I stole glances at one another, sharing a smile whenever our eyes met. It was a great feeling. The best! He could keep up with all the exercises, despite grinning his face off during the "bridge" position—in which you lie on your back with your feet by your butt and push your hips up into the air to work on those "buns"—and making me giggle. At one stage, Monica shot me a look—the first time that'd ever happened in all my years of coming to this class. But I didn't care. I was having a wonderful time with Parker, my boyfriend, sharing something I loved with him.

And, what's more, I didn't fall over, say something wrong, or come across as an idiot. I was poised and in control the whole time. Other than the giggle, that is. But that was neither here nor there.

Parker, on the other hand, struggled through the more advanced abdominal section, flopping in a heap on his mat. I persisted, shooting him a supportive smile, all the while enjoying the feeling

I was better at something than him. Paige was right; Pilates was a great idea.

Afterwards, Parker suggested we go to Alessandro's for brunch. Although I've never been a fan of its high ceilings, endless chrome and glass—too cold and sterile for my liking—I agreed, and we drove the short distance into the city.

Alessandro's was heaving, and we were lucky to get a small table near the huge coffee machine, which was in constant use, squirting and steaming and generally making a racket. We both chose eggs benedict, coffee, and juice. I smiled to myself, another thing we had in common.

"So, how did you like your first Pilates session?" I asked between bites. "God, this is good!"

"I told you! You'll learn to love Alessandro's, trust me."

I scanned the café, my mouth full of the delicious combination of egg, ham, and hollandaise. It was a very chic place and clearly popular with a mixture of the city's well-to-dos and hipsters alike. I could see why Parker liked it. But it wasn't the Cozy Cottage.

"Pilates was all right," Parker said, bringing my attention back to him. "Those ab exercises were a little more intense than I'd expected. I do crunches at the gym, but not hundreds with my legs flailing about in the air like an ant."

I laughed. "Your legs didn't flail. You looked good." My eye twitched as an image of him in a collapsed heap on the mat sprung into my head.

"You were watching me, were you?" He smiled, looking at me through his lashes.

"Maybe a little." I smiled back. We were doing a lot of smiling at each other today. It was beyond wonderful.

Oh, yes. I could get used to being Parker Hamilton's girlfriend.

CHAPTER 9

I SPENT THE NEXT week in Parker Bliss Mode, now officially my favorite brain setting, the one I hoped would stick around for the rest of my life. And it really was spectacular. We talked and kissed, strolled through the park, kissed, ate, and kissed, and kissed some more. It was pure, unadulterated, dating nirvana.

By the time my interview for the Regional Sales Manager's job rolled around, I felt completely ready. I had been blessed by Lady Luck: how could I not get this job, the icing on my already sizeable cake?

I collected my compendium from my desk and headed out the door and up the flight of stairs to the twelfth floor, trying to steady my nerves with each step. At the top, I pulled the stairwell door open and came face to face with none other than "Poop Boy" himself, Will Jordan.

"Well, well, well. If it isn't Dunny Dunhill."

I nodded at him, my mouth terse. "Hello, 'Poop Boy'."

He chuckled. "What are you doing up here on the exec level? Been a naughty girl, have we?"

I crossed my arms and glared at him. "I have an appointment, actually." My air was defiant. And what was it with this "naughty" rhetoric? Couldn't he think of anything new, for crying out loud?

He raised his eyebrows. "An appointment, huh? Intriguing." He tapped his fingers on his chin.

"Not really. Now, if you wouldn't mind?" I gestured at the door he was currently blocking.

He stood back for me and bowed. "Of course, Duchess Dunny. I am, as always, your most humble servant."

I rolled my eyes. *I wish.*

I approached Rottweiler slash Spoodle Brian's desk. "Morning, Brian." I smiled at him when he looked up from his computer.

"Cassie. What, no treat for me today?"

Totally thrown, I bumbled, "I . . . err, no. Sorry."

"That's okay. I hardly need it." He patted his protruding belly.

He was totally correct, but I wasn't about to say anything about it. "Shall I just wait here? I've got an appointment to see Laura at ten."

He held his finger up, telling me to wait. He stood up and knocked on her door, and I watched as he poked his head through a crack. A moment later, he turned to me and told me to go in.

I took a deep breath and walked through the door. I was met by Laura and Hugo from Human Resources, both sitting on those plush leather sofas I covet, notepads on their knees. They both stood and greeted me with handshakes.

We took our seats, and the interview began. And I nailed it. I was completely prepared for everything they threw at me. They complimented me on my successes, including the recent Nettco win, talked about my leadership potential, and even laughed at my jokes.

Afterwards, I sailed down the stairs, my head filled with the interview and the possibilities it offered, back to my desk in the sales department.

"How did it go?" Marissa asked eagerly, almost before my butt hit the seat.

I grinned at her. "It went well. Really well."

She perched her aerobicized butt on the edge of my desk. "Oh, I really hope you get it. Then, I can get your job!"

"That would be so great!" I had an image of Marissa and me working together, her my star Account Director, me her gracious and magnanimous boss.

"When do you find out?"

"They told me they're putting their short list together over the next couple of weeks. I'll know if I'm on that list soon. Oh, I hope I am."

Marissa brushed my momentary doubt aside with her hand.

"You will be. No worries."

I smiled at her as my excitement rose once more. Marissa's confidence was impressive. She was one of those people whose self-belief was unshakeable, who always believed things would work out, despite having a sizeable dollop of cynicism thrown into the mix.

"Now, are we going in your car on Tuesday to Napier or do you want me to drive?"

I felt a sudden stiffness in my neck. The sales team retreat. I'd forgotten all about it in the wake of everything that had been happening with Parker and at work. We did it annually at the end of the financial year. Kind of like a reset for the upcoming twelve months. This year, Richard had arranged for the sales team to spend a few days in Napier, a city in the beautiful wine-growing region of Hawke's Bay. The idea was that we would take some time out to talk about our sales strategies, how to improve the team, and to have some much-needed fun.

"I'm happy to drive."

Marissa grinned. "Road trip!"

I shook my head. "You're funny. It won't be the same without Paige, though."

"It'd be great if she could come. We'll have to get her to change her career to sales."

I smiled. "Just so she can go on the retreat?"

"Exactly. Then, she won't have to miss out on anything. Have you told Parker?"

"That Paige is not in sales?" I asked, a cheeky grin on my face. "Yeah, I told him I had to go away. We're seeing each other once I get back."

"So?" Marissa lead, her eyes sparkling.

"So, what?"

"Have you done it yet?"

If I'd been drinking coffee, I would have chocked on it. I felt my face warm. My eyes darted around the room. No one appeared to be listening in. "We, ah . . . I think that will happen after the Napier trip."

Marissa smirked at me. "Wow. Big night."

I smiled back at her as my tummy did a flip—out of excitement and nerves. "Yeah."

"And?" She raised her eyebrows at me.

"And what?"

"Have either of you dropped the L-word yet?"

"No," I replied in a quiet voice as Marissa leaned down to my level. "It's too soon."

She scoffed. "Too soon for your *plan*?"

I shrugged. Of course, she'd hit the nail on the head. In my plan, we didn't say "I love you" until we'd been on a minimum of twelve dates. Any sooner and it may just be lust talking, any later and I might be wasting my time.

You see, my life plan worked on both a macro level and a micro level. My macro plan was career, home, marriage, kids. My micro plan mapped out when each step to achieve these larger goals took place. In the romance stakes, Date Twelve was "I love you," and meeting one another's parents needed to happen by Date Twenty at the very latest. And a marriage proposal? Well, I could be a little more flexible with that, although it needed to happen before a full year of dating was done. Because otherwise? Well, let's just say I was on a tight schedule with this.

Our eleventh date was just around the corner.

"The date after next is the big twelfth date. It'll happen by then." I glanced at the ginger cat, sitting next to my computer screen. A smile teased at the edges of my mouth as a sense of peacefulness pervaded my chest. "I have no doubt."

Marissa smiled back at me. "Look at you. You're already in love."

I blushed. "Maybe." I thought about all the things we'd done together, about the kind of man Parker was, about how he seemed to feel about me. He was as close as anyone I had ever met to being my perfect man. Was I in love? Well, if I wasn't, I was very well on my way to being so.

* * *

Marissa and I drove through the entrance gates of the beautiful old Monastery Estate Winery late on Tuesday afternoon. We'd had the classic road trip experience: eating junk food, singing along to our favorite playlists, talking about anything and everything, and stopping to shop whenever the whim took us. So maybe it was more of a *girls'* classic road trip experience. Girl road trip heaven, even. Just the way we liked it.

"I need to be your maid of honor," Marissa insisted as she searched her phone for our next pop-tastic music compilation.

"Well, I have to think of Paige, too. I know, how about I make you both maid of honor?"

Marissa laughed. "I'm not sure it works that way."

"It can if I want it to. It's *my* wedding, you know." Or it would be, once Parker had asked me to marry him. Which I knew was on the cards. We had been on our eleventh date on Saturday night, and he had told me I was unlike any other girl he'd dated and that he really, really liked me (his words). With the all-important twelfth date coming up on Friday night, I knew that was about to turn into the big L-word.

"Okay. That's fine with me, but you have to let me choose the bridesmaids dresses. I don't want Paige and her kooky hippy ideas anywhere near it."

I laughed. "Sure. Ooh, look. There's that place we stopped at last time we were at Lake Taupo. I call a shopping stop!" I pulled the car over and parked. And so began the third shopping expedition of our road trip. So far, the trip to Napier had taken twice as long as it ought.

As I said, it was girl road trip heaven.

An hour and a half later, we drove through the suburban streets of the city of Napier, looking for the winery. Marissa looked out the window. "The sat nav is saying it's two blocks away, but this looks too much like suburban paradise for there to be a winery here."

Sure enough, two blocks later the suburb came to an end and we were faced with a magnificent view. We looked up a hill to a large, white colonial building, nestled amongst established gardens, looking out over the valley stretching out to the bay below.

"Wow, this place is amazing." I drove up the long, tree-lined driveway. I took in row up row of vines, stretching as far as the eye could see across the flat and up over the rolling hills.

Marissa read from her brochure. "It says here it was built by the Catholic Church in the eighteen hundreds for European monks to grow grapes to make wine." She looked back up. "This place is magical."

The dappled sunlight danced on the windscreen as we wound our way up to the main building, bright in the famous Hawke's Bay sun. I pulled the car into an angled parking spot and peeked out the window at the impressive colonial building before us. "I can't believe we get to stay in this amazing house. It's how old?"

"Very. Like, older than your nana." Marissa opened her door, climbed out of the car, and stretched. "That's Will's car. He must have beaten us here."

I closed the car door and put my sunglasses on top of my head. "Marissa, I think a team of elderly grandmothers on a Sunday drive would have beaten us, we took so long getting here."

She shrugged, playing with her newly acquired bead necklace slung around her neck. "Important things to do."

"Welcome, ladies." Will, dressed in shorts and a polo shirt, walked out the entrance to the grand old building. Accompanying him was Sally Saunders, another member of our team, wearing a pretty sundress and floppy hat.

"Hey, guys," Marissa said. "Not a bad spot here."

"I know, right?" Sally replied. "You should go and have a look at the view from the restaurant through there. It's incredible."

Will sidled up to me. "Glad to see you made it, Dunny. We were worried about you."

Sure you were. I shrugged. "We had things to do."

He peered in the window of the backseat of my car, taking in the shopping bags and discarded junk food wrappers. "I can see that. Where did you go?"

"Places." I deflected his line of questioning. "I can't wait to see our rooms. This house is amazing."

"Actually, we're staying in the old monks' quarters out the back." He nodded his head toward the hill behind us.

I raised my eyebrows. "Monks' quarters? Are you serious?"

"Yup. It's not bad. A bit like a boarding school, I guess, but nice enough."

"Shared bathrooms. You need to tell her that part, Will," Stephanie added.

"Oh." My heart sank. I had been swept away by the romance of staying in the main house, imagining myself taking tea on the terrace, playing croquet on the lawn. Now I get a dormitory where monks, who weren't exactly known for their lavish luxury, used to sleep.

"Don't worry, Dunny." Will punched me playfully on the arm. "We each get our own room, it's not like we're bunking or anything. And our meeting room is in the main house. We're having dinner there tomorrow night."

"What are we doing tonight?" Marissa asked.

Will wrapped one arm around my shoulder and one around Marissa's. "Tonight, my minions, we're going bowling."

I grinned, pushing the image of us as little yellow people in dungarees from my mind. I gave Marissa a sideways smile. Bowling? Oh, yes.

Bring. It. On.

* * *

"I need three people to volunteer for team captains," Will said as we were seated on the coach, transporting "his minions"—*don't get me started*—to the bowling alley.

Marissa nudged me in the ribs. "Volunteer! You want to be the boss, right?"

I needed no further encouragement. I shot my hand up.

"Great, thanks, Sally and Raj. Anyone else?"

I pushed my hand as high as I could. If I'd added, "ooh, ooh!" I could have been on a school bus on a trip to a museum. Yes, I had been a bit of a nerd in school.

"No one?" Will asked.

I shot darts at Marissa. "Is he seriously doing this?" I hissed at her.

"Maybe you should stand up."

"I'm not that short! My hand does reach above the top of the seat, you know." With a huff, I stood up, and said with a clear voice, "I'll do it, Will."

"Great. Didn't see you there. Thanks. So, we have our team leaders. Now, I'll number you off from one to four."

I looked around at Sally and Raj, then back at Will. "Why four?"

"You, Sally, Raj, and me."

Silly me.

Will pointed at each of us, giving us our team number. He then proceeded to walk down the bus pointing at each and every person, giving them a number. When he was finished, he announced which number went with which leader. I hoped I had a good team but knew it wouldn't be clear until we were off the bus.

"Oh, Cassie. You've *so* got this," Marissa said.

Marissa was right. I had virtually grown up at the bowling alley. My dad used to take my big brother and me there every Thursday evening from when I could walk. It was my favorite time of the week: Dad Time. We'd eat junk food, laugh, and bowl. Dad was the king and taught us all he knew, which was a lot.

I narrowed my eyes at Will as he took his seat at the front of the bus. *Yeah, I've got this.*

My phone beeped. My heart gave a little squeeze when I saw it was a text from Parker.

Missing you! xx

I smiled. I texted back.

Me too. Going bowling! xx

A reply came within seconds.

Lucky you.

My smile broadened. I didn't know Parker liked to bowl. This would be another thing we could share together.

Once we all had our rented bowling shoes in hand, I sized my group up. I didn't get Marissa, but that was okay since she had bowled precisely twice in her life and had taken the prize for Worst Player with her persistent gutter balls in our last match. She wasn't what could be called "a natural." I did get Big Jake, however, one of The Cavemen, as we referred to the gang of back-slapping, loud, trash-talking men from the sales team. And he was good. Really good. He and I had been on the same side a couple of years back when we beat Richard's team in the final. It was an epic victory. Would history repeat itself tonight? I certainly hoped so.

The bowling began. My team was good. We all either had strikes or spares nearly every bowl. I congratulated them all. We were on fire!

I eyed the other teams' scores. We were ahead of all but one of them: Will's team. I ground my teeth. He was *not* going to beat me and my team.

It was down to Big Jake's last bowl. He'd managed so many

strikes and spares, no one dared doubt his ability. And then he bowled his worst bowl of the night, hitting only the four middle pins, creating a huge gulf, right down the middle. Big Jake knitted his brows together. He was determined, he was focused, but we all knew that was one tricky bowl.

"You can do this!" Prue shouted, followed by "Yeah!" and "Come on!" from the rest of our team.

I watched as Big Jake's shoulders tightened. He was feeling the pressure. He lifted his ball. He eyed his target, appeared to glance to the heavens—with the scores this close, we needed all the help we could get—looked back at the pins, and then bowled that ball.

We all watched in agonizing silence as it scuttled down toward its target. It smashed through the pins, making that satisfying clank, only hitting the three pins on the left, missing the ones on the right entirely.

Our team's collective hearts sank.

Big Jake slunk back to us and plunked his large frame down on his seat.

"Don't worry about it," Prue said kindly as she patted his back.

"Yeah, man. It could have happened to any of us," Tim reassured. "It's up to you now, Cassie."

I took a deep breath. Will's team had finished, posting a final score of 198. That meant I needed to get a strike to win. Nothing less would cut it.

"Come on, Dunny. Let's see what you've got," Will goaded from across the tables.

I glared at him. He had that self-satisfied smile on his Poldark face I so dearly wanted to wipe off. With a piece of sandpaper. Or a chainsaw.

I raised my chin. It felt so important to win this, like my future depended on it. Win this and I would win the job. And then I could wipe that irritating grin off his face once and for all.

I collected my ball from the rack, slotting my clammy fingers into the holes. I eyed my target. Ten pins, waiting for this ball to knock them over.

"You've got this!"

"Come on, Cassie!"

I stepped up to the edge of the alley, eyeing my target. I could hear my dad's voice in my head, telling me to stay calm, block out any distractions, and bowl like I meant it. I took a deep breath, swung the ball behind me, and bowled. It shot down the alley. I could barely look, my heartbeat loud in my ears. Within seconds, it hit the pins with a *PAWOCK!* sending them clanking in all directions. I held my breath as the last pin on the right wobbled precariously.

Drop! Drop! Drop!

It wobbled from side to side, as if on a string commandeered from above. Eventually, painstakingly, it fell to the floor.

We had won.

My teammates whooped, erupting from their seats and crowding around me, congratulating me and themselves on our epic win. Big Jake lifted me up onto his shoulder as though I were a bag of feathers. Despite potential vertigo—you don't get the nickname "Big Jake" without being one large, tall guy—I beamed at my teammates below. I was on top of the world, not just Big Jake's shoulder.

"You were lucky, Dunny," Will said, once I was back on *terra firma.*

I squared my shoulders. "Luck had nothing to do with it, actually. It was skill, pure and simple."

He smiled. "Well, you've certainly got that." He turned to the rest of my team. "All right, Team Dunny. Victory drinks are on me at the bar!"

Everyone cheered and drifted over to the bowling alley bar to claim their prize.

"Where did you learn to bowl like that?" Will asked as I sat, slipping my bowling shoes off.

"I used to bowl as a kid."

"Me, too! My dad used to take us most weeks. My brothers and I got pretty competitive."

Knowing Will as I did, I commented, "I bet you did." I stood up, bowling shoes in hand.

He punched me playfully on the arm. "Well, it takes one to know one. You're pretty good. Remind me to organize a different activity next team retreat."

I narrowed my eyes at him. "You think you've got this job in the bag, don't you?"

"Maybe. Why, have you applied?"

I pursed my lips. "What's it to you?"

He shrugged. "Just asking, that's all. It doesn't make any difference to me."

My hackles rose. Was he really writing off my chances of getting the job? "Actually, Will. I did apply. And I think I have a pretty good chance of getting it."

He nodded, studying my face. "Game on?" He raised his eyebrows as he extended his hand.

I crossed my arms, ignoring it. I nodded, my jaw set.

"Game on."

CHAPTER 10

THE FOLLOWING MORNING, I woke to the birds chirping their cheery song outside my dormitory window. I stretched, reaching my arms above my head and pointing my toes under the covers. My mind skipped around, settling on Team Dunhill's famous win at the bowling alley last night. We had celebrated, basking in our well-deserved glory, through drinks and dinner. Man, it had felt good—especially beating "Poop Boy".

And now I'd outed myself to him. He knew I was running against him for the Regional Sales Manager job. Good. It was better to have it out in the open. No need to pretend. We were clear adversaries, and we could treat one another as such.

I threw the bed covers off, swung my legs over the side of the bed, and slipped them into my UGG boots to protect them from the ice-cold hardwood floorboards. I collected my towel and toilet bag and padded down the hall to the communal bathroom. With any luck, I would be the first up and could luxuriate in a long, hot shower.

I put my hand on the bathroom doorknob and pushed the door open. I took a step into the room, stopped, and stood in shock, taking in the naked torso of a man with his back to me, wearing nothing but a towel tied around his waist. His head was down as water poured into the sink before him. I gripped the doorknob, rooted to the spot.

How embarrassing!

I needed to get out of here before he raised his head and saw me in the reflection. Without taking my eyes from his broad, toned back, I took a step back, just as his head rose.

"Cassie?"

Our eyes locked in the mirror.

It was *Will*? I gave him a weak smile. "Ah . . . hi."

He turned to face me, a half smile on his face. "Good morning."

Don't look at his chest! Don't look at his chest! My eyes didn't listen, skipping over his broad shoulders, his defined pecs, down to his taut belly.

Oh, my.

I bit my lip as my hand darted to my own chest in an attempt to still my heart. I forced myself to drag my eyes up to his face. Will's half smile had turned into a full grin, his eyebrows raised in question. "Nice pj's."

My eyes shot down to the teddy bears on my T-shirt. Self-consciously, I hugged my towel and toilet bag against my body. Like they were being dragged by some sort of magnetic force, my traitorous eyes returned to Will's chest. "I'm . . . ah . . . sorry to disturb you," I managed. I took a step back, let go of the doorknob, letting the door fly shut.

I heard a chuckle. "No worries. I'll be done in a minute," came Will's muffled reply from within.

I stared at the door.

Well, that was weird.

I shook my head, breaking the spell. Clutching my towel and toilet bag to my chest, I hurried down the hall, back to the safety of my dormitory, closing the door firmly behind me.

My eyes flicked to my phone. Parker. I'll call Parker. I picked my phone up and pressed his number.

"Good morning," Parker's voice answered after a few rings. "You're up bright and early."

"Yes, I . . . I just wanted to say hello."

"Well, hello then. How was your night?"

I thought of the fun we'd had winning the bowling and the subsequent celebrations. "It was really good, thanks."

"You managed to get through the bowling all right?"

What does he mean, "get through the bowling"? "Yes. In fact"—I paused for dramatic effect—"my team won!"

"That's fantastic!"

There was a knock on my door, causing me to levitate off the narrow bed by about two feet. My heart rate kicked up again.

"It's all yours," Will called from outside in the hallway.

"Err, thanks," I replied, my hand over the mouthpiece. "Sorry, Parker."

"Who was that?" Parker asked.

"Oh, just . . . Marissa, telling me the bathroom's free."

Why did I just lie to him?

"You have to share a bathroom? Well, that's not ideal."

"I know, right?"

A few moments later I had said goodbye to Parker and snuck down the hallway on light feet to the bathroom. Tentatively, I opened the bathroom door and peered around, eternally grateful there was no sign of anyone—let alone a scantily clad Will Jordan.

Another encounter like that I could do without.

* * *

Later that morning, I walked into the conference room. Its walls were wood-paneled, with large dormer windows, and there was a large oak table in the middle of the room, surrounded by about twenty chairs.

I had gone to the bathroom after breakfast to freshen up and was one of the last to arrive in the grand, old room.

"Over here, Cassie!" Marissa called. "I've got you a seat."

Will was standing at the front of the room, checking his presentation. I had two options to get to Marissa: either walk right past him or go the long way around and avoid him completely. I took the second option.

As I plunked my laptop down on the table next to Marissa, Will called out, "Hi, Dunny. Are you all better now?" He had an amused look on his face.

I jutted my chin out and turned to face him as my cheeks burned with embarrassment. Will Jordan was not going to get the better of me. "Yes, thank you, 'Poop Boy'. I'm doing great."

Damn him! He probably now thought I was one of those women at AGD who was half in love with him. Like Paige.

I sat down, heavily.

Marissa narrowed her gaze at me. "What's up with you and

Will?"

"Nothing. What?" I snapped. My palms began to sweat.

She studied me for a moment. "You're a bit . . . uptight."

I shrugged, trying to appear unfazed, despite the growing holes her eyes bored into my face. There was no way I was going to make mention of any half-naked men in bathrooms. "I told Will I'm in the running for the Regional Sales Manager's job last night," I said quietly in her ear.

Why am I lying to one of my best friends?

Marissa's eyes got big. "You did? Why?"

I glanced over at Will. He had his back to me. It was so much easier when he had his shirt on. "Because then it's out in the open. I don't have to pretend. He knows who he's up against"

"I guess," she replied, sounding as sure as a lemming being led to the cliff's edge.

"Right, everyone. Let's get down to it. We've got a lot to cover today," Will began, smiling at us all from the front of the room.

I rolled my eyes. Having to listen to Will talk all morning was hardly my idea of a fun way to spend my time. "Here goes nothing," I said to Marissa.

And it dragged. Oh, how it dragged. We talked about our goals for the year, our strategies and tactics, and new products in the pipeline. I watched with a bad taste in my mouth as half the women in the room flirted their faces off with him and the men joked around with him, enjoying their caveman camaraderie. It was enough to make me vomit.

We finally broke for lunch. We sat down at a long table outside on a brick patio. It was one of those cool, crisp, sunny winter days. The view of the city below and on over the sparkling blue of the bay from our elevated position was breathtaking. We were all bundled up in our warm coats—well, the women anyway, the men were, as ever, seemingly impervious to the cold— with heat lamps dotted around us.

Our first course delivered, Marissa leaned in, and whispered, "Why is there an empty seat next to Will?"

"Perhaps no one wanted to sit next to him?" I smiled at the thought.

"Oh, I get it." Marissa nodded at Will. Laura had arrived. Will leaped up from his seat to shake her hand, welcoming her.

She addressed us all. "Hello, everyone. It looks like you've got a pretty spectacular spot here."

Will—suck-up that he was—pulled the chair next to him out for her to sit down. Everyone settled into conversation as we ate.

After dessert of a delicious lemon and raspberry cheesecake that could almost meet the Cozy Cottage Café's high standards, Laura stood up from her seat and clinked her glass. "May I have your attention, please? Thank you, thank you. Well, it's been quite a year for you all. I wanted to come here personally today to share with you the excellent news. Your team as a whole has achieved target!"

We all applauded. Big Jake and some of the other guys whooped and cheered.

"We have a few outstanding performers I would like to take the opportunity to acknowledge. First of all, Will. Not only have you stepped up to the plate as Regional Sales Manager—and done an amazing job, I might add—"

I clenched my jaw.

"—but you are also our top salesperson of the year! Well done, Will."

The team applauded again, and a grinning Will bowed his head, lapping the attention up.

"But that's not all. Cassie Dunhill was a close second with her wonderful Nettco Electricity deal. Well done to you, Cassie."

Marissa squeezed my hand. "Awesome!"

I grinned at her through clenched teeth. Coming second to Will Jordan grated.

"Other stellar performances this year have come from Tamati Southie, Marissa Jones, and Sally Saunders. Well done!"

It was my turn to squeeze my friend's hand in congratulations. "You're a total star."

After the applause had calmed down, Laura raised her glass. "To a wonderful year. Well done, all of you."

After lunch, Laura called me over to where Will and she were standing at the end of the lawn, overlooking the rows of vines below.

"Cassie. Thanks for joining us. I have a task for you both."

I looked at Will. He looked back at me and shrugged nonchalantly. *Does anything rattle this guy?*

I took the lead. "Of course. What can I help you with, Laura?"

"I need two strong leaders to work with Marketing on delivering a new solution they've been working on for some time now. We need input from a sales perspective, and to be honest, they need some direction. It will need to be in addition to your day jobs, of course. Are you up for the challenge?"

I opened my mouth to speak, but suck-up Will got in there first. "Of course, Laura. I'm always ready for a fresh challenge."

"Great. I knew you would. Cassie?"

My muscles tightened. "Absolutely. I'm there for you one hundred percent."

"Thank you. It will be for a good couple of months, starting the moment you're back in the city. I'll have Brian email you both the relevant background information today and schedule a meeting with Dwight Barlow. We need to get this solution packaged up and ready to hit the market yesterday, so time is of the essence."

This time I got in first. "I won't let you down, Laura."

"No, *we* won't," Will added with that smarmy half smile of his, raising his eyebrows at me.

My smile was pinched. Working with Will Jordan? I knew I was going to need all the tolerance I could muster—and leave him for dead.

CHAPTER 11

THE MOOD WAS UPBEAT at our usual table at the Cozy Cottage Café on Friday morning.

"Here you go, ladies." Bailey placed our sweet treats on the table in front of us. "I see you've broken with tradition today, Cassie."

I smiled up at her from my seat. "What can I say? I'm a sucker for a good sugar cookie. And yours are the best."

She beamed. "Thank you. It was my mother's recipe." A shadow passed over her face momentarily before she broadened her smile once more. "I've got a moment. What's the latest?" She pulled a spare seat out from the table and sat down, looking at me expectantly.

"Well," I began, enjoying the chance to talk about recent events once more, "my boss's boss has asked me to work on a special project. She said she needs good leadership. I met with the Marketing Manager today, and I've got a lot of work to do. Although, I have to work with a guy I don't like." I glanced at Paige. "Sorry, but I don't."

She shrugged. "No worries. Hey, do you think this is Laura checking you both out to see who would be best for the Regional Sales Manager job?"

"Of course it is." Marissa nodded. "This way she gets to directly compare Will with Cassie."

I gave a severe nod. "So, I have to totally kill this."

Paige and Marissa both nodded along with me. We all looked

grim, contemplating my task.

Bailey furrowed her brow. "I meant with your boyfriend. The one you're going to marry?"

"Oh. Right. Well, we're on date twelve tonight."

Paige and Marissa's faces both lit up. "It's a big one," Marissa said.

"It is?" Bailey asked.

"Oh, yes. This is the one where they profess their love for one another," Paige confirmed.

"Really?" Bailey raised her eyebrows. "That *is* a big one. But . . . how do you know that's what's going to happen? Are you planning on saying it first?"

"God, no!" I guffawed.

"He will." Paige's confidence matched mine.

Bailey's eyes darted between the three of us. "I don't get it. How do you know?"

"Because Cassie has it all mapped out," Marissa explained.

Bailey's face was still a study in confusion. "If you say so." She looked up as the bell above the door chimed. "Customers. Gotta go." She stood up and pushed her chair under the table. "You have to tell me everything on Monday. Promise, Cassie?"

"I promise."

With Bailey gone, Marissa, Paige, and I drank our coffee and ate our treats, talking about my new project and Parker.

"How about you, Marissa? Anyone you've got your eye on for your One Last First Date?" I asked between mouthfuls.

She let out a sigh. "No. I mean, I meet these guys and they seem really nice, then I find out something terrible about them. It's in the too hard basket for me."

"The right guy will come along when you least expect it," Paige commented with a smile. "You'll see."

Marissa harrumphed, clearly not convinced by Paige's optimism. "I'm not even sure I'm buying into this whole One Last First Date thing, anyway."

"Well, you should," Paige replied. Marissa rolled her cynical eyes and Paige changed the subject back to me. "Where are you going for the big twelfth date tonight?"

"Nowhere. He's coming over to my place, and I'm cooking him dinner."

Paige's eyes got huge. "Is that a good idea? I mean, *I* love your cooking, of course. Yum yum." She rubbed her tummy. "But maybe Parker . . . won't?" She looked to Marissa for support.

"I've already told her," Marissa said, shaking her head. "She won't listen."

I laid my hands flat on the table. "Look, I know I'm not the best cook in the world. But Parker is a traditional kind of guy. I want him to see I can cook."

"Can you? Cook, I mean?" Marissa asked, looking innocent, like it was a genuine question, which it most certainly was not.

"I can," I replied firmly. My mind darted to the last time I cooked for Paige and Marissa. I had been very ambitious and invited a number of people over for a dinner party to celebrate my birthday. Cutting a long story, a bout of salmonella, and minor weight loss short, we ended up ordering pizza. It was very good. "It will be just for him and me. No grand plans. Just a simple dinner for two."

"That sounds lovely." Paige smiled at me, that dreamy look in her eyes once more.

"Well, it sounds to *me* you're making yourself into some sort of Stepford Wife for him," Marissa added.

"It's just one dinner! If I turn up at work on Monday as a blonde wearing a fifties frock with a vacant look in my eyes, then feel free to start worrying."

Jeez. I could always count on Marissa to tell me like it was. Well, the way *Marissa* saw it, I should say.

Paige usually had more tact. "I think it'll go really well. And Parker will confess his love for you and you will for him and it'll be so romantic and wonderful." She let out a sigh.

"Thank you, Paige." I looked pointedly at Marissa.

"I hope it does, too," she conceded. "Only, please don't give him food poisoning. My clothes are still a little loose on me, thanks to your non-Stepford Wife culinary skills."

I put my hand against my heart. "I won't. It's going to be . . . perfect."

* * *

Still on my sugar and Parker-was-about-to-say-he-loved-me

high, I arrived back to a meeting with Will and the project team over in the Marketing Department. Everyone was already sitting around the large wooden table when I walked through the door.

Will looked up at me, one of those smarmy grins plastered on his face. "Afternoon, Dunny!"

It was eleven o'clock in the morning.

I resisted the urge to call him "Poop Boy" in front of an audience. *Some* of us have a sense of decorum. Instead, I ignored him. "Good *morning*, everyone. Although some of the less mature members of this team prefer nicknames, I would like it if you could all stick with 'Cassie.'"

There were murmured greetings from the others in the room. I sat in one of the empty seats next to Melanie, a member of the Marketing Department I knew, ensuring I was as far away from Will as I could be without leaving the room.

"We've been brought up-to-date this morning on the progress of the project by Dwight, but we'd like to get a feel for how things are sitting with you all. Wouldn't we, *Cassie*?" Will looked at me pointedly.

I narrowed my eyes at him. "Yes, we would, *William*."

"I've put together a project spreadsheet with milestones and progress to date, if we'd like to start there?" Melanie offered.

I knew I'd sat next to the right person in the room. "That sounds great, thanks, Melanie," I replied, taking the sheet from her.

"Before we do that, how about we get to know each other a little?" Will said. "I mean, I see all of you around the office, but I wouldn't say I knew you very well. How about a little ice breaker?"

Everyone agreed, and Will continued. "Let's all take turns telling everyone two unusual things about ourselves, only, one of them has to be something embarrassing."

I cocked an eyebrow and gave him a glassy stare. "Why do we have to tell each other something embarrassing?"

Will shrugged. "It's fun. Plus, it helps to create a rapport."

I tapped my foot.

"Melanie? How about you go first?"

I crossed my arms. "No, why don't *you* go first, Will. I'm sure we'd all like to hear Mr. Perfect's take on himself."

He raised his eyebrows. "Mr. Perfect?"

I shifted in my seat. Will clearly hadn't heard the nickname some of us gave him when he first joined the company and blew us all away with his success. Even though "Poop Boy" was eminently more suitable for him, I was committed. "Yes." I was resolute.

He looked unconcerned. "Sure. I'll kick things off. Let me think." He paused, tapping his chin. "One unusual thing about me is that I'm a little OCD. I always have to have my shoes lined up neatly in my closet, organized by type. And my embarrassing thing is that I listen to eighties rock in my car and have been known to sing along, which I do very badly. My personal favorite has to be Meatloaf. I love me a bit of Meatloaf." He grinned at us.

Everyone in the room chuckled. The image of Will dressed in his slick suits, driving his fancy car, and rocking down to *Bat Out of Hell* was amusing.

"Okay, Melanie? Your turn."

"Well, I'm a bit of a whizz at chess, winning competitions. That's something unusual people here don't know about me. Plus, I was born in the backseat of a taxi."

"You were?" My eyes were huge.

"My mom was on her way to the hospital, but, apparently, I came out too fast and, hey presto, baby delivered in the back of the taxi."

"So, that's your embarrassing thing?" Will asked.

Melanie shrugged. "Yeah, I guess. Probably more embarrassing for my mom, though."

After the laughter and comments had died down, Will turned to me. "Your turn, Dunny."

I pursed my lips. "Okay. One unusual thing about me is that I was born without any wisdom teeth. So, I don't have to go through the pain of having them extracted. Lucky, huh? And my embarrassing thing?" The image of walking in on a shirtless Will sprung instantly to mind. *No, not that one.* I cleared my throat. I decided to make a Parker reference, to ensure everyone, including Will Jordan, knew I had a boyfriend. A very special and *significant* boyfriend. "I guess that would have to be my first date with my boyfriend where I kind of flashed him my underwear by accident when my dress got caught on a barstool."

There was a general titter in the room.

"And, what's more, I ended up whacking myself in the nose—

which hurt like crazy, I might add—as I tried to work my dress loose."

"Oh, that's terrible!" exclaimed Melanie to various other comments.

"Interesting. I felt sure you were going to go with the teddy bear pajamas," Will said, smirking at me.

All heads in the room swiveled back to me. "I . . . ah . . . yes, I guess some might see teddy bear pajamas as embarrassing. Personally, I don't." I glared at Will. Great. Now he had everyone in the room wondering how he knew about my preferences in nighttime attire.

"No, you're right, Dunny. Falling over and flashing your underwear on a first date is loads more embarrassing than choosing to wear teddy bear pajamas as a grown woman."

"Anyway, let's move on, shall we? Who's next? Danny, how about you?" I said, trying my best to ignore the rising heat in my cheeks.

Luckily, everyone was more than happy to contribute their unusual and embarrassing things, after which we all got down to some work. I hated to admit it, but Will's idea worked out great. The ice was well and truly shattered and we were buddying up to our new project team in no time, sharing jokes and anecdotes and going through the minutia of the project, highlighting all the areas that needed attention. I, personally, identified two key points that meant selling the solution would be tricky, which became lengthy discussion points.

Of course, Will and I disagreed over virtually everything, but that had become our *modus operandi* these days. And I couldn't see it changing any time soon.

* * *

I felt thoroughly prepared for the all-important twelfth date with Parker on Saturday night. I had channeled my inner Nigella Lawson—who I had secretly suspected was just waiting to come leaping out, looking a-mazing in a floral apron, cooking up exquisite culinary delights—and decided on a Thai-themed meal, with vegetable spring rolls to start, followed by a red chicken curry, fragrant rice, and cucumber salad. The meal would be finished off with mango with sticky rice for dessert.

I had googled how to make a Thai banquet at home and had scoured the Asian markets for the weird and wonderful ingredients required to dazzle Parker with my cooking skills.

I'd found a clip online with instructions on how to make everything on the menu, so I figured, how hard could it be? So what if I'd never actually *cooked* Thai food before? I'd eaten it plenty of times down at The Thai Elephant on a Friday night, so I knew how things should look and taste. I had this.

I stood in my small kitchen, the ingredients I'd purchased laid out on the counter before me. I bit my lip. Perhaps I'd been a little ambitious? *No, I can do this.* I glanced at the clock. It was only three fifteen and Parker wasn't due until seven. That gave me three whole hours to whip up dinner and forty-five minutes to get myself gracious-hostess ready. Easy.

Or so I thought. The woman presenting the show online went too fast, and I had to keep pausing and rewinding with mucky hands. I got bits of food on my laptop, including some shrimp paste stuck between the *f* and *g* on my keyboard I just knew was going to have its own special kind of stench within a day or two.

The woman presenting the show looked as fresh as a daisy, so very serene, and positively thrilled to be cooking. Me? I'd worked up a serious sweat, had blobs of food stuck in my hair, and was feeling anything but serene. She was beginning to get on my nerves.

I paused Little Miss Know-It-All and tasted the red curry sauce. It didn't taste the way it did at The Thai Elephant. In fact, it tasted a lot like red-colored coconut milk. I added more of everything and gave it another stir. I dipped a spoon in and took another mouthful. My eyes popped open wide. It was hot with a capital *H*! *Water! Need water!* I seized a glass from the cupboard, filled it with water, and slugged it back. Still burning. A voice in the back of my head said "milk." I grabbed a carton of milk from the refrigerator and poured it into my mouth, not even caring as it ran down my chin and onto my top.

Still holding the milk carton, I sunk to the floor, defeated. Eventually, my lips stopped feeling like large slabs of rubber, my eyes stopped watering, and my mouth began to feel less like my tongue had taken over, swelling to twice its actual size.

This was so much harder than I thought it would be!

To add insult to injury, my cat, Zig, wandered past me and flicked me with his tail. How to kick a girl when she's down, Zig.

Little Miss Know-It-All's chirpy voice blasted out from my laptop, telling me to julienne a carrot. I sighed. Zig must have stepped on the keyboard. I pushed myself up off the floor. Zig was licking between the *f* and *g* keys, purring his fluffy head off. Great, shrimp paste and now cat slobber; my favorite combination.

By five thirty-seven I was on the phone to Bailey—one of only two of my friends who could actually cook (Paige being the other, but she was out of town for the weekend)—with the spring rolls looking more like a Jackson Pollock painting, the sticky rice not sticking, but the fragrant rice so stuck I couldn't get it out of the pan without the use of a power tool or two.

"You've got to help me, Bailey. It's not working, and he'll be here in less than an hour and a half. *Please.*" I'd resorted to pleading now.

I heard her yawn down the phone. "I'm really tired. I only just locked the café up at four."

"Please, please, please!" I knew I sounded pathetic, but she was all I had and this date *had* to go well.

Bailey laughed. "Sure. I'll be over in fifteen."

"You are an angel."

By the time she arrived, I had managed to make the cucumber salad, tasted it, and was actually impressed by my efforts. But then there was no cooking involved in making a salad, was there? Simply cutting and compiling. Probably where my culinary talents lie. Maybe I could consider becoming one of those raw foodists? The salad even looked pretty in the bowl. I hoped Parker would think so, because at this rate, a pretty cucumber salad was the sum total of our dinner for tonight.

The intercom rang, and I buzzed Bailey up. She burst into laughter at my disheveled appearance when I opened the door. Self-consciously, I wiped the hair away from my face. I closed the door behind her as she struggled for breath. "Oh, honey. I'm sorry," she said, wiping her eyes. "Have you seen yourself?"

I'd had no time for anything but cooking, let alone looking at my own reflection. "That bad, huh?"

Bailey nodded. I walked to the bathroom. She was right. Not

only did I have food in my hair, my mascara had run from my watering eyes, I had smudges of curry paste on my cheek, and even some julienned carrot in my hair. Absentmindedly, I plucked the carrot out and chewed it.

When I got back to the kitchen, looking considerably more like a human being than a walking culinary disaster, Bailey was surveying the meal, aka the now squalid state of my kitchen, aka the culinary disaster zone.

"So." She rubbed her chin. "Is there anything here that's salvageable?"

With pride, I told her about the cucumber salad.

"That might not be enough for dinner though, right?" She lifted the pot lid on the stove. "Is that a Thai red curry?"

"It sure is." I was encouraged. If it looked and smelled like a red curry, it couldn't be all bad. Could it?

She dipped her finger in to taste it.

I leaped across the kitchen. "No! Don't!"

Too late, she sucked on her finger. Like mine before, her eyes bulged as her face turned pink. "Milk," she croaked, fanning her face.

I poured her a glass and watched as she drank it down, slowly returning to her normal color. "So that's a little on the spicy side."

"Yeah, sorry about that. It didn't taste right, so I added more. Can we save it?"

She thought for a moment. "Have you got any more coconut cream?"

"Yes!" I opened my pantry and dug around in the cans until I found one. "Here."

"Okay, we'll pour some of this . . . actually, we'll pour *all* of this into the sauce and see if that fixes it."

I let out a breath and smiled. With Bailey and her incredible cooking skills here, everything was going to be all right.

She opened the can, poured the coconut milk in, and gave it a stir. She shot me a nervous glance before dipping her pinky in once more. "Here goes." She tasted the sauce, pulled a face, and said, "We may need to start again."

"Start again? I was just about to add the chicken. Little Miss Know-It-All said to add that at the end."

Bailey arched her eyebrows. "Who is Little Miss Know-It-All?"

I gestured toward my laptop. "The bossy chef on my video. I officially hate her."

Bailey nodded, as though it was thoroughly reasonable to get angry with a person I've never met on a screen.

"You get the chicken out and I'll chop it up. Do you have any ingredients left over?"

I shook my head, furrowing my brow. "I used it all up."

"What time is Parker here?"

"Seven."

She glanced at her watch. "Okay, so we have twenty-eight or so minutes."

"What?" My eyes shot to the wall clock. "Twenty-eight minutes? Are you serious?" My tummy did a flip-flop. "I'm not dressed, I have to wash this goop out of my hair, and the rice is . . . well, it doesn't look like rice anymore, that's for sure." I rubbed the back of my neck. This was *not* going to plan.

Bailey lifted the lid on the rice pot. "You're right with the rice, honey." She turned the pot upside down, and the rice stayed firmly and resolutely stuck to the bottom. Not even a solitary grain made its escape. "You could build furniture with that."

Despite my increasing stress levels, I let out a giggle. And then another. They must have been catching, because before too long, Bailey was laughing, too. We laughed and we laughed, holding our sides and gasping for breath.

Eventually, wondering if I'd ever be able to stop after almost wetting my pants, we calmed down. I glanced at the clock: we had wasted a good four minutes laughing, four minutes I needed to be cooking or getting ready!

"I've got an idea. Why don't you go and get all glammed up and I'll pop down to The Thai Elephant and buy a red chicken curry? I know it's not what you'd planned, but it's better than the alternative."

My eyes softened. "You're amazing, do you know that?"

Bailey grinned at me. "If you could get me a Parker who thinks that, too, I'll be set." She pulled on her jacket. "Now, I'll go and get the curry." She looked at the spring roll disaster on the counter. "Did you want an appetizer, too?"

"They're meant to be vegetarian spring rolls. I tried to roll them up, but the rice pastry kept tearing."

Nigella Lawson I was quite clearly not.

"I'll get some of those, too. What were you planning on doing for dessert?"

I plucked the mango from the fruit bowl and handed it to her. "Sliced mango with sticky rice." I glanced at the pot of rice cement. "I'm pretty sure even I could manage to slice this baby, but maybe you could pick up the sticky rice?"

She smiled. "That sounds like a good idea to me."

I handed her my credit card and thanked her profusely before I dived into the shower to wash off some of the goop hardening in my hair and make myself twelfth date ready.

At exactly seven, the intercom buzzed, and I yelled in a panic for Bailey to let Parker in. "Tell him I'll be out in a couple of minutes, okay?"

"No worries."

I slipped on my black pencil skirt and sleeveless top, saying a silent prayer of thanks to my past self I'd already laid out my outfit for the evening. I pushed my feet into my heels and surveyed myself in my full-length mirror. *This is it, the night we tell each other how we feel, and . . . other things.* My tummy flip-flopped.

I heard Bailey letting Parker into my apartment. One final check in the mirror and I opened my bedroom door and walked out into the living room. "Hi, Parker."

He was holding a single red rose—so *The Bachelor* romantic—and dressed as he always did when I saw him, in khaki pants and a crisply ironed polo shirt. He pecked me on the cheek. "Hi, Cassie. You look beautiful and something smells delicious."

Bailey and I shared a look. "Thanks," I said, taking the proffered rose.

"Well, that's my cue to leave." Bailey collected her purse from the table, which I noticed she had set beautifully, complete with napkins and a lit candle in the center. She'd placed the steaming hot curry, my cucumber salad, and rice in bowls on the table, no sign of any telltale takeout packaging to be seen.

I mouthed an indebted "Thank you" to her, and she winked back. "Great to meet you, Parker. See you soon, Cassie. Have a fun night!"

With Bailey gone, I poured Parker a drink and we sat down to the meal.

"This looks amazing. You have hidden talents, Ms. Dunhill."

I beamed at him, ignoring a pang of guilt. Should I tell him I was a disaster in the kitchen and it was all Bailey—and The Thai Elephant? I settled for, "Thanks." My eye began to twitch.

We served ourselves the food and chatted about our weeks. We hadn't seen one another since I'd been to Napier, so I had a lot to tell him about the retreat and working on the new project.

"You're a great cook," he commented between mouthfuls. "This tastes just as good as that place down the road from here. What's it called?"

"Which place are you talking about?" More eye twitching. I didn't make eye contact with him, focusing on my dinner instead.

"Something about an Elephant. I've only been there a couple of times. We should go sometime."

"Sounds like a great idea!" I replied a little too enthusiastically.

"I'm going to keep you on." He smiled at me, his eyes twinkling.

I almost cracked and told him the truth. *We'll laugh about it together one day . . . when we're married.*

"Tell me, how was the bowling?" he asked.

"It was so great. My team won! We totally smashed the opposition. Very satisfying."

He grinned at me. "It sounds like it. You like bowling, do you?"

"I love it."

He shrugged. "Each to their own."

I drew my eyebrows together. "You don't like to bowl?" He had taken a new mouthful, so I waited for him to swallow.

"What's to like? It's just throwing a heavy ball at a bunch of white things at the end of an alley. It might be fun every now and then, but it's hardly a sport, is it?"

I nearly choked on my curry. *Hardly a sport?* If my dad could hear him, he'd be spinning in his grave! And he's not even dead. "Umm, I guess." I pushed my dinner around my plate. "Are you saying you wouldn't go bowling with me?"

"Well—" He paused when he looked into my eyes. "You know what? If you like it, I'm certain I would, too."

"You mean you've never bowled?" I was incredulous. How could you live in the twenty-first century and never have been ten-pin bowling?

"My family was more chess and tennis, I suppose. And golf. We all love golf."

In comparison with golf, tennis, and chess, bowling suddenly seemed pretty lowbrow. My eyes got huge. "You played golf as a family when you were a kid?" Who *did* that?

"Of course. My parents are avid golfers, and they wanted to bring us up to love it, too. I got my first set of clubs when I was four years old."

I smiled at the mental image. "I bet you were very cute. Did you wear plus fours?"

He laughed. "No. There's a dress code, of course, but no plus fours."

After dinner, we kicked off our shoes and sat cuddling up on the sofa together. It felt so right. I just knew those magical three words were about to leave his lips, changing my life forever. I decided to come clean about dinner—well, at least partially.

"Parker, I need to tell you something. Bailey, my friend, was here to help me out in the kitchen. She's a great cook, and so we didn't end up eating pizza, I called her to ask her to help me when things didn't quite . . . go to plan."

"Oh, I see."

I turned and looked at him. "Sorry."

He gave me a kiss. "Don't apologize. It's so great you tried to make me this dinner. It's just another thing to adore about you."

I smiled as warmth spread across my chest. Parker adored me? *Adoring someone is very much like loving them, isn't it?*

"How come Bailey's such a good cook?" He wrapped his arms around me as I lay against him.

"She runs the best café in the city."

"Alessandro's?"

I pushed myself back up to face him. "No. The Cozy Cottage Café, of course!" How could he think Alessandro's was the best café in Auckland? Their coffee was middling at best, their muffins were dry, and they didn't even do flourless chocolate and raspberry cake.

"I've never been to that one. Where is it?"

"Heaven."

He chuckled. "That good, huh?"

"Oh, yes. Marissa, Paige, and I go there all the time. It's our special place."

"Are boys allowed?" he teased.

I crinkled my forehead. "Well—"

"Oh, I see. It's out of bounds, is it?" He tickled my tummy, causing me to break into peals of laughter. I'm really very ticklish.

"Okay, okay!" I conceded.

"Okay what?"

"Okay, I'll take you to my café."

"Good. And I'll take you to mine." He extended his hand, and we shook on it.

"Now, I'd much rather do this than argue about whose café is the better one." He put his hand under my chin and pulled me in for a kiss. It was a deep, long kiss, that had me melting at the knees.

When Parker stood up and held his hand out toward me, I knew exactly where this evening was heading. And I was more than happy about it. I reached up and took his hand, gazing into his eyes as I stood up next to him.

"Did you want to . . . ?" he asked, his voice deep.

I bit my lip and nodded.

He smiled back at me. "I do. So much."

My mind darted to the state of my bedroom. Even though I had planned for this evening with fresh sheets, candles and a perfectly made bed, I'd virtually exploded in there in my haste to get ready before Parker had arrived. "Give me one second."

I rushed into my bedroom and grabbed my speedily discarded jeans, sneakers, and T-shirt from the floor and stuffed them under the bed. I grabbed the matches from the top of my nightstand and lit the candles, almost burning myself, my hands were shaking so much. I smoothed out the bed and checked myself in the mirror. Then I did one final glance around the room to ensure it was up to first-time-sex-with-my-future-husband standards. It was.

I took a deep breath. This was it. I returned to Parker, who was still standing where I'd left him. He looked as nervous as I felt. Without a word, but with my belly in knots, I led him past the sofa and through my bedroom door.

"Nice room," he commented.

"Thanks."

He pulled me into him and kissed me once more, tugging at my top to loosen it. I did the same to him, running my hands up under his top, feeling his firm back.

"I've wanted to do this for so long," he breathed into my ear.

"Me too," I breathed. His . . . err . . . *interest* pressed up against me confirmed his words.

We fell onto my bed, pulling our clothes off, hands everywhere, kissing, wanting. And it was amazing. He was so gentle and thoughtful, and loving. Just the way I'd hoped he would be. The perfect first time with my perfect One Last First Date.

But time was ticking by. We were nearing the end of the date, and yes, things had moved along very nicely, but this needed to get to the next level. A declaration needed to be made. Stat!

As we lay in my bed together, my mind darted to the embarrassing things conversation Will had got us to do during our first meeting with the Marketing team. That had worked so well, all of us having fun with it and getting to know one another better, too. Will was onto something. Maybe it could work with Parker.

Back up the bus. What was I doing thinking about Will "Poop Boy" Jordan while in bed with Parker?

I pushed myself up on my elbow and looked into his sleepy eyes. "Tell me something weird about yourself. Something embarrassing."

He furrowed his brow. "Something embarrassing?"

"Yeah, like . . . something you don't usually tell people."

He pushed a stray hair from my face. "Like I had acne as a teenager?"

"No, something unusual. Here's something about me: I sing in the shower. Probably really, really badly, even though I secretly suspect a top music producer will happen to hear me from the place next door and offer me a multi-million-dollar record deal."

He looked at me with what appeared to be a mixture of surprise, interest, and, quite possibly, a touch of fear. "I see."

Undeterred, I replied, "Your turn."

"Umm, let me think. Something embarrassing." I could almost see the cogs whirring in his smart doctor brain. "Well, I guess I got a flat tire a few months ago and didn't know how to change it."

"And?" I led.

"And phoned my friend Hunter. He changed it for me."

Okay, not quite getting it here. "How about something you do when you're on your own and no one knows about it? Like me singing Taylor Swift songs in the shower."

"Well, there is this one thing."

My eyes were wide. "Yes?"

"Even though I'm a doctor and have to use them some of the time, I'm kind of scared of needles."

I kissed him on the lips. *"That's* what I'm talking about! See? That's something weird about you."

He grinned at me. "Don't tell anyone. I've got a reputation to uphold, you know."

"Oh, I won't, Doctor. I promise."

His face changed as our eyes locked. "Cassie, I—" He hesitated.

This is it. This is the moment.

I swallowed. "What is it, Parker?"

"I . . . Can I say something?" He looked nervous. This was good. Very good.

Come on, Parker, say it!

"What is it?" I encouraged as hope rose in my belly.

"Do you want to play golf with me next weekend?"

Kersplat! My heart hit the floor. "Oh . . . err . . . golf?" *Golf? He wants me to play golf with him?* I was lying naked in bed with this man after our very first time together, and he wanted to ask me to play golf with him?

He smiled. "Yeah, golf. You know, clubs, balls, green. That kind of thing."

"Sure. That sounds fun." *What happened to "I love you"?*

"It's kind of a big deal for me to ask a girl to play, to be honest. I've only ever played with one girl, my ex. You see, I really love golf."

Well, at least he used the word "love." My heart got up off the floor and pricked up its ears. *This is a good sign.* "I would love to play golf with you."

He looked relieved. "Great! Have you played before?"

"Yes, absolutely. I'm pretty good, actually." I failed to mention the words "at Nintendo Wii Golf." Semantics. How hard could golf be?

"You are awesome."

I smiled at him, waiting for more. I waited. And waited. In fact,

I waited right through the night and into the next day. By the time he went home, I knew I would have to completely dazzle him with my golfing prowess and force him to tell me he loved me.

CHAPTER 12

PAIGE WAS AT MY desk first thing Monday morning, waiting for me to arrive. "How was it?"

Although I wasn't about to delve into any of the sordid details, Paige was my friend and deserved to hear about this important development in mine and Parker's relationship. After all, I was the first one of us who took the pact to take the leap.

I grinned at her. "Amazing."

She beamed back. "Oh, I'm so happy for you!"

"Yeah, me too."

"And? Did he say it?"

I smiled, despite the persistent sinking feeling that appeared to have taken up residence in my belly since Saturday night. "No, but he will." I tried to sound upbeat, despite my mood.

Paige's face fell. "I thought he would have. I was sure of it." She furrowed her brow. "What are you going to do?"

I placed my laptop bag on my desk with a sigh and slipped my jacket off. "I'm not sure yet. He did ask me to play golf with him, though."

Paige laughed. "Golf? Really? That's not much of a consolation prize."

"I guess not." She was right. Although Parker had only ever played golf with one woman before, it was but a mere tiny footstep in the right direction. By now I needed giant leaps for mankind.

"Morning, ladies." Will breezed past us on the way to his—my future—office.

"Hi, Will." Paige's face flushed pink, right on cue.

"Hey, Millsey," Will said over his shoulder. He disappeared into his office only to pop his head out a moment later. "Dunny, do have a moment?"

I rolled my eyes at Paige. "Gotta go."

I walked into my future office, temporarily occupied by Will Jordan. "What's up?"

He was already sitting back down at his desk. He looked up at me. "How's your calendar looking this morning?"

I narrowed my eyes at him. "Not too bad. Why?"

"You know how we talked about engaging a graphic design company in our last project meeting?"

"Yes." I sat down on the other side of the desk from him. "You mentioned you had a contact at Design Zoo."

"Exactly. We've got an appointment with them in"—he glanced at his watch—"twenty minutes."

"You're giving me twenty minutes to prepare for this? Really?" I tapped my foot. This was so typical of Will, always leaping at things, not bothering to see if it suits others around him.

"It'll be a cinch. We know what we need them to do, we just need to get them on the same page with us."

"Well, I don't know if I'm free in twenty minutes." I knew I was being obstinate. I did not care.

He smiled. "Nineteen."

I crossed my arms. "Nineteen then."

He peered at his screen, moving his mouse around. "It looks to me like you're free."

I opened my mouth to speak. Will had access to my calendar? What was I thinking? He was my manager, of course he did. *Damn him.*

Looking thoroughly self-satisfied, he stood up. "Grab your things and let's go." He slipped on his suit jacket and slid his laptop into its bag.

With a sigh of resignation, I pushed myself up and left his office. Back at my desk, Paige was gone, leaving a message with "Cozy Cottage at ten?" written on a Post-it note stuck to the side of my laptop bag. I pulled it off and stuck it on my desk, collecting my purse and jacket as Will appeared at my desk.

Of course he wanted to drive, so I sat in the passenger seat of his flashy, high-status German car to Design Zoo in the upmarket inner-city suburb of Ponsonby. I suggested that I would lead the meeting—for a change—and Will seemed happy with the idea. Odd.

We were met in reception by Bri, someone I had expected to be a woman, but a tight man-bun, bright paisley shirt, and elaborate facial hair confirmed he was most definitely male. And a total hipster at that. He was very enthusiastic about working with us and offered a ton of ideas, some of which could fit very nicely with our brand.

At the end of the meeting, we said our farewells to Bri and his ironic hair and climbed back into Will's car. He turned the ignition over. The car thrummed, low and deep. "After that level of man-bun enthusiasm, I could do with a caffeine top-up, how about you?

I couldn't help but chuckle. "Sure. We could grab a takeout."

Will hit the accelerator, and the car rumbled off, back toward the central city. "I've got a better idea. Let's go to my favorite café."

"Sure." Judging by his car, his favorite café would be some sort of ritzy place with funky music, walls of mirrors, and a cooler than cool clientele. I sat back in the plush black leather bucket seat, watching the houses, shops, and trees whizz by. "That went well. I think Bri had some useful ideas. I especially liked the third campaign he suggested. The aesthetic was really 'now.'"

"Do you think all graphic designers have ridiculous beards and buns on top of their heads?" he asked, completely ignoring anything I'd said.

"Possibly not the women."

Will laughed. "You're funny, Dunny. Ha! And that rhymes."

I glared at him, although my heart wasn't in it. It was getting exhausting being Will's arch nemesis. Sometimes a girl simply needed a break. "He's just creative. They're all a bit like that. It kind of goes with the territory."

Will slowed the car and performed an expert parallel park in a space I would have deemed too tight, even for my little hatchback. He switched off the ignition. "Attagirl."

I shot him a look. "You talk to your car?"

He shrugged, undeterred. "Why not? She's a beauty."

"Do you take her on dates? Buy her pretty things? Ooh, maybe this is your international supermodel girlfriend!"

He arched an eyebrow in response. "Jump out."

I laughed. Why hadn't he listed *that* as an embarrassing thing? I closed the door behind me and stood beside the car on a very familiar street, looking at the building in front of me, openmouthed. The Cozy Cottage Café was Will Jordan's favorite café?

Will looked back to me over his shoulder. "Are you coming?"

Rendered speechless, I simply nodded and concentrated on putting one foot in front of the other. Will reached the door and held it open for me. As I walked in, I was instantly hit by the familiar and inviting aroma of coffee and sweet treats, the place warmed by the fire, crackling under the old wooden mantle.

"You're going to love this place. The food is fantastic and the coffee second-to-none. I don't come here much because it's so far from the office, but when I worked around the corner, I came here pretty much every day."

I nodded as he spoke, trying desperately to marry the arrogant Will Jordan of my experience with the man whose preferred café was also mine.

From behind the counter, Bailey spotted me and waved, a confused look on her face as her eyes darted to Will. I smiled at her as though this was perfectly normal and I came here with random men every day of the week.

At the display cabinet, Will pointed at the flourless chocolate and raspberry cake. "I'm going to buy you a slice of this. It will blow your mind. Seriously."

"Sure. Great." I smiled weakly at him.

Why did this feel like such a big deal? So what if Will liked this café? It's not mine; anyone can come here. He has just as much right as the next person. And so what if he loves the same cake as me? It's a great cake!

"Good morning, what can I get you?" Adeline, one of Bailey's staff members asked when we reached the register. "Oh, hey, Cassie."

I mumbled a greeting. Bailey caught my eye and smiled.

"The usual?" Adeline turned to Will. "Cassie likes the flourless chocolate and raspberry cake. Like, a lot. Right, Cassie?"

I nodded. "Mm-hm." Not using actual words somehow made

this experience less confusing.

Will raised his eyebrows. "You know this place?"

I nodded. "Mm-hm."

"Isn't it the best?" His voice was tinged with excitement, like we were now both in on some fantastic secret.

Finding my voice, I replied, "You're right, it's the best café in Auckland."

"I'm very glad you see it that way," Bailey said, appearing behind Adeline. "Hi there. I'm Bailey. I've seen you here before, right?"

Will took Bailey's outstretched hand. "Yes. I used to come here a bit. I'm Will."

"Great to meet you. Has Adeline taken your order?" Bailey asked.

"I think it has to be two slices of flourless chocolate and raspberry cake, right, Dunny?"

Bailey and Adeline raised their eyebrows at the mention of my despised nickname. I decided it was best to act as though it was no big deal. "Yes, please. And a latte."

"Make that two," Will added.

"Why don't you grab us a table and I'll be over soon?" I said to him.

With Will out of earshot, Bailey asked, "What's happened to the 'no men allowed' rule you three have here?"

"It wasn't my idea. Will chose it. I had no idea he even knew your café existed."

I watched as Bailey looked over at Will, sitting at a table for two near the fireplace, scrolling through his phone. "I remember him. He used to come in a couple of times a week with this pretty brunette."

I glanced over at Will. A pretty brunette?

"To be honest, I thought the first man you brought here would be Parker."

"It is. I mean, it will be. Technically, I didn't bring Will here, he brought me. So . . ."

"Well, he's cute. If you want me to cook for him, I'd be more than happy to." She flashed me her beautiful smile. "How did the dinner go with Parker, anyway?"

I gave Bailey a quick rundown on the date.

"Any news?" Her eyes twinkled.

"He asked me to play golf with him, which is really special."

"Fantastic!" she said a little too loudly, making it obvious she was faking her excitement. "Hey, I'll bring these over for you."

Will was still looking through his phone when I sat down in the comfy armchair opposite him and shrugged off my jacket. As usual at this time of year, it was toasty warm inside the café, adding to its homey, welcoming atmosphere. I pulled my own phone out and scrolled through my emails. My interest was piqued when I spied an email from Laura, asking to meet with her at the end of next week to "take the next steps in the interview process."

I glanced at Will. He was still engrossed in whatever he was reading. I quickly bashed out a response, agreeing to one of the times she had offered. By then, at the rate we've been working, Will and I would have moved the project along nicely.

"Anything interesting in there?" His eyes had a hint of mischievousness in them.

"No, nothing out of the ordinary." I stared him down. There was no way I was going to let on I had a second interview for the job.

"Are you sure?" he prodded, a smile teasing the corners of his mouth.

"Yes." I turned my phone facedown on the table. A quick change of subject was required. The first thing to pop into my head was Will's supposed supermodel girlfriend. "How's your girlfriend? Still in Milan or Tokyo or somewhere exciting?"

He shifted in his seat. I narrowed my eyes at him. Did he look uncomfortable? "She's back here for a bit. Doing some modeling, then heading off again soon."

"It must be hard to have a relationship with someone who's never really around."

"I guess. She's here enough. Oh, look, here's our food."

Adeline placed the cups of coffee and slices of chocolate heaven in front of us, and for the next few moments, Will and I sat in silence as we devoured them.

"How's lover boy?" Will asked once his plate was mere crumbs.

"He has a name, you know. It's Parker."

"Parker sounds more like a name for a dog. Or incontinence pads." He chuckled at his own lame joke.

I rolled my eyes. God, he was so immature. "Don't be so ridiculous. Parker is a fine name."

A smile teased the edges of his mouth. "A 'fine name,' is it? Have we been transported back to the nineteenth century? Next you'll be complimenting his rifle skills and how well he keeps his oxen."

"I could, but he wouldn't need any of those things. He's a *doctor*, don't you know." I felt a surge of pride as I thought of Parker, my boyfriend, doing something as important as caring for people's health.

"Good for him. Does he like this café?"

I shifted in my seat. "Ah, actually, I haven't brought him here yet."

Will took a sip of his coffee. "Why not?"

I played with the handle of my coffee cup as my mind darted to our last date—and the distinct lack of any L-word usage on Parker's behalf. "I don't know. It's kind of a girls' hangout, I guess. I come here with Paige and Marissa. I had planned on bringing Parker here soon, though."

"So, when's the big day?"

My heart banged against my ribs. "Excuse me?"

"He's the guy you're going to marry, right?" I nodded. "When's the big day?"

"We haven't got to that stage yet. We've only been on twelve dates. These things take time, you know."

He smirked. "You've been counting?"

I bristled. "So what if I have? Some of us have a plan for our lives."

He leaned back in his chair. "Oh, really. What's your plan? No, don't answer, I bet I can work it out." He paused, assessing me through narrowed eyes. "You're what? Twenty-eight?"

My back stiffened. "Twenty-seven."

"Okay, you're twenty-seven. I bet you devised a life plan when you were a tweeny-bopper and you first began to fantasize about your big white wedding. You probably practiced walking down the aisle with your teddy bear."

I shook my head. "No."

He cocked his head, his brown eyes boring into me.

"It was my stuffed rabbit, Wilbur."

Will chuckled. "Of course it was. So, you've got the big day nailed, and you decide, being the A-Type, overachieving chick you are, you needed a 'Life Plan.'" He did air quotes to emphasize his point. "You probably even wrote it up with a pencil with some sort of fluffy animal on the top."

I drummed my fingers on the table in agitation. *How is he doing this?*

"I'm guessing"—he rubbed his chin with his fingers—"climb the corporate ladder to get to your dream job by twenty-eight; meet Mr. Right; get married no later than twenty-nine; first kid of two or maybe three by the time you're thirty." He shot me one of those self-satisfied smirks I knew only too well.

I looked at him, openmouthed. It was almost as though he'd read my diary from when I was eleven and first devised The Plan. I needed to collect myself; no way was I going to let Will Jordan in on something as personal as my life plan, regardless of whether he was right or not. "Something like that," I sniffed. "Although, you have a few of the details wrong."

"Something *exactly* like that. Everything going to plan?" He pulled an innocent face. I wanted to throw the rest of my coffee at it, stand up, and stomp out of the café.

I jutted out my chin. "Yes, thank you."

He studied me again. After a pause, he said, "I broke up with Samantha. Well, to be honest, she broke up with me."

The penny dropped. That's why he looked uncomfortable. "I'm sorry to hear that. What happened?"

He shrugged. "Too hard, I guess. She was away a lot. Plus, she's totally hot, like the hottest chick around, you know?"

I rolled my eyes. *Of course* she was.

"She could have any man she wanted."

The look of vulnerability in his eyes took me by surprise. "You're a pretty great guy, you know. Any woman would be happy to be with you, I bet." I was tempted to put my hand on his to comfort him but thought better of it. This was Will Jordan I was talking to, after all.

He chortled, shaking it off. "Yeah. Anyway. These things happen. It's no biggie. What about you and what's-his-name?"

"Parker." I shook my head. I didn't know whether it was the fact Will had shown me some vulnerability, my sugar high from that delicious cake, or the magic of the Cozy Cottage Café, but I decided to open up to him. If he loved the Cozy Cottage, he couldn't be all bad. Could he?

"It's pretty good, I guess," I said, looking down at my coffee cup.

"Sounds like a problem."

I let out a puff of air. "You were kind of right about me having a life plan."

He nodded, clearly not surprised.

"And, well, I kind of expected things to have . . . I don't know, moved on a bit. Emotionally."

"Ah-ha. He's dating other women?"

I recoiled. "God, no! Nothing like that. We're exclusive. He just . . . hasn't said those three magic words yet."

He arched his eyebrows. "Have you?"

"No!" The thought of saying "I love you" to someone— *anyone*—and not having it reciprocated made me want to run and hide, or shrivel up and die—perhaps both.

"Why not? Why does he have to be the first one to say it?"

My hands felt warm and sweaty. "He just does. Anyway, I thought he was going to, but instead he asked me to play golf."

Will leaned back in his chair and roared with laughter. "Golf?"

I shot him a tight smile. "He doesn't usually ask girls to play golf with his buddies, so it's a big deal," I protested, my voice whiney, even to my ears.

"But still, *golf?*"

I waited, my lips pursed, as Will continued to chuckle to himself. "Finished?" I enquired when he'd finally begun to calm down.

"Yes, thank you. Did you say yes?"

"Of course I did!"

"Can you even play golf?"

"Yes." I was indignant.

"Well then, that'll be a nice thing for you to do together. And maybe he'll even say those three little words you want him to say on the green."

I twisted my coffee cup around on its saucer. "Okay, so here's the thing. I've never actually played real golf."

He raised his eyebrows. "*Real* golf? You mean on a green?" I nodded. "So just mini golf?"

I grimaced. "Try a golf video game. Wii."

"Are you seriously telling me you think you can play 'real' golf, as you call it, because you've played it on Nintendo Wii?"

I crinkled my eyes. "Yes?" It suddenly seemed utterly preposterous that I could do something because I'd played a game on a screen in the comfort of Marissa's living room.

He shook his head, smiling. "You are one of a kind, Cassie Dunhill. Look, I'm a handy enough golfer. How about I take you to the driving range and give you a few pointers?"

I looked at him, agog. Will Jordan wanted to help me with something? *Who is this guy?* "You're offering to help me out with Parker?"

He raised his hands, palms up, shrugging his shoulders. "Sure. Why not? Just because I'm sad and lonely now doesn't mean you need to be."

"You're not sad and lonely. At least you won't be for long." I nearly added the fact half the female staff were in love with him but thought better of it. Will Jordan's ego did not need stroking.

"We'll see about that," he replied mysteriously. He leaned in toward me. "Look, I know I'm a guy and not into all this emotional stuff, but maybe you need to just bite the proverbial bullet and say it first? What's the worst thing that could happen?"

"He could not say it back!"

"Don't you think he loves you? I mean, if you're going to marry this *doctor* of yours, shouldn't that come first?" He glanced at his phone. "Hey, we need to get back to the office. I've got an eleven-thirty with Marissa."

"Sure." I chewed on my lip. Maybe Will was right? Maybe I needed to simply man up and tell Parker how I felt?

And maybe I would end up watching my whole life plan blow up in my face.

CHAPTER 13

WILL WAS GOOD TO his word. One evening after work, I followed him in my car to a driving range—a place I had heard about, of course, but had never had any desire to visit in my entire life. It hadn't been too hard to recruit my friends to come with me. I had Paige at the mere mention of Will's name, but Marissa took a little more persuading. Marissa and ball sports didn't see eye to eye. When I explained it was to prepare me for my next date with Parker, she reluctantly tagged along. "As long as I don't have to hit anything," she had warned.

After a drive through the dodgier end of town, we arrived at the driving range and parked next to Will. As we walked into what was, for all intents and purposes, a large shed with a netted area over a big lawn out the back, I noticed all but one of the clientele were men. Undeterred, we hired a booth and Will began the expected lecture on the equipment. Paige hung on his every word, Marissa appeared to be scouting the surrounding men for her One Last First Date, and me? I spent my time fantasizing about how my imminent golfing prowess would undoubtedly elicit those three little words from Parker come Saturday morning.

"Dunny?"

I blinked, coming back to earth.

"I may need you to concentrate here, okay?" Will pulled one of his golf clubs out of his bag. "See this one? This is called a five-iron. I suggest you start with this because it's heavier and you should be able to get some good height with your shot."

Marissa scoffed, having given up on her man quest. "If Cassie can hit the ball at all, that is."

"Thanks for the vote of confidence! Just you watch. Pass me the bat, please." I stretched out my hand toward Will.

"Hang on there, tiger. First off, it's a *club* not a bat. Secondly, I think I should show you how to hit a ball before you go careening off, wielding a heavy metal golf club. And thirdly"—he grinned at us all—"I thought you ladies might like to check out my form."

I shook my head as Marissa laughed and Paige looked like she needed a fan and a lie down.

He pulled a golf ball out of the tub the driving range had provided and placed it carefully on a little bit of plastic poking out of the floor.

"This is the tee," he explained. He stood with his legs parted, holding the club by the ball and shifting his weight slightly from foot to foot.

I sniggered. He looked like an oversized cat about to pounce on invisible prey. Only he was a 6'2" man, trying to hit a small white ball with a long metal bat.

Will ignored me. "I'm in position now and ready to hit the ball. I'm aiming for that flag at the one-fifty line."

"You look great, Will," Paige said with a smile.

I rolled my eyes. She'd think he looked great covered in mud and stinking of cat poop. I snorted. That would mean he'd live up to his "Poop Boy" moniker nicely.

He lifted his club high up behind him and swung through, the ball and club making a *thunk* sound when they made contact. We all watched as the ball sailed high in the air, landing near the flag.

"Nice shot!" Paige called.

"Thanks, Millsey. Now"—he handed me the club—"your turn. Grip it like this." He placed my hands on the club.

I copied Will, standing the same way as he had—only I skipped the amusing cat jostling.

"That looks great, Dunny. Now, aim for the flag right there." He stood next to me and pointed at a flag in the middle distance, the one he'd almost hit a few moments ago. "It's about one hundred fifty yards. That's about how far you should be able to hit a ball with this 'bat.'" He smirked at me, and then stepped away.

I looked down at the ball. *Get ready for a whooping.* I eyed the flag, lifted the club up behind me, and swung it down toward the ball. Only, instead of hitting it, I whacked the club into the ground, shock waves ricocheting up my arm and down my body.

I swallowed. That wasn't quite the plan.

"No worries. It's your first try. Here, let me fix your grip." Will adjusted my hands on the club. "Why don't you practice swinging a couple of times before you hit the ball?"

"She already did that," Marissa said with a snigger, leaning up against the wall.

I shot her a look. "Not helping." I got myself back into position, lifted the club behind me, and swung through. This time it was going to be different: this time I was going to show off my skills, honed by many games of Wii Golf. My club whacked the ground once again, making my arms shake.

On my next attempt, I missed the ball and the ground all together and ended up spinning full circle around. I was thankful for small mercies: at least I didn't hit the ground, and I had managed to hold on to the club. Baby steps.

Will moved in and took the club from me. "Okay, now you've damaged my five-iron, let's move onto something else." He fished another club out of his bag, returning the five-iron—a lethal weapon in my hands, it would seem—to his bag.

"This is a three-iron. You can hit further with this one, up to about one hundred seventy-five yards. Well, I should probably say *I* can hit further with this one." He grinned at me. "Have a couple of practice swings and see how it feels."

"Are you sure you should be giving her another one?" Marissa asked, looking dubious.

He shrugged. "It's worth a shot."

As I got into position above the as yet untouched ball, I noticed all three of them took several large steps away from me and my new weapon of choice. I could hardly blame them. This golfing hogwash was proving much harder than I'd expected.

"Okay, when you're ready, Dunny, take a shot and aim for the next flag back."

I bit my lip. "This is a lot harder than Wii Golf."

"You mean you actually have to get up off the sofa," Will replied.

"Cassie's the reigning Wii Golf champion, you see," Marissa

explained.

"Yeah. No one can touch her when it comes to that game. Not that she'd ever brag about it, right, Cassie?" Paige added.

"*Moi?*" I laughed. It helped release the tension. As I lifted the new club up behind me, I held my breath, closed my eyes, and swung through. As my club made contact with the ball and shot off the tee, I got such a surprise I let go. Will's three-iron hurtled after the ball, bouncing along the grass until it came to an abrupt stop.

I was torn between elation and embarrassment. I had just hit my very first real golf ball, but I'd also possibly broken one of Will's clubs. I turned to look at Will, Marissa, and Paige. They were all watching me, agog. No one said a word.

I gave them a shy thumbs-up. "Yay. I hit the ball."

"Yup. You did that," Will replied, looking at his club, lying on the grass.

I followed his line of vision. "Sorry about your club, Will."

He let out a sigh, shaking his head. "I think we have a lot of work to do here. When are you playing with this boyfriend of yours?" He used those annoying air quotes around the word "boyfriend."

"Parker." I shot him what I hoped was a withering look. "We're playing next Saturday."

Will let out a puff of air. "Can you delay it, maybe make it sometime later?"

"I don't think so. Is it that bad? I mean, I just hit the ball pretty well, don't you think?"

Marissa and Paige laughed. I pursed my lips at them.

"Sorry, Cassie," Paige had the grace to say. "You've just started learning. I think it takes a long time to get really good at golf. Right, Will?"

Will scrunched up his face. "More than ten days, that's for sure."

"How long do you think I need?"

"Err . . . a while," Will replied evasively.

"What's 'a while'? Do you think we should come here again?"

Will put his hand on my arm, smiling down at me. "Let's put it this way, Dunny. Either you have some serious, *serious* beginner's luck when you play your round with him or you need to spend every waking moment between now and when you play with him practicing."

I bit my lip. "Oh." I thought for a moment. As much as it riled me to do so, having Will teach me how to play would be incredibly helpful—and help me look good in front of Parker. "Will? Do you think you could . . . err . . . help me out?"

"I'm sorry, what was that?" he replied, leaning into me, cuffing his ear.

I kicked the floor. He was making me work for this. "Would you please help me?"

"Help you, did you say?" He crossed his arms as he looked at me. "Would you be willing to put the time in? Every day after work?"

I glanced at my friends. Spending every evening for the next ten days with Will "Poop Boy" Jordan was hardly my idea of fun. "Well, we have that girls' dinner on Thursday, right?"

"I'm sure we can reschedule that," Marissa commented, a smile teasing the edges of her mouth. *She's enjoying this!*

"Yeah, no problem." Paige shrugged and smiled. "We can do it in a couple of weeks. We might be able to get into that new place on the waterfront then, anyway."

"But . . ." I searched my brain for another excuse. Sure, I wanted to be good enough at golf to dazzle Parker, but spending that amount of time being told what I'm doing wrong by the person I'm competing against for the Regional Manager's job felt like cruel and unnecessary torture. I was torn.

Will slotted his iron back into his golf bag. "Put it this way, Dunny. You either take me up on my very generous offer to impart my golfing wisdom or you should go home and pray. A lot."

* * *

So that's what I did. I went home and visualized myself hitting that ball with style and elegance, impressing Parker with my golfing proficiency and natural charm. In my mind, I was the consummate golfer, hitting effortlessly great shots every time, congratulating Parker on his good shots, and commiserating with him on his bad. At the end of every visualization, Parker would take me by the hand, look deep into my eyes, and tell me he loved me and could see us playing golf together for many years to come.

As part of my prep, I flicked the channel over to one of the many sports channels I'd never visited before and fell asleep watching the not-exactly riveting world of professional golfers in bad clothing each night, making it look easy.

And because my mama didn't raise no fool, I took Will up on his offer, despite my reservations. We went to the driving range every evening after work. And I turned up prepared. I bought a set of clubs second-hand online and even purchased a shirt-skirt ensemble from the pro golf store I passed on my way to work each day—a store I never imagined I would ever enter, let alone exercise my Visa card in.

Will let out a whistle as I slipped my new, pink golf bag off my shoulder in the driving range cubicle. "Don't you look the business."

"Why, thank you." I turned and pulled my five-iron out of my pretty pink bag, removed its pink fluffy cover, walked over to the tee, and put my golf ball (pink, of course) in place. I was ready for my first shot.

Will leaned back against the wall of the cubicle. "Hit it, tiger. Let's see what you've got."

I got myself into position, did the little wiggle I noticed in my TV research all pro golfers seem to do, then looked from the ball to my target and back again. In short, I was feeling it. And it was good. I swung my club up behind me and let loose, hearing the satisfying *clunk* of club hitting ball. I watched my girly pink ball soar through the air, eventually landing close to the one-fifty flag.

A surge of pride rose up my chest. I tried my best to suppress a smile.

"Wow, Dunny. What an awesome shot! Are you sure this is your first time back at the range? You haven't been cheating on me with another coach, have you?"

"No. I guess I'm just a natural, that's all."

"A natural, huh? Okay, let's see that again."

"Sure. No problemo." I took another pink ball out of my bag, placed it on the tee, and got myself into position once more. This time, however, I clunked my club into the ground, entirely missing the ball and tee.

Will pushed himself off the wall and rolled up his sleeves. "Okay. We've got some work to do."

We spent the next hour and a half taking shot after shot, Will frequently offering advice, and me frequently scowling at him. But I listened to him and did what he said. My shots, although not exactly at pro level, had improved by the time we decided to call it a night, and we even began to have a little bit of fun together.

On our way back to our respective cars, Will proposed we grab a bite to eat together at a burger bar down the road. My tummy grumbled as I thought of the depressing state of my refrigerator back home. "Sure, why not? I could eat."

At the restaurant—a fifties-inspired American diner—a waitress showed us to a darkened vinyl booth near the bar. In my skirt, my bare legs stuck to the seat as I tried my best to shimmy around to the back. I picked up my menu, and my mouth instantly started to water at the long list of burgers, from vegetarian to fish to beef and everything in between.

"What are you going to get?" Will asked.

"I can't decide between the Tex Mex, the Double Cheese, and the Bacon and Avocado Burger." I looked at him over the top of my menu. "Do you think I could get all three?"

He grinned. "Why not?"

In the end, I ordered the Bacon and Avocado, a side of fries, and a lime milkshake. My excuse? I'd worked up quite an appetite at the driving range, not only playing golf, but having to be in Will Jordan's presence for an hour and a half more than was necessary. I deserved a medal.

"How did you know I loved burgers so much?" I asked.

"I took a wild stab in the dark. You and I have more in common than you think."

I guffawed. Will and I were poles apart as human beings. What was he thinking?

I changed the subject. "So, how am I doing with the golf?" I asked once we'd ordered and the waitress had delivered us our shakes.

"Actually, I know I give you a hard time out there, but you're doing great."

"Thanks," I replied, swelling with pride. "I do appreciate your help, you know."

Will nodded. "It's really important to you, impressing this guy. Right?"

I turned my glass around, feeling the cold condensation with my fingertips while thinking about Parker. "Yeah. It is." I looked up at him, suddenly embarrassed. "Is that so bad?"

"Of course not. I mean, you've got to make up for that first date underwear malfunction, right?"

I pursed my lips. "You can't be nice for more than a minute, can you?" I asked, my tone harsh.

Will looked surprised. "What? You're the one who told us about it. Remember?"

"Yeah. I really wish I hadn't told the whole team about it." What I meant was I wished I hadn't told *Will* about it. I should have known he would use it against me. "And anyway, it wasn't an underwear malfunction. They didn't fly off me or some other bizarre state of affairs." I squirmed in my seat, uncomfortable we were discussing my underwear.

"It's nothing to be embarrassed about. Really. He's a lucky guy."

I snapped my head up. "Why do you say that?" I looked at him out of the corner of my eye. This had to be the lead into some kind of dumb joke at my expense. Well, I wasn't going to fall for it. No way. Not this time.

He shrugged. "Just that you care enough about him to go to all this effort to impress him."

"And?" I lead. "What's the punchline?"

He shook his head at me, smiling. "Just that. What? Can't I say something nice, Dunny? Jeez."

"You can. It's just you don't. At least not to me." I knew I sounded like a wounded puppy, but I couldn't help it. Will was always teasing me and calling me by that stupid nickname. I found it thoroughly disconcerting when he was actually *nice* to me.

"It's just you're so easy." He waggled his eyebrows and grinned at me. I couldn't help but reciprocate. He was right, I was easy to wind up, especially where he was concerned. Perhaps I needed to loosen up a bit, join in the fun?

"And besides, we're archrivals for the job. I need to get in as many potshots as I can."

I frowned. I wanted the Regional Manager's job almost as much as I wanted to marry Parker. "So you can make my life a living hell before I get to be in charge of you and kick your butt into next week?

He laughed. "Something like that, Dunny."

"You know, it's kind of weird we're out to dinner together, when you think about it."

"I guess. We can still be friends, though, right?"

I nodded. Being Will Jordan's friend was never something I'd aspired to. But there was something about him that seemed genuine, different. I couldn't put my finger on it. "Sure," I said, smiling.

"You really want that job, don't you?"

"Of course. Why else would I have applied?" What was he, stupid? Of course, I wanted to be Regional Manager. It was something I'd been working toward since I joined the company—a long time before the likes of Will Jordan was on the scene.

The music changed to a song I recognized, "Jailhouse Rock" by Elvis Presley. Will started bobbing his head and tapping the table. I smiled. "Like the oldies, do you?"

"What? Oh, the music. Yup. Can't go past a bit of The King. My pops was a big fan, so it was practically the law to like him in my house."

"Mine, too. Must be an old guy thing. Did your grandpa live with you?"

"Well, *I* lived with *him*. He and my nan brought me up."

The atmosphere changed.

He continued to tap and bob his head as though it was no big deal.

"How old were you when you went to live with them?"

"I was seven. You see, my parents were killed in a car accident. My grandparents took me and my brother in. I lived with them until I left school."

My chest felt tight at the thought of Will as a seven-year-old, losing both his parents in one horrific, devastating blow. Just like that: gone. My eyelids felt hot. I blinked. "I'm sorry."

Will shrugged. "It's okay. Sure, it sucked at the time, but my brother and me? We were just fine. Our grandparents were awesome; we were just like a regular family, only they were a heck of a lot older than the other soccer parents. And look at me now?" His palms up, he leaned back against the booth. "You've got to say I turned out pretty good."

I smiled, shaking my head. "If I agree with you, I'll only feed your already enormous ego. And if I don't agree with you, I'm a heartless witch. Right?"

He grinned. "Exactly. So which is it?"

Stuck between a rock and a hard place, I replied, "You turned out great."

He slapped his hands together. "Yeah, I did."

We both laughed. Perhaps it was the fact he'd opened up about his family to me, or perhaps I just felt sorry for the little orphaned boy he was? But, in that moment, something changed between us.

I watched as Will got back to the serious business of looking like a total goofball, nodding and tapping to the music, this time adding in a bit of a shoulder jiggle.

I let out a chuckle. "Did you learn those moves from your pop?"

"As a matter of fact, I did. Join me out here, Dunny. Loosen up a bit."

I glanced around the room. No one I recognized. *What could it hurt?* Against my better judgment, I began to nod my head up and down. Elvis had moved onto "Hound Dog" by now, and Will had added hand movements to his repertoire, looking more and more like he had lost his mind. "Come on, Dunny!" he encouraged.

I shook one shoulder, then the other. Before I knew it, I was shimmying to The Pelvis complaining about his hound dog crying all the time, enjoying myself. Of course, we looked like a couple of patients who had escaped from a loony bin, but in that moment, I couldn't have cared less.

Our seated dance off was interrupted by our waitress delivering our burgers. "You two look like you're having a good time," she commented as she placed my burger in front of me.

I gave her an embarrassed smiled. "Ah, yes. Thanks. It looks great."

"Well, you two enjoy."

"Oh, we will," Will said. The waitress turned and left. "Dig in."

"Try and stop me, 'Poop Boy'. These look amazing." I picked up my burger and took my first bite. "Oh, my god. This is so good!" I exclaimed, my mouth still full.

He grinned at me. "I know, right?"

We sat in companionable silence as we devoured our burgers, pausing only to comment on how good the food was.

"Is it just that I'm ravenous or is this the best burger the world has ever known?"

Will chuckled, wiped some sauce from his lips with a napkin. "They are pretty good. I'm surprised you haven't been here before, being such a burger connoisseur."

"I don't come to this side of town much, to be honest."

"Well, you will be for the next seven days."

Every last crumb of my burger consumed, I sat back in the booth, my hands on my full belly as I rested my head against the vinyl backing. "That was divine," I declared with a sigh.

Will grinned at me. "I'm glad you enjoyed it."

For the first time since we arrived, I looked around the restaurant as Will finished off his plate of fries and I sipped my shake. I took in the booths, the fifties-style jukebox, the Tiffany rip-off lampshades. Even though it was after nine, the place was packed with people, clearly enjoying the food as much as we did. It felt comfortable, relaxed, cozy. Like the Cozy Cottage. "This place has a great feel to it. I like it."

"Yeah, me too. I've been coming here for a while now. Best burgers in town."

I grinned at him. "Amen to that!"

For the next few nights, we followed the same routine: Will telling me what I was doing wrong at the driving range, then dinner together afterwards before heading home. My golf was improving, although not at the rate I'd have liked. I may not be a gifted sportswoman by any stretch of the imagination, but I could usually pick up a new sport quickly. Golf, however, was proving to be trickier than most.

Will continued to make jokes at my expense, but instead of biting, I gave it straight back. And you know what? It was liberating. I was having fun, and I liked it.

But, of course, he persisted in calling me Dunny, even when he introduced me to some of his friends when they took a cubicle next to us one evening.

"Actually, my name is Cassie," I corrected, raising my eyebrows at Will as I quietly clenched my fists at my sides. Will might be Mr. Nice Guy these days, but he could at least use my proper name when introducing me to new people.

"Really? Well, it's nice to finally meet you, Cassie," Will's smooth-looking friend, The Joffster—another nickname, so who knew what the name his parents gave him was?—said.

I looked at him in alarm. "What do you mean, 'finally meet me'? What's Will said about me?" I looked from The Joffster to Will. He glanced down at his feet momentarily before looking back up. I narrowed my eyes at him. Of course, he's feeling sheepish. He'd told his friends about this lame chick he needs to train, the one he thinks he's going to beat to the Regional Manager's job.

"Is that the time?" Joffster said, glancing at his watch. "Wow, I should really get on with taking some shots here. Got to get back to the Missus by nine. Nice to meet you, Dunn—Cassie."

I watched as The Joffster—I mean, what a stupid name!—spun back to his friends in the cubicle and started rummaging through his golf bag. I turned to face Will, crossing my arms and fixing him with my steely glare.

He avoided eye contact with me. "Well, I think we should call it a night, don't you? It's been a good session, but it's getting late."

I clenched my jaw. "Sure." I packed up my bag as Will chatted with The Joffster, making plans to play pool on Saturday night.

We walked in silence back to our cars.

"Well, this is me. See you tomorrow."

Will paused, hovering next to my car as I flung my bag in the backseat. "Aren't you hungry?" he asked, puzzled.

I let out a sigh. "Look. You've been great, helping me out with all this. And I appreciate it, really I do."

"Why do I sense a 'but' coming up?"

I pursed my lips. "I don't appreciate being the butt of the jokes with your friends."

"That wasn't the 'but' I was referring to." He shot me a cheeky grin.

I rolled my eyes and slammed the car door firmly shut. "Okay, whatever."

He looked unexpectedly serious in the evening dusk. "Don't worry about what The Joffster said. You're not the butt of any joke."

Hands on hips, I asked, "Really?" my voice dripping in sarcasm.

"Really."

I studied his face for a moment. He looked genuine, but what did I know? Will Jordan had gone from being the bane of my work existence to my golf tutor and friend and back again. If you asked me which way was up, I'd get it wrong. Confused didn't begin to explain the current state of my brain. "All right. I'll give you the benefit of the doubt. And, err, thanks for the lesson tonight."

"You know you're doing great."

"Thanks."

"Still can't tempt you with a bite to eat? I know a great Thai."

My tummy rumbled. "Thanks, but no thanks. I'm going to have an early night."

"Your loss. There's a green chicken curry with my name on it. Let's work on your short game tomorrow after work."

"Sure, thanks."

He turned to walk away, calling, "See you, Dunny," over his shoulder in his usual light-hearted tone.

"See you, Man of Mystery," I said to myself as I watched him reach his car, throw his bag in the back, get in, and drive off.

* * *

We "worked on my short game" the following evening in the office once everyone had gone. Will set up an obstacle course with cups for me to putt my pink golf balls into, which proved so much harder and more irritating than whacking the heck out of a ball at the driving range. It was a whole different skill, one of which I was unlikely to get the hang of before I played with Parker on Saturday morning—three short days away.

Will was his usual sarcastic, joking self, and I tried my best to hold my own and not react the way I used to. But something had changed. Although I tried to let it go, I couldn't get The Joffster's comment out of my head. I didn't like being some laughable charity case one little bit.

"Hey, Will?" I asked once we'd packed up the cups and returned the office to its proper order.

"Yup?"

"I can't make it for the next couple of nights. I've got a dinner and a . . . another dinner. But I wanted to say thanks for all you've done for me. I may not be as good as you, but I think I can hold my own now. So."

"Hey, no worries. The big game's on Saturday, right?"

"It is. So, I'll see you tomorrow at work?"

"Sure. Have a good night."

I shrugged my jacket on, collected my purse, and walked to the elevator. Once I'd pressed the button, I looked back. I could see Will through his office window. He was already sitting at his computer, reading his screen intently, clearly accepting my story about two dinner engagements over the coming evenings. I let out a sigh. That man was beyond confusing. One moment he was going out of his way to be incredibly nice to me, dedicating hours of his free time to help me learn golf. The next moment, he'd talked to his friends about me, no doubt telling them all about how I'm some clueless charity case. I cringed. They probably all knew about my first date underwear fiasco, too!

And then there was the fact we were rivals for the Regional Manager's job. No. This was getting too hard. As the doors opened and I stepped into the elevator, I made a decision: keep Will Jordan at arm's length. Anything else was simply too bamboozling for me.

CHAPTER 14

BY THE TIME MY golfing date with Parker rolled around, I knew I wasn't going to set the golfing world on fire and become the next . . . whoever a famous female golfer was (Tiger Woods's sister? Mother? Cousin? Oh, I know, Lydia Ko! That's who). That said, I could hit the ball while holding on to my club, which, let's face it, was a major milestone for me.

Despite our weirdness and my decision to back away, Will had written out a list of which club to use when, and I had studied and studied it, even practicing pulling each club out for different shots in my living room at home.

Early Saturday morning I sized myself up in my bedroom mirror, taking in my new, sensible pink golf polo shirt and matching skirt combo and my long auburn hair, which I had swept up into a high ponytail. A pair of white ankle socks and uncomfortable, deeply unattractive golf shoes completed the ensemble. A bit on the cutesy slash preppy side of the fashion equation—in fact, add some makeup so I looked like a doll and this look would go down pretty well in Harajuku circles in Japan— but I certainly looked the part.

A beep of a car horn from outside my window told me Parker was waiting. I collected a sweater and visor from the end of my bed and slung my clubs over my shoulder. I headed out the door, down the stairs to Parker in his sensible, marriage-material Volvo. No flashy, rumbling status symbol for him.

"Good morning, beautiful," Parker said with a kiss once I was safely in my seat. "Are you all set?"

"Absolutely. This is going to be so much fun." *And, potentially, a complete disaster.*

"I know. The fact you play golf makes this all feel so . . . so right."

I looked into his eyes as my heart gave a little squeeze. Today could very well be The Day. Date thirteen might just be the charm.

We arrived at the club, a stately building with large columns set on, well, a golf course. Having never actually been to a course before, I was immediately swept up in the romance of the place, with its perfectly-manicured lawns and big old trees. Parker had a regular "tee off" at seven a.m. every Saturday with a couple of old medical school pals. I was nervous about meeting them; this would be the first time I had met any of his friends, other than Marissa's brother, who wasn't invited as he apparently was, and I quote, "a total hack." I tried not to wonder what he would think of me by the end of the morning.

Once inside the club, we were approached by two men about my age. They slapped Parker on the back and greeted me with enthusiasm. It felt nice.

"Cassie, this is Hunter and Geoffrey. Friends from medical school and pretty poor golfers."

They chorused their hellos, and I watched as Parker and his two friends enjoyed some friendly banter about golf, most of which went completely over my head.

As we walked across the lawn to our tee, Hunter and I chatted. He was the shorter and dumpier of the pair, with a kind smile and round, tortoise-shell glasses. "How long have you been playing golf?" he asked.

"Not long." *Eleven days, to be precise.*

"Oh, I thought Parker said you were a golfer? I must have gotten that wrong."

I smiled at him and changed the subject. "You're a doctor, too, Hunter?" *Doctor Hunter.* I almost giggled.

"Yes. I did my training with Parker and Geoffrey at the University of Auckland back in the day. I moved into obstetrics, though." He raised his voice so the others could hear. "None of this easy general practitioner stuff. Obstetrics is actual work."

"Ha! Try strep throat, possible bird flu, and a bad case of

hemorrhoids. And that was all before lunch."

And so the doctor banter continued until they all fell silent when the important business of teeing off rolled around.

"Would you like to go first, Cassie?" Parker asked. "This hole is a par three, so shouldn't be too taxing to start off."

"No, no. You all go first. I'm crashing your regular match." My smile dropped when I noticed all three men shared a look. Did I say something wrong?

"All right. In that case, Hunter, you tee off first, followed by myself, and then Geoffrey. You'll need to go last, Cassie, is that okay?" Parker's eyes were soft, encouraging.

"Fine by me." I smiled at him. That way I could study their form and copy it. Perfect.

Hunter placed his tee in the ground and the ball on top. I watched as he plucked a bit of grass out of the ground and threw it in the air. Some weird golfer's ritual, I assumed. Something to do with wind. In Wii Golf, they tell you the speed of the wind. This could be tricky.

I watched as Hunter pulled out a club and got into position, doing that same cat-on-a-hot-tin-roof move Will had done at the driving range. With his plump midriff, white pants, and black golf shoes, he looked a lot like a penguin about to dive into the ocean. I was forced to stifle another giggle.

Hunter swung and hit the ball with a *tap*, sending it flying up and away into the air, landing near the flag. I was so impressed with his accuracy and grace I burst into applause, slowing and eventually stopping only when Parker and Geoffrey shot me sideways glances. I clutched my hands in front of my body. Note to self: clapping must be reserved only for the professional golfers on TV.

After an awkward moment, Parker took his position, pushing his tee into the ground and the ball on top of it. Just like Hunter, he swung through and hit the ball beautifully, although his didn't get seem to get as close to the flag.

This time I resisted the urge to applaud.

"Bad luck," Hunter said with a grin.

"I'll make up for it with my short game," Parker replied stiffly. He seemed miffed. Perhaps he was as keen to impress me as I was him?

Geoffrey followed suit, again his ball landing close to the flag, and, finally, it was my turn. Three sets of eyes watched as I prepared to hit my first ever ball on a golf course—not that any of them knew that. Everything in place, I stood next to the ball, sitting on my tee, my driver in my hands—*thank you, Will*—and eyed my target. This was the shot I had practiced and practiced at the driving range. I visualized myself hitting the ball so it landed right next to the flag, making me look like I'd been playing for years. *You got this, Cassie.*

I took a deep, steadying breath. It was now or never. I swung my club behind myself and swung through, hoping, praying I didn't humiliate myself by hitting the ground or missing the ball. I almost dropped the club in surprise when I heard the satisfying *ping* of club and ball making contact. I stood still, holding my breath, my feet concreted to the spot. I watched the ball sail through the air. It climbed and climbed, and then, after hanging in the air like a tiny pink ball on a string, it dropped. I squinted, barely believing my eyes. Had it landed almost on top of the flag?

I leaped off my spot and punched the air. "Yes!"

The three men's heads swiveled around to look at me.

Parker blinked. "That was quite the shot, Cassie. I didn't realize how good a golfer you were."

I beamed back at him, my chest expanding. Hunter and Geoffrey both congratulated me.

It's official; I'm a golf genius.

"I can see we're going to have to lift our game to beat this one, Parker," Hunter said, slapping him on the back. "You didn't mention she was a budding Lydia Ko!"

Parker's smile was broad, his eyes sparkling bright. "No, I didn't." He looked so proud of me, I could burst, right there on the fairway.

On a high, we slung our bags over our shoulders and walked down toward the flag, Parker taking my hand as he walked beside me. I was eager to see where my ball had landed, but just as eager to bask in the admiration of my boyfriend.

"I had no idea you were this proficient a golfer, Cassie," he said quietly to me.

I shrugged. *You and me both.* "Oh, I like to keep a thing or two up my sleeve, you know," I replied with an air of mystery.

"Hey, maybe we could play a round with my parents? They're pretty good players. They're coming back from their cruise in a couple of weeks. I've told them all about you, of course."

Warmth spread through my belly. "That would be wonderful." Meet the parents? Check!

He gave my hand a squeeze. "I'll set it up. They're really going to adore you, my golfing queen."

"I hope so. You'll have to meet mine, too."

"Okay."

A smile spread across my face. We walked hand in hand to the green. Sure enough, my girly pink ball was sitting pretty, only a few feet from the flag, leaving everyone else's boring old white balls for dust. *Wait until I tell Will about this!* I smiled to myself. Good at Wii golf does equal good at real golf after all.

I took a mere one attempt to putt my ball into the hole, and the three men applauded my effort. I took a curtsey, basking in the adulation. The three men putted their balls into the hole—Parker missed his first, had to take another two shots to do it, and looked very grumpy with himself as a result—and we moved onto the next hole.

I was still as confident as could be as I watched the men hit their balls. It was my turn. I stood at the tee, preparing to hit the ball, fully expecting to perform just as dazzlingly as I had on my first shot. I was a natural, how could I possibly *not* kill this shot, too?

I gripped the club the way Will showed me. I had this. I swung up behind myself and prepared to follow through. Too late, I realized something wasn't right. I twisted my body too far around, and when I swung downward to hit the ball, I missed, stabbing the ground with my club, pain jarring up my arms. My mouth slackened as I watched the scene before me unravel in slow motion, like a home video you see on those funny TV shows. Although, this was far from funny for me. My club sailed out of my hands and bounced head to tail, head to tail, across the fairway in front of me. It finally came to a stop with a humiliating *thud,* a good ten feet away.

The ball remained on the tee.

I looked down at my palms accusingly, as though they had decided to let go of the club without my brain knowing about it.

My heart sank down, deep into the pit of my stomach. *I guess the cat's out of the bag now.*

Parker wrapped a comforting arm around my shoulders. "What happened, Cassie? Are you hurt?"

"No, no. I'm fine." *Merely unbearably embarrassed.* "I . . . err . . . I don't know what happened, exactly. One minute it was in my hands, the next it . . . wasn't." I looked up into his eyes. I could tell he was working hard not to laugh.

He pressed his lips together, but the smile broke free. He let out a chuckle, his arm shaking around my shoulders. "That was quite something." He reached down and brushed a stray hair that had escaped from my ponytail away from face.

His laughter was contagious. Within seconds, I began to giggle. I glanced at Hunter and Geoffrey. Their eyes were shining as they tried their best not to laugh. They too gave in, and we all stood together, laughing out of sheer surprise—and how ridiculous I had looked.

"We all have a bad shot every now and then. Yours was . . . well." Parker was too gracious to continue.

"Horrific," I confirmed, because it was. There was no other word for it. I wouldn't be telling Will about this one, that was for sure.

The three men smiled. Although no one said it, I knew they all agreed.

"How about you take the shot again and we'll finish the day's play off with just nine holes?" Parker asked.

My heart melted. Parker really cared for me, and nine instead of eighteen sounded fantastic to me. I grinned at him, my eyes misty. "Perfect." *Just like you.*

The rest of the game proved resoundingly that my first shot was just fantastic beginner's luck. I didn't fail to hit the ball quite so spectacularly on the next seven holes, but I wasn't exactly Tiger Woods or Lydia Ko, either. Nevertheless, I managed what Parker referred to as a "quite decent" total, so I could at least hold my head up high at the end of the game—and heave a sigh of relief no one filmed my epic golf fail.

As we drove away from the club, having enjoyed a post-game cup of coffee with Hunter and Geoffrey, Parker put his hand in mine. "You don't play often, do you? You can be honest with me."

I bit my lip, my eye twitching. "Some?"

He gave my hand an encouraging squeeze. "It's okay. The fact you gave it your best shot, and got that incredible first shot, is amazing." He slowed the car and pulled over next to a playground, where toddlers were bounding around, watched by their parents, chatting to one another, holding cups of coffee. "You did it for me, right?"

I looked into his soft, gentle eyes. I bit the inside of my mouth. The game was up: he knew. And I knew he knew. I decided to come clean. "Today was my first ever time. I mean, I'd practiced at a driving range and watched golf on TV, but I've never actually been on a golf course."

His mouth fell open. "Really?"

I nodded as my belly twisted into a knot. What would he think of me now?

He leaned over the gearshift and collected me in a kiss. He looked into my eyes. "Cassie, you're incredible. Thank you."

I shrugged, self-conscious. "For what?"

"For caring so much you learned how to play golf and put yourself through all that."

I hung my head. "But I lied to you."

"So what? You were trying to impress me, trying to relate to me."

He leaned across and took my face in his hands, looking deep into my eyes.

Oh, my god. Here it comes. He's going to say it!

My heart hammered in my chest like an overenthusiastic bongo player who had drunk too much coffee. The anticipation of the moment was almost too much. I could barely breathe. I nodded at him, hoping to encourage him to say those three little words I knew he was about to say. Inside, my head was screaming, *Just say it!!*

"Thank you." He kissed me.

Oh, for the love of God, say it!!

He took my hand in his. "I love that you'd do that for me."

He loved that? He used the L-word? *Oh, my!* Things were definitely going in the right direction.

He swallowed. "Cassie, I . . ."

"Yes?" I leaned in, ready and waiting. He was going to say it. I just knew it!

He smiled, his face glowing. "I really like you."

My eyes welled with tears as my heart clenched. I sprang across the seat and hugged him in close. "I love you, too!" I declared in a gush.

He flinched, as though I'd threatened him with a hot poker. "What? Oh, yes. Great. Thank you. That's . . . ahhh, just great."

That's just great? *What?* With a sickening thud, my heart hit my belly as his words rung in my head. It wasn't the "I love you" I'd expected. He liked me. *Really liked me.* Not loved me.

I recoiled from him, my eyes darting around the car, a wild animal frantically searching for an escape. I didn't know what to say. "I . . . umm . . . yes."

Parker took my hand in his again. It was warm against my suddenly cold flesh. "Cassie, please. I really like you, and I love spending time with you. Please accept that for what it is. It's no small thing."

"Sure," I replied, my voice unnaturally chirpy. "No problem. Consider it accepted." I forced a smile. I couldn't quite bring myself to look him in the eye.

"And I so love that you love me. Really, I do. And I'll get there. It'll probably just take me a little more time, that's all."

My hand felt like a log in his. "Of course! No worries." I tried to make my tone confident and breezy—like I hadn't just made a declaration of love for a man who simply "really liked" me. "Take your time. As much time as you want, in fact."

What am I saying?

He looked entirely unconvinced. "Really?"

"Yes, really. Take as long as you need."

What?!

"I mean, you feel what you feel, right? I can't make you feel something you don't feel just as much as you can't make me feel something *I* don't feel."

Somebody stop me.

He nodded at me, looking a little skeptical. "That's true."

"Like for instance, if you loved the Blues and I was like, no way, I hate the Blues and loved the Hurricanes instead, you couldn't change my mind, could you?"

Why was I talking sports?

"Actually, I don't really care for rugby," he replied hesitatingly.

"Whatever!" I shouted, my voice reverberating loudly around inside the car. "I mean, that was just an example to illustrate my point."

"I see."

"Or maybe you like apple strudel and I'm like 'apple strudel, are you freaking kidding me?' And you're like, 'yeah, apple strudel is the best' and I'm like, 'it sucks,' and you're like, 'it does not,' and . . . stuff."

Oh, good Lord.

Now he was looking at me as though I was possessed by some sort of teenager with verbal diarrhea. "Yes, of course." He cocked his head. "Cassie? Are you all right?"

"I'm good. In fact, I'm great! We've got this whole 'like-love' thing out in the open, and you know what?"

He shook his head.

"I feel so much better. A weight has been lifted from my shoulders. A weight, Parker! I know where you stand and you know where I stand. It's all good. Now, why don't you take this baby on the road so I can get back home and get on with my day, thinking about how much you really like me?"

"If you're sure."

"I am."

He started the engine and glanced at me once more. I shot him my best Guy Smiley smile, and he drove me home through the busy streets of Auckland. As I sat in the passenger seat, watching the buildings and parks whiz by, I wondered how I had I gotten myself into this mess. This was not the way it was supposed to happen. *No way, José.*

If I could have wiggled my nose and disappeared in a puff of smoke, never to return, never to have to see Parker again, in that moment, I knew I would have.

CHAPTER 15

I STOOD IN THE stairwell of the twelfth floor, my knuckles clenched at my sides. I took some deep breaths. It was seven minutes before my scheduled second interview with Laura, and I was as nervous as a deer with a neon target on its head in hunting season.

After "the conversation" with Parker on Saturday, I'd said goodbye to him in his car, pleading a headache—unoriginal, I know, but I'd had a horrible experience and needed an easy out—and retreated to the sanctity of my home. I dumped my stuff on the floor and threw myself on my bed. I sobbed all my carefully applied, golf-appropriate makeup off onto my pillow. By the time I was finished, it looked like some small animal had been brutally murdered on it.

After a long weekend, closeted away in my house, I woke up on Monday morning, resolved I was going to allow Parker the time "to get there" and not twist myself up in knots about it all. But the thought rung in my head: I'd said I loved him and he hadn't said it back. A sick feeling in the pit of my stomach seemed to have taken up residence, and I had little hope I would manage to shake it today.

I took a deep breath. I needed to be on my game. Today was the second interview. No thoughts of Parker. No thoughts of unreturned feelings. No thoughts of my humiliation. No thoughts of anything except nailing this sucker. *You can do this, Cassie.*

I reached for the door only for it to be pushed open, my

fingertips cracking with the impact. I jumped back, clutching my hand, my laptop bag swinging perilously from my shoulder. It was Will "Poop Boy" Jordan. Again. Why did he always seem to barge through this door when I was here?

"Oops, sorry, Dunny. I didn't see you there." He took in me nursing my hand. "Did you hurt yourself?"

I shook my head in irritation. "It was the door. That's all."

Concern was etched on his face. "Here, let me look."

Before I could protest, he held my injured hand in his and examined it. "Can you move your fingers?"

With tentative movements, I twitched my fingers. They throbbed but there was no searing pain. They weren't broken, thank goodness. "I think they're okay. Thanks."

"Good." He still held my hand in his. "I may not be your doctor boyfriend or anything, but I'm glad I could help." He looked at me, smiling, like he was in on some kind of secret I didn't know about.

I glanced down at our hands. "Can I—?"

He dropped my hand like it was a hot coal. "Sorry." He cleared his throat. "Are you here for your second interview?"

I glanced at the stairwell door, then back at Will, feeling awkward. Did he really expect me to talk about my second interview with the person I'm up against for the job? "Ah, yes."

He nodded. "Well, good luck. Laura may come across as a tough old bird, but she's a softie at heart. You'll do great."

"Okay," I replied, eyeing him uncertainly.

He stood looking at me for a moment before flashing me his smile and taking off down the stairs, two at a time. I watched him leave and heard the door to the sales floor slide closed behind him.

Well, that was weird.

I raised my chin and took a deep breath. I reached for the door and pulled it open, plastered on a smile and approached Brian's desk. "Good morning, Brian."

Brian looked up from his computer screen at me, peering over his glasses. "Cassandra Dunhill. Right on time. Take a seat, I'll let Laura know you're here."

I did as I was told because, even though I knew Brian was really a Spoodle of a man, he didn't have the reputation of being an uncompromising Rottweiler for nothing.

A moment later, Laura stood at her door, smiling at me. "Come in, Cassie."

"Sure. Thanks."

As the door closed behind me and I said my hellos to Laura and Hugo, the Human Resources Manager, my nervousness kicked up a notch or ten. Will must have been up here for *his* second interview when I saw him in the stairwell a few moments ago. Had he dazzled them with his confidence and expertise? Was I the irritating second interview they needed to conduct, although their minds were already set on Will for the role?

We sat around the coffee table, overlooking Auckland's sparkling blue harbor. I crossed and uncrossed my legs, thought better of it, and crossed them again. Laura shot me an encouraging smile. I relaxed a hint.

"We are really interested in how the Marketing project is coming along, Cassie. Can you take us through where you are with it?" she asked.

"I'd be happy to." I pulled out my laptop, opened it up, and double clicked on the presentation I had prepared for this very question. As I talked, I noticed Laura nodding and Hugo jotting down occasional notes. Laura asked a number of questions, although I suspected she already knew the answers to many of them. They'd just finished their interview with Will, after all. I answered all of her questions, highlighting how well I was leading the team, and what we had achieved to date.

"How do you think you and Will Jordan worked together?" Hugo asked once I had finished my presentation.

"Fine." I smiled at them both.

Laura and Hugo shared a look. "Care to elaborate?" Hugo asked.

My mind raced. I had avoided working directly with Will, preferring to manage my own tasks and responsibilities and not have to deal with his know-it-all confidence. "Well, I . . . I think we've worked well together. He and I tend to deal with different aspects of the project. I believe our time is more effectively utilized that way."

"I see." Hugo nodded. He resumed scrawling in his notebook.

Laura furrowed her brow. She picked up a pile of papers that had been lying facedown on the coffee table in front of us. She scanned a page. "Some in the project team have mentioned you have a tendency to dominate proceedings at times." She looked up at me. "What do you think they mean by that?"

Dominate? My palms began to sweat. My mind darted to the numerous times Will had decided on a point and I had overridden him or raised something that rendered his point moot. I did it so the team would see me as their leader—and not Will. Irritating him had been simply a fringe benefit. "Well, at times I've felt the direction Will has wanted to take the project hasn't been quite right. I want to deliver the work on time and in the best shape I can, so sometimes I feel I need to step in."

An image of Will helping me at the golf driving range flashed into my head. I swallowed my unease. Hugo crossed his arms as he sized me up. I tapped my foot. I had no idea members of the project team were reporting back to Laura. What else had they said?

"What about teamwork? It is important to lead but equally important for the Regional Sales Manager to be able to work with others in a consultative way," Laura said.

I furrowed my brow. Consultative? "What do you mean . . . exactly?" I didn't like where this was going.

"How well do you think you and Will work as a team? Is it going well, are there areas to work on? Take us through it."

My heart rate picked up. Will and I as a team? "Err . . . pretty well? I mean, we have different styles, but I don't see how they can't complement one another."

"I see." Laura nodded at me.

I swallowed as Hugo wrote yet more notes in his notepad.

Mercifully, Laura changed the subject to something else, and we moved on. For the rest of the interview, I couldn't shake the feeling me dominating Will in the project had directly impacted my chances of winning this job.

After almost an hour of answering questions and asking a few of my own, we three stood up and shook hands.

"Thank you, Cassie. Hugo and I aim to make a decision once this Marketing project is delivered. We'll be honest with you, we have eliminated all options other than you and one other candidate."

Will Jordan.

I shook her hand. "That's . . . good to know." *Was it?* "Thank you, Laura. And you, Hugo."

I walked out of Laura's office with a sense of disquiet in the pit of belly. Yes, for the most part the interview had gone well. Yes, I was one of only two candidates for the job. But had I self-sabotaged? Had trying to outsmart and out-lead Will damaged my chances?

And, I realized with a start, had I been unfair to Will?

* * *

"Morning, ladies," Bailey called with a bright grin from behind the counter. "Only two of you today?"

"Paige is going to be late. How are things?" I explained. I listened absentmindedly as Marissa and Bailey chatted about their weekends. Having come straight to the Cozy Cottage Café from my interview, my mind was too full for small talk today. That and the not-quite-I-love-you calamity from the weekend.

"How about you, Cassie? The usual, I assume?" Bailey smiled as she pushed a plate with a slice of flourless chocolate and raspberry cake toward me on the counter.

I looked down at it as though it were a moon rock. "Yes, sure," I mumbled.

"Okay," Bailey replied uncertainly. She and Marissa shared a look.

"Come on, you. Let's grab a table and debrief." Marissa pulled me by the arm over to our usual table by the fireplace. I noticed it wasn't lit as it was a mild spring morning. With a pang, I wished it was. I could do with the comfort of a fire about now.

"Spill," Marissa instructed in her matter-of-fact way.

I didn't know quite know where to start. I opened my mouth to speak, but no words came. This was an extremely rare occurrence for me.

"Is it the interview? Parker?" Marissa's voice was soft.

I let out a long breath and pushed my hair behind my ear. "The interview, I guess. Parker's . . . Parker wants me to meet his parents." My smile was weak, to say the least.

"That is so exciting! Big step in the right direction."

"What is?" Bailey asked as she placed our order in front of us.

Marissa smiled up at her. "Parker wants to introduce Cassie to his parents."

"Oh, my. Cassie, that's fantastic news." She pulled a chair out from the table and plunked herself down. "Tell me everything."

I took a deep breath. I told them about my fantastic first shot, the case of the flying golf club, and Parker's almost-proclamation in the car. I left out the fact I'd blurted out the L-word without it being reciprocated—I didn't want to dwell on that. And anyway, it felt good to concentrate on something positive.

Bailey scratched her chin. "I have to admire you, Cassie. You set out to marry the next guy you dated and now look at you. You've gone and fallen for the next guy you dated."

I smiled at them both as I ignored that persistent sick feeling in the pit of my stomach. "You're right. It's all working out to plan."

"Give me enough warning before I need to buy a hat, though," Bailey added.

"Oh, I don't think we're in that ballpark just yet," I replied quickly.

"You will be. I give it a couple of months." Bailey grinned at me.

"Oh, you know, it could be a lot longer. I mean, we haven't said 'I love you' yet or anything." Which was, strictly speaking, true. *We* hadn't said it. Just dumb old me.

"But you're about to meet his parents. Guys don't do that unless they're serious about someone," Marissa affirmed.

Bailey nodded in agreement.

"You're right," I replied, a hint of a smile spreading across my face as hope rose inside me. Why would he introduce me to his parents unless he thought he might be falling in love with me?

"Which is why I need the warning. I've got a few pounds I could do with losing." Bailey patted her belly.

I sized my friend up. Sure, she was no anorexic stick insect— she had thighs and breasts and all the things a woman was supposed to have—but she was voluptuous and gorgeous just as she was. Why do we women do this to ourselves? "Don't you go losing anything. Promise? And anyway, how could you not eat all these amazing things you bake? If I had your cooking skills, I would be the size of a house."

"An apartment block," Marissa confirmed, nodding.

Bailey stood up and pushed the chair back into the table, a smile on her face. "You girls are the best." She looked over at the counter. "Gotta go. Customers are calling."

Once Bailey was back dazzling her customers with her sweet treats and beautiful smile, Marissa leaned in conspiratorially, as though the café walls had ears, which would be a really freaky thing if they did. "So, did you hear about Will?"

My heart skipped a beat at the mention of his name. "What?"

"Apparently, he broke up with his girlfriend because he's in love with someone at the office." Her eyes danced.

My breath caught in my throat. "He is?" I squeaked, giving my best Minnie Mouse impersonation as my breath caught in my throat.

Why does this matter to me?

Marissa nodded, her mouth forming a thin line. "Mmm-hmm. And we all know who *that* has to be." She shot me a meaningful look.

My banging heart was almost deafening. "Who?" My voice came out in almost a whisper.

Marissa regarded me as though I was some sort of idiot who'd been living under a large rock. "Paige, of course! Who else could it be?"

I forced a smile. *Paige.* "No one. Paige. Yes, it has to be Paige."

"It all makes sense. He must know how she feels about him, and over time, he's developed feelings for her, too."

I swallowed. Paige is an awesome person. She's single, available—hasn't declared her love for anyone else in a parked car at the side of the road lately—and thinks the sun goes out when Will sits down. He could do a lot worse than Paige Miller.

I played with my coffee cup. "How did you hear about Will?"

"Being in love with Paige? I put two and two together. Apparently, he went out for a few drinks on Friday night with The Cavemen, had a few too many, and admitted he'd broken up with his girlfriend because he wanted to be with someone else. Cassie, it *has* to be Paige." She leaned back in her chair, satisfied with her conclusions.

"But he didn't actually say that."

She shook her head.

Cogs whirred in my brain. "Does Paige know?"

"I thought I'd tell her the good news when she gets here. She is going to be so excited, you know how she feels about him."

"Yeah. Yeah, she will."

As if on cue, I spotted Paige closing the café door. I waved at her, and she waved back. A few moments later, she arrived at the table, her order placed with Bailey. She sat down next to us in a cloud of Dior. "Sorry I'm so late. Princess Portia droned on and on for what felt like a lifetime. I'm in serious need of coffee or I'm at risk of falling into a coma."

Marissa and I watched her intently. Once she noticed, she narrowed her eyes at us. "What?"

Marissa glanced at me, a smile teasing the edges of her mouth. "Should we tell her?"

Paige's eyes darted from Marissa to me and back again. "Tell me what?"

Neither of us said anything—Marissa because she enjoyed the suspense, and me? I couldn't quite work that out.

"Come on. You guys are freaking me out."

I shrugged, nodding at Marissa. "She'll tell you. It's her news."

Marissa's face broke into a full-blown grin. "I think Will's in love with you."

Paige's mouth dropped open, and her eyes got huge. "Wh . . . what?" The color drained from her face. She looked like she might bolt for the door at any second.

Marissa grinned at her. "It's all coming together for you, Paige. He *loves* you."

Paige's eyes whizzed from Marissa to me and back to Marissa. She swallowed hard.

I tried to temper her confusion. "What Marissa's trying to say is she's heard Will has feelings for someone at work."

"He does?" Her voice was so squeaky it beat mine hands down in the Minnie Mouse stakes.

"And it's you." Marissa was so confident in her summation it was hard for me not to believe her—let alone confirm everything Paige had ever hoped for.

"But he . . . he hasn't said anything, and I only just talked to him before coming here." She looked like she might cry. "Are you sure?"

I bit my lip.

"Who else could it be? It *has* to be you, Paige. We're so happy for you, aren't we, Cassie?"

"Yes, yes we are," I replied.

Paige's flushed face broke into a grin that would put Julia Roberts to shame. "I could ask him out, couldn't I?" She bit her lip. "Will could be my One Last First Date."

"I know!" Marissa's excitement was almost a match for Paige's.

I nodded, trying to join in. But I couldn't help thinking Marissa was making a big leap with this

For Paige's sake, I hoped she was right.

CHAPTER 16

THE FOLLOWING AFTERNOON, I sat with the project team around a large table in the Marketing Department, discussing the project's status and upcoming action points. As I listened to Will making suggestions as to how we could approach our next milestones, I watched as others in the room listened intently to him, nodding along, occasionally interjecting with ideas of their own. Will listened respectfully to everyone in the room, and when he disagreed with someone, he got his point across gently but firmly.

Since Laura's suggestion I wasn't working well enough with him, Will kept popping up in my head when I least expected it. Like out to dinner with Parker when one of us ordered a burger. Or doing squats and crunches at Pilates class. Even when I was in the bath! He totally ruined my soaking zen, that was for sure.

Every time he waltzed into my thoughts, an unpleasant sense of guilt hung in the air around me. I had been so intent on making sure I looked good to the project team, a much better leader than Will, I'd ended up damaging my chances at the Regional Manager's job. And been unfair to him.

Then, there was Marissa's assertion he was in love with Paige. I don't know what it was, but something told me he wasn't, that Marissa had put two and two together and come up with a banana.

I chewed the inside of my lip. It was obvious to me Will was a decent guy. He'd had a tough time in childhood, but he'd come through it and, in his own words, turned out great. He treated people well. He *led* people well. What's more, he'd helped me out with my short-lived golfing career without me even having to ask—potentially putting his life at risk as I inexpertly wielded a golf club. That *had* to mean something.

Sure, he could be a total know-it-all and a complete show-off, and then there was that weirdness with his friend, The Joffster, that night. But doing what he had done for me was going beyond the call of duty. At his core, Will Jordan was okay.

I swallowed. *His favorite café is my favorite café.*

"Anyone want to add to that?" Will asked, surveying the faces in the room.

I put my hand up. "I would." All eyes turned toward me. I was certain I detected a moan from someone in the room. I ignored it. "I just wanted to say . . . that is, I believe wholeheartedly . . ." I cleared my throat, nervous. "What I'm trying to say is, I for one think what Will has said sounds really great." I smiled and nodded at him encouragingly. "Don't you think, everyone?"

The others in the room shot me looks ranging from agreement to puzzlement to downright hostility.

Will furrowed his brow. "Which part, exactly, Dunny?"

I threw my hands up in the air. "All of it! Don't you think, you guys?" I looked around at the faces in the room. "Will has *such* good ideas. I think we should definitely go with these ones and consider revisiting some decisions we've made in the past, too."

Will leaned back in his chair and regarded me through narrowed eyes. "You want to revisit past decisions?"

I looked at him, my eyes bulging. "I do! I've reviewed some of my input and I have come to believe, in the best interests of the project, we should have gone with a few more of your suggestions, Will. You see, I've been thinking lately I can sometimes dismiss your ideas too quickly. And I want to change that." I stood up, pushed my chair back, and started to pace the room. I was getting into the swing of things now. "In my mind, leadership isn't all about being the person who makes the decisions. It's about making the right decisions and working successfully as a team. From here on out I want to be more"—I searched for the word Laura had used—"consultative. Yes, that's what I want to be. More consultative. With you, and with everyone." I opened my arms in a dramatic gesture to show just how very consultative I planned on being.

I looked at Will, awaiting his reaction. He tried and failed to suppress a smile. "Is that so?"

"Yes, yes it is. I believe we can all work together and achieve great things." I was unwavering in my commitment. If Laura wanted me to show leadership through inclusiveness, then I was going to include the life out of each and every person in this room. Starting with Will.

"Sure, that sounds . . . reasonable," Simon, one of the project coordinators, said hesitatingly, looking around at his colleagues.

"Yes. Being consultative is . . . err . . . a good thing, right?" said another, looking at Will for confirmation.

As I sat back down at the table, I noticed Melanie typing something into her phone. I narrowed my eyes at her. So, she was the mole who'd told Laura and Hugo I didn't work well with Will! An image of Melanie with a long, pointy black nose and whiskers, burrowing happily in the dirt, flashed into my mind. I had to work hard to suppress a rising giggle.

"Okay. Great." Will was still looking at me as though I was speaking in tongues or something. "Consultative Cassie. It has a ring to it." His smile was quizzical. After a beat, he added, "So, to recap, you're happy with changing the date for phase four to the twenty-first, despite your protestations at our last meeting?"

"Yes. Absolutely. Bring on the twenty-first, I say." I punched the air.

He nodded at me as if in slow motion. "And you're happy to work with me and Design Zoo on the final graphics?"

"If that's what *you* think best, Will, then yes. Of course." I smiled and nodded at everyone in the room. They were all watching me closely.

I turned back to Will. He raised his eyebrows in question.

"Will, what matters here is teamwork. Leadership, yes, but teamwork first and foremost." I turned and looked directly at Melanie. "I don't need to be in charge. It should be shared."

Melanie flashed me a weak smile and shrunk in her seat. Good. *Scuttle back to your mole hill where you belong, missy.*

Will eyed me for a moment, clearly trying to work me out. "All righty then. It looks like we can wrap this thing up for the day. We've all got our actions, Cassie more than others, it would seem."

I nodded at him and smiled, happy with the new me. Consultative Cassie.

"Shall we meet up again on Friday at nine?" Will continued.

Everyone around the table pulled out their phones to check their calendars. There was a chorus of "Sounds great," "No problem," and "See you then." People stood up, collected their things, and filed out the door. I was about to follow the others when Will asked, "Can I talk with you for a moment, Dunny?"

I smiled at him brightly. "Sure." Not even that ludicrous nickname could sway me from my new path. I followed his lead and sat down opposite him. I plastered on a smile. "What can I do for you, Will?"

He eyed me for a moment. This was becoming a habit. "You could explain what that was all about for a start."

I knew exactly what he was referring to. I decided to act innocent. "What *what* was all about?"

He shook his head. "You know what I'm talking about. Usually you fight me on every point and try to take over." He shrugged. "Sorry, but it's true."

"You're right. But that's now all in the past. I've decided you're not all that bad and maybe I should give you a chance."

"'Not all that bad,' huh? High praise." He raised his eyebrows and smirked at me. For the first time in recorded history, I didn't want to wipe that smile off his face.

"You know what I mean. I . . . I guess I've been a bit tough on you. You have some great ideas, and I don't really give you a chance. Plus, you've been really nice to me with the golf thing. I'm—" The word stuck in my throat. "I'm sorry," I managed in a croaky voice.

"You're *sorry*?" His eyes got huge.

I lifted my chin. "Yes. I'm sorry," I sniffed.

He watched me for a moment. He narrowed his gaze, crossing his arms as he leaned back in his chair. "Your golf date with what's-his-name went well, didn't it?"

I felt heat in my cheeks. "Yes . . . but that's not what this is about." I shifted uncomfortably in my chair. Talking with Will about Parker felt . . . wrong, somehow.

"How did it go? Did you maim anyone? Or yourself?" He studied my face closely for a moment. *Again*. It made me want to squirm. "No re-broken nose or anything. Must have gone okay."

"No one got hurt. And it went well." *Other than the lack of love.*

"Oh. Well, I'm glad I could help." He stood up abruptly, rolling his chair out from behind himself. "I'll see you later. Got a meeting to get to. Keep up the . . . consulting." He collected his things and put his head down as he headed out the door. He was gone in a flash, without a backward glance.

I was left, sitting on my own at the oversized table in the empty meeting room, wondering what in the world had just happened.

CHAPTER 17

FOR THE NEXT COUPLE of weeks, life ticked over predictably enough. I continued to meet with clients and work with the team as Consultative Cassie. It was turning out great, and even Will seemed to accept the new, improved me, despite his initial weirdness. I had a much heavier workload now, of course, but it seemed a small price to pay in the pursuit of the Regional Manager's job. I made sure Melanie the Mole saw me in my teamwork-magnificence whenever possible and tried my best to befriend her to show her what a nice person I was. It seemed to be going well.

Paige, Marissa, and I kept up our regular Cozy Cottage Café sugar-fests—if it ain't broke, don't fix it, right?—and Parker and me? Well, once I convinced myself his lack of a declaration of love was a mere speedbump and he would be true to his word and get there in his own time, things got back on track. We were seeing one another a couple of times a week, going out for dinners, going on forest walks, taking picnics to the park in the warm spring air. My Instagram feed was littered with happy couple photos that were probably making my single friends want to vomit. I was in my almost-love-bubble with my future husband, so I didn't care.

"Are you ready to go?" Parker adjusted his tie in the mirror, concentrating on creating the perfect Windsor knot.

"Just give me three more seconds," I called from the bathroom. I studied myself in the mirror. I was wearing a pale pink dress with white detailing, pearls I'd borrowed from Marissa at my neck, and a pair of Mary Janes on my feet that made me want to break into a fifties Hollywood dance routine. I'd swept my hair up into a relaxed bun, allowing a few strands to hang loose around my face. My makeup was fresh and natural. In short, I looked like the future Mrs. Cassandra Dunhill-Hamilton. Today was the day I was meeting Parker's parents. And tomorrow, he was meeting mine. It was a big weekend.

"Cassie? We really should get going," Parker called, a hint of stress in his voice.

I switched the light off and stepped out of the bathroom. "Ready."

Parker turned and looked at me. Instead of the expected compliment, a cloud crossed over his face.

"What?" I asked uncertainly, glancing down at my dress.

Parker blinked and shook his head. "Nothing. You just . . . nothing. You look wonderful."

I did a little twirl, feeling—and I hoped *looking*—like Kate Middleton's red-headed sister. Equally classy, equally gorgeous.

"They're going to love you."

I smiled weakly. *Not like you . . . yet.*

He glanced at his watch. "We'd better go or we'll be late."

Twenty-seven minutes later, we were still sitting in Auckland's legendary traffic, a good handful of miles from the swanky country club where we were due to meet Parker's parents for lunch. He had told me his parents were Annette and Dickie—no, seriously— although he advised I call them Mr. and Mrs. Hamilton for starters, that they were keen golfers, and that they were active patrons of the arts. His dad was a retired surgeon and his mother a former nurse who spent most of her time either playing golf or attending lunches with similarly well-heeled society ladies. Although he didn't say so, it was clear to me they had more money than God and lived the life of Riley—who, by all accounts, had a pretty good time of it.

"Got it." I smiled at him and glanced down at my dress. *They're going to love me.* God, I hoped Parker was right.

For the past few minutes, we'd been sitting in silence since Parker had yelled at a driver in front of us who had failed to notice the lights turning green, causing us to miss the light all together. He drummed his fingers on the steering wheel in agitation as he stared at the red, unchanging light. I reached across and placed my hand on his arm to try to comfort him. He jumped in his seat, and I instantly pulled it back.

He turned to look at me. His face was tense and drawn. "Sorry. It's just my parents are very punctual and they expect the same of me."

I softened my voice. "We're only a few minutes late. They live in Auckland, they know all about the traffic. They'll understand. Plus, they'll be really happy to see you. They've been away for a month."

"Sure." He sounded as convinced as Sully's copilot probably did when his captain announced he was going to land their plane on the Hudson. I watched in concerned silence as he gripped the steering wheel, his knuckles turning an unnatural white.

His obvious nerves permeated my skin. I began to tap my foot, worrying exactly why he was so uptight. Sure, meeting your partner's parents for the first time can be nerve-wracking, but we were right for each other. I was his future wife. And he had already said they were going to love me. Where was the problem?

Sixteen silent, uptight minutes navigating traffic later, Parker parked the car at the country club. As he bounded out and slammed his door, I did a final check in the mirror, decided to apply some more lipstick, and zipped open my purse. Mid-application—a crucial moment, as any woman could attest—Parker flung my door open, making me jump. I snapped my head in his direction, drawing a line of lipstick on my upper lip.

"Argh!" I peered in the mirror. Great. I looked like I had a five-year-old child with an unsteady hand for a makeup artist. I rummaged around in my purse, looking for a tissue.

"What are you *doing*?" Parker demanded, still holding the car door open.

Hadn't he ever seen a woman put on makeup? "I was trying to apply some lipstick. Have you got a tissue?"

Parker pursed his lips. "You've had all trip to apply lipstick, Cassie. You look fine. Let's go." He offered me his hand.

"But it's smeared over my top lip," I protested, taking his hand nonetheless.

"No one will notice." He walked off with speed toward the entrance to the country club, pulling me by the hand behind him.

With my free hand, I rubbed frantically at my top lip. I suspected I looked like I'd just lost a bar brawl—not the look I was going for right now.

We virtually ran up the steps, through the large wooden doors, and into the reception area. The contrast between the blazing sun outdoors and the dark interior had me blinking like I was in a dust storm.

"Mr. Hamilton! How nice to see you," said an attractive young woman with a chic blonde pixie cut and a thousand-watt smile at reception.

"Hello, Angelica. How are you?" Parker said in a tone he hadn't used with me since before we got in the car.

I couldn't help but shoot him an annoyed look.

"Very well, thank you." Her smile didn't drop. "Are you here to meet your parents? They're sitting out on the terrace."

"Yes, thank you. Lovely day for it."

As Parker and Angelica shared pleasantries, I scanned the room for a mirror. I spotted one, walked over to it, and peered at my lip in the half-light. There was a definite lipstick-on-upper-lip situation going on. Why did I decide to wear my ruby red permanent lipstick today? I licked my index finger and rubbed. Better. Not great, but better.

"Cassie?" Parker enquired.

I gave my lip one further surreptitious rub, turned, and faced him and the ever-smiling Angelica. Parker stretched his hand out to me. I took it, and we walked out onto the terrace together, as ready as I'd ever be to meet the parents who make my boyfriend so uptight. There was a smattering of tables on the terrace, shaded by large, cream umbrellas. The view down the lawn to the golf course below was breathtaking. Parker scanned for his parents. Nervous, I concentrated on my breathing.

You can do this, Cassie.

He spotted them sitting under one of the umbrellas at the edge of the terrace. I sized them up in record-breaking speed. Father: late-fifties, recently cut gray hair, perfectly pressed polo shirt, the sort of tan you get from having enough time to spend in the sun across the hemispheres each year. I thought of my own dad, his year-round pasty Irish complexion, his rapidly receding hairline, his slight paunch, his ready laugh and twinkling eyes. I swallowed.

So far so intimidating.

I turned my attention to his mother: probably also late-fifties but harder to tell, thanks to probable "work"; short, perfectly coiffed brunette bob cut; large, dark glasses in sharp contrast with her diminutive frame; crisp white shirt, red cardigan, and pearls at her throat. Her resemblance to Anna Wintour, the *Vogue* editor with the fearsome, cool-as-a-cucumber reputation, was not lost on me.

I was beginning to understand why Parker had been so edgy.

I gave his hand a quick squeeze. He snapped his head in my direction, shot me a slightly feverish look, and pulled me along faster in their direction. I plastered on my best "I'm your future daughter-in-law and I know you will just love me" smile and walked with as much confidence as I could muster at Parker's side. I may have been dressed like I belonged here, but Parker's nerves, his scary-looking parents, and the plush surrounds had me feeling like a country bumpkin on her very first visit to the big smoke.

We reached their table.

"Mother, Father. How are you both today?"

I narrowed my eyes at Parker. He called his parents "Mother" and "Father"? What was this, a Dickens novel? Had we been transported to nineteenth century Britain and I had somehow failed to notice?

Parker leaned down and kissed his mother on the cheek. "You look wonderful, Mother. As always."

"Oh, thank you, darling," she simpered.

Parker's father sprang up, pushing his wicker chair back. "Parker! Good to see you, lad."

I watched as they shook hands. Not hugged. It felt . . . odd. But then, it must be refreshing not to have to endure endless hugs like I do with my family. Hug Mom, hug Dad, hug Granny and Pop, hug Bella. Frankly, it's exhausting. A handshake is probably much more civilized. Perhaps we'll teach our children to shake our hands once they're adults? I wouldn't need to worry about creasing the linen slip dresses I'm sure to be wearing then when Parker and I host family lunches in our gracious home.

"Father" turned to me, his teeth standing out against his tan so clearly the coast guard could use him in their arsenal. "How are you, Sara?"

I opened my mouth to speak. *Sara? Who the heck is Sara?* I

closed it again, not knowing exactly what to say.

Parker's dad took me by the shoulders, grinning down at me. "It's lovely to see you again."

What? Before I had the chance to correct him, he leaned in toward me, puckering up. I turned my cheek so he could kiss it and began to pull back, but he was going in for another, European style—naturally—so I turned the other cheek, only to meet him in the middle. Our lips locked. My eyes sprung open in astonishment as his crinkled into a smile. He pulled away and let go of my shoulders.

My cheeks flushed red hot. "Mr. Hamilton. I, err, I'm . . . I'm sorry about that," I stammered.

"Don't be, Sara." He turned to Parker, and said in a deeper tone, "I do like this one."

Mortification crept across my chest. I shifted my weight.

"Oh, Dickie. You are an old goat sometimes. This is *Cassie*, Parker's new girlfriend," Parker's mother responded on my behalf from her seat at the table. If she'd noticed the big smacker her husband had just planted on me, she didn't let on. "Sara is someone else entirely."

Parker's dad smiled at me. "Of course it is. My mistake. Although, you do look a lot like Sara, doesn't she, eh, Parker? You clearly have a type, lad."

I watched, agog, as Parker's dad elbowed him in the ribs, as though me looking like Sara—and I was still utterly in the dark as to who she was—had somehow become quite the joke of the day.

Parker slipped his arm protectively around my waist. "Yes, I suppose. I hadn't thought about it actually, Father." He gave me a little squeeze, instantly assuring me.

"Well, *Cassie*," Parker's mother said, emphasizing my name for Mr. Hamilton's benefit, "it's very nice to meet you. Parker's told us very little about you, of course. It's nice to see you actually exist and you're not just some sort of online girlfriend or something."

I blinked at her. *He hasn't told them much about me?* Panic seared through me in a flash. "Well, I do! I exist! Cassie exists! And she's not Sara, she's *Cassie*! Yay for Cassie!" I blurted loudly, as though I was headlining a pep rally to a cast of thousands. I looked from Parker to his parents. They all had inquisitive, puzzled looks on their faces—yeah, like *I* was the weird one here.

"Well, that's just great. Good for you for . . . existing," Mrs. Hamilton said. "Why don't you both take a seat? You are rather late."

"Yes, we're sorry about that. Traffic," Parker replied.

"We managed to arrive on time," she replied with a smile.

Still grinning like a lunatic off her meds, I sat down in a wicker chair Parker pulled out for me. He sat opposite me and shot me a look that asked whether I was okay. Either that or he was determining whether he needed to call the men in the white coats to take me away before we ordered our appetizers.

I took a deep breath and nodded at him, hoping to reassure him that I'd not flicked the lid on my brain and certainly didn't require any sort of medical intervention. Normal, calm, in-control Cassie was back. And sitting in silence. No one was talking. I watched as Parker smiled, his mother nodded and smiled, his dad smiled and winked at me. *Back up the bus!* Parker's dad winked at me?

"So, Cassie. Tell us about yourself," Mrs. Hamilton said, breaking the awkward silence at the table.

"Oh, well, where to start?" I managed.

"How about you tell us about your family?" Mrs. Hamilton blinked as she smiled.

"Sure. Well, my parents live in Auckland, which is where I grew up with my—"

"Where?" Mrs. Hamilton enquired, cutting me off mid-sentence.

"I'm sorry, what?" Remembering the sort of manners one would expect at a country club, I said, "I mean, I beg your pardon, Mrs. Hamilton?"

"Where exactly did you grow up?"

"In Onehunga." I thought of my middle-of-the-road childhood suburb, with its strong community spirit and affordable housing—a far cry from the city's chi chi streets Parker and his family inhabited.

"Onehunga? Been there a few times over the years," Mr. Hamilton said.

I perked up. "You have?"

"Yes, that's right," Mrs. Hamilton replied, nodding at her

husband. "We had that place there."

"Really? How long ago did you live there? You may know my parents. My dad's a bit of a bigwig locally. He runs the pharmacy on Rocket Road. You've probably met him." I thought of my dad's big, booming laugh as he shared a joke with his regulars, advising on treating itchy bites and rashes, selling hot water bottles in the winter months, sun hats and sunscreen in summer.

Mrs. Hamilton looked incredulous. "*Live* there? Oh, heavens, no. We owned a building there, as an investment. We've lived in central Auckland for many, many years."

Chastised, I replied, "Oh. I see."

"Cassie doesn't live there anymore, do you, Cassie?" Parker said, his face bright. "She bought her own place closer to the city. Right?"

"Is it one of those high-rise blocks?" Mr. Hamilton asked, a scowl on his face.

"No, it's not. It's a townhouse, actually."

"Good, good. Don't want to touch some of those towers. Not a good investment right now."

"Okay. I'll . . . ah, bear that in mind." You know, when I'm next *investing* in property, that is. "Thank you, Mr. Hamilton."

"No, it's a great place. And really handy for everything. Cassie's up for a promotion at work actually, aren't you?"

I shot Parker a puzzled look. He was rapidly taking on the guise of Public Relations Manager for Cassandra Dunhill. I kinda liked it. "Yes. I'm hoping to become Regional Manager at the technology company I work for."

"Good for you," Mrs. Hamilton commented. "Now, tell me more about your family. Your father is a pharmacist, correct?"

I nodded.

"And your mother?"

"She works in the pharmacy, too."

She raised her eyebrows. "Two pharmacists in one family? My, my."

"No, she just helps out in the store. You know, serving customers, ordering stock, that kind of thing."

"I see." Mrs. Hamilton seemed singularly unimpressed.

To my relief, a waiter in a white shirt and black pants materialized at the table. I'd been so busy dealing with Parker's family—the accidental lip kissing, the interrogation, the consequent looking down their noses at me—I hadn't even opened my menu. Luckily, Parker stepped in, saving my butt.

"I know the menu pretty well here. How about I order for you? Smoked salmon followed by a Caesar Salad sound good to you?"

My heart filled up as I smiled at him across the table. "Yes, that'd be great, thanks."

No sooner had the waiter departed with our order when, much to my dismay, the interrogation resumed.

"How old are your parents?"

"How many brothers and sisters do you have?"

"Are your grandparents still alive?"

"Are there any serious medical issues in your family, such as heart disease or diabetes?"

I felt thoroughly sociologically and biologically vetted. I tried to look at the bright side, all these questions suggested she wanted to ensure I was good enough for her son to breed with, which must mean Parker was inching closer to "I love you." At least, that's what I was hoping. If not, his mother was lousy at small talk for a lady-who-lunches.

"What about herpes?"

"Herpes?!" I guffawed, almost choking on my Caesar Salad.

"Well." Mrs. Hamilton gestured toward my upper lip.

My hand flew to my mouth, half expecting to find a large, crusty cold sore, despite never having had one in my life. I patted my face, felt nothing. The smudged lipstick, of course! I rubbed frantically at it, shielding my mouth with my other hand.

"That's just some lipstick, Mother. Cassie doesn't have herpes, or anything else for that matter," Parker said, springing to my defense.

"Smudged lipstick, eh, lad?" Mr. Hamilton waggled his eyebrows suggestively at Parker.

Meanwhile, I was totally mortified.

Mrs. Hamilton fell short of giving me a physical examination, but I wouldn't have put it past her to offer up a syringe for a blood sample. Eventually, after it was clear to everyone I was beginning to crack under the harsh light of interrogation, Parker jumped in to help me. "Mother, don't you think that's enough questions for now? You'll tire poor Cassie out."

Mrs. Hamilton looked alarmed. "Why? Does she tire easily?"

"Mother!"

Mrs. Hamilton sat back in her seat, raising her hands in surrender. "I'm only taking an interest in your new girlfriend, darling. Any mother would ask these sorts of questions."

"It's fine, Mrs. Hamilton. I don't mind," I said. My eye began to twitch.

"That's right, Sara was that excellent golfer. Shot a six handicap," Mr. Hamilton commented from out of the blue, looking impressed.

I turned to look at him. Sara? *Again?*

"Yes, Father," Parker said, a tight expression on his face.

"What about golf, then, eh? Do you play?" Mr. Hamilton asked me.

My mind shot instantly to the mortifying events in Parker's car following our one and only golf game together. "Oh, well, yes. A little," I replied, darting a look at Parker, my eyes pleading with him not to share my golfing catastrophe from a few weeks ago. Or remind him how he hadn't said "I love you" to me afterwards.

I needn't have worried. "Cassie's an excellent golfer. We played a round only a couple of weeks ago. Didn't we, Cassie?"

"Yes, I—"

"Does she shoot a six handicap, though? That's what I want to know," Mr. Hamilton questioned.

Whoever this Sara person was, she was beginning to get on my nerves. "No, I don't, Mr. Hamilton."

"Cassie's very good at Pilates," Parker offered as he squeezed my knee under the table.

I shot him a grateful look. "I'm okay at it."

"Flexible, is she?" Mr. Hamilton asked, as though I wasn't sitting right next to him at the table. "That's what a man likes to hear."

"Dickie!" Mrs. Hamilton looked offended. "That's snooker room chat, it's not appropriate luncheon conversation."

But asking me about herpes is?

I cleared my throat. "So, how was your trip? I understand you were in Europe?"

And that was it for the rest of the meal. Three courses. Mrs. Hamilton complained about the weather and the people, even the

165

cobblestoned streets. Mr. Hamilton drank his weight in chardonnay, occasionally winking at me as his wife droned on. As boring as it was, and as difficult as it was to pretend every word she said was fascinating, at least the bright light of interrogation had been lifted from me. I could relax. A little.

I heaved a sigh of relief when we bid them goodbye.

"That went well," Parker commented as we walked to the car.

I nearly tripped over in astonishment. "It did?" I blinked at him in wonderment. Mr. Hamilton thought I was a poor second to this Sara person; I kissed him smack-bang on the lips, and he *liked* it; neither of his parents knew *anything* about me until today; and Mrs. Hamilton's line of questioning made me feel like I was auditioning to be an egg donor for an online service.

"Yes, silly. Don't seem so surprised. I know my mother can be a little full on, but it's only because she loves her only son." His smile was so cute I almost forgot about Sara.

"She put me through the third degree, you know."

"Yes, she does that. It's just her way, that's all. And my father thought you were terrific."

I thought of Mr. Hamilton winking at me across the table and his suggestive comments to his son. "I certainly got that impression."

"So," he said, leaning in to kiss me, "even if it was tricky for you, it went well and you can relax. You passed."

"I passed?" I asked, startled.

"Yes, you passed. You may proceed to the next level." He grinned at me, and my heart melted. Sure, it was probably a nerdy reference to some sci-fi movie I didn't know, but Parker cared enough about me to introduce me to his parents and he thought they had liked me.

He may only "really like" me so far and "needed more time," but that had to count for something.

* * *

Back at my place after the lunch, I asked Parker about something that had been bothering me all day. "Who's Sara?" I kept my tone light as I handed him his coffee and sat down next to him on my sofa.

"Oh, err, sorry about that. That was pretty awkward, I know. My dad isn't great with names."

"Ah, no." When no response to my question was forthcoming, I asked, "So? Who is she?"

"Ah, Sara's my ex-girlfriend."

I knew it!

"Oh. And your parents obviously knew her?"

"Yes, yes they did. We dated for a while. They're friends with her parents, that's how we met."

"Oh."

Parker put his coffee down on the table and wrapped his arm around my shoulders. "Cassie, don't worry about Sara. We broke up quite a while ago."

Telling me not to worry about Sara made me do exactly that. "I'm not worried," I lied. I took a sip of my coffee and smiled at him, just to show him precisely how relaxed I was about this Sara ex of his from quite a while ago. "How long did you date?"

"A few years."

A few years?! I jerked, spilling some of my hot coffee on my hand. "Ouch!"

"Oh, you clumsy thing. Here." Parker took my mug from me and put it on the table. He reached behind the sofa and pulled a couple of tissues out of a Kleenex box I kept on a side table.

I took them and wiped my hand. "Thanks." I tried to sound nonchalant when I asked, "Out of interest, how long is it since you broke up?"

"Ages, really."

Is he being elusive on purpose?

"Are we talking months here, or years? Give me a ballpark to work with," I persisted. For some reason, it seemed vital for me to know.

"Why do you want to know about her? It's not relevant to us," he said.

"Humor me?"

He let out a sigh. "Okay. Let me think." He looked out my living room window to the street outside. "I guess about six months. Give or take."

"Six months!" I replied far too loudly. I was pleased I wasn't holding my coffee for *that* particular little gem of information.

Recovering, I cleared my throat. "Oh, yes. That is quite a while ago." I did some frantic mental arithmetic. That would mean Parker and Sara had broken up—after dating for *years*, the precise amount of time yet to be determined—only a matter of mere weeks before he and I started dating. My tummy twisted into a knot.

Did that make me a rebound?

"So, she was a good golfer, huh?" I asked leadingly, desperate for any clue about how he felt about her now.

"She is. Was. Yes. Hey, Cassie? Let's talk about something else, okay? We both have exes, but we don't need to delve into one another's past, right?"

"Sure, of course." My tone was light while my mind was going a mile a minute, and my tummy was involved in some sort of energetic trampoline convention. It wasn't a pleasant combination. I sat next to Parker, listening to him telling me about some patient or another, brooding. Why had they broken up? How many years exactly did they date?

"Parker? Can I ask something else?"

"Look, if it's about Sara, I'd prefer you didn't. It was a tough breakup and I'd really rather not get into it."

Alarm bells clanged in my head like it was Sunday morning. Tough for whom? For him? Did Sara dump Parker? Although breakups can be difficult for all concerned, it's a universal truth it's much harder on the dump*ee* than the dump*er*. Parker may have expressed his desire not to talk about this anymore, but I was in imminent fear of becoming obsessed.

CHAPTER 18

THE NEXT AFTERNOON, WE stood together on the doorstep of my old family home, dressed in much less formal attire.

"Ready for this?" I asked Parker with a grin.

Up until I had met Mr. and Mrs. Hamilton yesterday, I had thought it would be much easier for Parker to meet my family than me his. Even though I knew Mom and Dad would be happy for me in whatever person I chose to be with—unless he was a drug lord or leader of a terrorist organization or the like, clearly—as I stood next to Parker, I was suddenly anxious *he* wouldn't like *them*.

"Yes," he confirmed with a smile.

It was now or never. I turned the knob and pushed the front door open. "Hi, it's me!" I called out.

As though they had been lurking around the corner, awaiting our arrival—and I wouldn't be surprised if they had—both my parents materialized in the hallway at once, wide grins on their faces.

I greeted them with hugs, as was the Dunhill way. "Mom, Dad? This is Parker Hamilton. Parker, this is Cheryl and Joe Dunhill."

I watched as Parker extended his hand and gave my dad a firm handshake. "It's a pleasure to meet you, sir."

"Sir?" Dad roared with laughter, his belly wobbling like a bowl of jelly in an earthquake. "Call me Joe. We're not in the military, you know. And what's with this handshaking? Come here." He pulled Parker in for a hug, slapping him on the back the way men do, as if half maiming one another was perfectly acceptable.

"Of course . . . Joe." Parker extracted himself from the hug, looking distinctly uncomfortable.

"It's a pleasure to meet you, Mrs. Dun—ah, Cheryl." He greeted my mother with a kiss on both cheeks.

"Oh, look at him, all French," Mom said to me, still clutching onto Parker's arms. "Aren't you the fancy one? But then, you are a doctor." She pulled him down for one of her famous bear hugs, squeezing the living daylights out of the poor guy. I swallowed as I noticed Parker's eyes bulge in surprise.

I closed mine in silent mortification. Why did Mom and Dad have to be so . . . so *not* Parker's parents?

"Well," Mom said, her cheeks pink. "Why don't you come on in? We don't stand on ceremony here, Parker."

Dad slapped Parker on the shoulder. "No, we don't. Come and put your feet up, have a nice cup of tea, Park. Can I call you Park?"

"Ah, Parker," he replied.

Oh, god.

Dad's smile didn't drop. "Parker it is then."

I followed the three of them down the hall and into my parents' living room. I glanced at the eighties-inspired sofa, with its plastic arm covers that crinkled when you touched them, Mom's extensive plate collection, and the large TV dominating the room. Over time, it became clear to me my parents weren't overly interested in moving with the times in interior design. I'd never felt this quite as keenly as I did today. Where once I had simply thought of this as my childhood home, suddenly it looked old, tired, and in serious need of a style injection.

Is Sara's family home like this?

"What a lovely room you have here. Very relaxing," Parker said, looking about as relaxed as a lamb in docking season.

"Thank you," Mom said, brimming with pride. "Come and have a look at this." She signaled for him to go to the far wall and look at a collection of photos of me and Bella at various stages of growing up. I closed my eyes, knowing what was about to come next.

"Is this you, Cassie?" he asked, pointing to a photo of me, dressed in my girl guide's uniform, aged about eleven.

"Yup. Embarrassing, huh?" I shot Mom a look. *Why didn't we meet at a café somewhere instead?*

"Oh, I don't know. I think you look pretty cute with your long plaits and knee-high socks," he replied, shooting me a teasing smile.

"Oh, well, if you like that one, you should see this one over here," Dad said, standing in front of what was quite possibly the most embarrassing photo of me ever taken. Period. "Cassie hates it, but I think it's just wonderful."

Parker took in the photo of me, dressed up for my first ever school formal. I was wearing an orange knee-length dress with a full skirt, complete with ruffled puff sleeves and sewn-on flowers. I was grinning, clearly feeling like a princess in my get-up, my mouth a flash of metal. My hair fell about my shoulders in soft auburn waves, which should have been my one saving grace, but it clashed so perfectly with the orange of the dress it made me physically ill just looking at it.

"I hate that picture, Mom," I said, shaking my head. And now Parker had seen just how awful I looked back then. *Wonderful.*

"I know you do, sweet pea, but you look so happy. You know how much you loved that dress."

"Yes, when I knew zero about fashion and what suits me." I took a handful of hair and brandished it toward Mom. "Orange, Mom? Really?"

She put her hands up in surrender. "You insisted on it."

"You looked adorable. I never understand why you don't like that photo," Dad added. Yes, you guessed it: my dad was color blind.

I rolled my eyes. "Look at what I've got to put up with!" I said to Parker, hoping he wasn't considering bolting to the hills. "Parents who love to embarrass me at every turn."

To my relief, he smiled back at me, looking a little less like a rabbit in headlights. Perhaps the walk down bad-fashion-choice-lane had taken the edge off his discomfort?

Parker and I sat down on the sofa next to one another. It was so old we sunk down into it a good half a foot more than we should. I suppose it *was* bought new in 1988, back when it was probably the height of fashion.

Mom handed Parker a photo album. "Here."

Parker raised his eyebrows in question at me, a smile teasing the edges of his mouth. "A family album?"

I tried to smile. I knew what was coming next.

He opened onto the first page. There were cute baby photos of me with the dog, my Dad at a picnic. So far so good. Then, he turned the page and saw me, sitting in all my naked glory on a potty in the very room we were sitting in today, laughing my head off with a diaper on my head.

Parker chuckled. "How old were you?"

"Three."

"I bet you were adorable."

"Oh, she was!" Mom gushed. "Here, let me show you."

And so the troll through the family photo albums continued, with Mom explaining every photo, Dad chipping in with the odd bit of background on various events, Parker making all the right noises, and me? Sitting on the eighties nightmare of a sofa, wishing it would swallow me whole.

When Mom finally put the albums away and toddled off to the kitchen to make us all a cup of tea—despite the fact Parker was a committed coffee drinker—I watched as Parker surveyed the room once more. "Your parents like plates, don't they?" he said in my ear.

I stifled a giggle. My mom and her plate collection go way, way back—back to when she was a little girl and her grandmother gave her her very first plate. Or so the Dunhill legend goes. She now has nothing less than about thirty adorning the walls of the living and dining rooms, and at least another dozen in the kitchen. They come from all over the world, and Mom would be more than happy to tell Parker the story behind each and every one of them. I think I'll save that treat for another time. He'd had more than enough to contend with for one day.

"Now that you know everything you need to about Cassie, why don't you tell us a bit about yourself?" Dad said as Mom placed a tray of tea and cakes on the coffee table. My mouth watered as I spied her famous chocolate mud cake.

"Here you go, sweet pea. I made your favorite." Mom handed me a plate with a large slice of cake and a dollop of cholesterol-laced cream on the side.

"Thanks, Mom. You're the best." Mom's chocolate mud cake never lasted more than a couple of hours in the cake tin, it was so good.

"Thank you. This looks delicious," Parker said, taking a slice of cake from Mom, who looked as pleased as punch. "Tell you about myself? Of course, Mr.— I mean, Joe. Well, I'm an only child, I grew up in Auckland, I like fine food and wine, and, of course, spending time with your wonderful daughter." Parker gave my hand a quick squeeze, and I beamed.

"Fine food and wine, eh?" Dad asked, taking his slice of cake and leaning back in his leatherette chair. "Have you been to Davey's? Now there's a place that knows how to fry chicken!"

"Oh, yes," Mom confirmed, a fried chicken glaze in her eyes.

I cringed. Davey's had been Mom and Dad's favorite place for a "slap up meal," as they called it, since I could remember. Run by Dad's friend, Davey—no surprises where he got the name for the place from—they specialized in deep-fried anything, including the vegetables, and desserts with enough sugar to give you diabetes on the spot. The paleo, low carb, clean food movements had completely passed Davey and his cronies by, that was for sure.

"I don't believe I've been there. Where is it?" Parker replied politely.

"You haven't been to Davey's?" Dad sounded astonished, as though it was beyond human understanding why someone, who had lived their whole life in Auckland, had never been to Davey's for an artery-clogging meal. "Cheryl, did you hear that? Parker's never been to Davey's!"

"Well, we'll just have to remedy that, won't we?" Mom chirped, licking her lips at the prospect of some of that deep-fried crapola.

Oh, great. That was all I needed, a "slap up meal" with Parker and my parents in a place that smelled of rancid fat—on a good day. On a bad? You don't want to know. Davey's was about as far-flung from the refined and elegant surrounds of Parker's parents' country club as could be. I squirmed in my seat. A change of subject was needed, stat!

"So, Dad. What's happening in the world of the Rocket Road Pharmacy?"

As Dad launched into stories from the store, with Parker listening, I leaned back in my seat and tried to see my parents through Parker's eyes. The hugging when we arrived got us off to a difficult start, but he seemed to have recovered since then. My parents, with their stories and cups of tea and endless props (I'll have a word with them later about that photo of me in the orange disaster), were at least friendly. But they weren't refined like Parker's parents. I wondered what Sara's parents were like, whether they were like Parker's, all high class and stiff.

For the first time since we began dating, Parker was seeing where I came from—not just the person he thought he knew. As I watched him nod along to my Dad's story about a customer having a fainting spell by the hand lotions, I wondered if he liked what he saw.

CHAPTER 19

WILL FLASHED A STRIP of card in front of my face, interrupting my work. As mildly irritating as it was, he caught my attention. And I'd been going cross-eyed from all the project figures, so it was a welcome break.

"What's that?"

He hopped onto my desk, making himself right at home—as usual. "This, Dunny, is a ticket to the one and only Lady Gaga concert."

"What?! But those are like hen's teeth! Where did you get it?" I reached out to grab it. Will snatched it away before I got the chance.

"Hey, hands off! This is mine."

I cocked my head. "*You're* a Lady Gag fan?"

"Any self-respecting, safe-in-his-manhood Kiwi guy is a Lady Gaga fan. Have you lost your mind?" He smirked at me, and I let out a laugh.

"Who are you going with? Whoever it is, I'm jealous. You know how much I wanted tickets to that concert."

He shrugged. "A bunch of friends. All chicks, of course."

I rolled my eyes. *Of course.*

"And . . . I thought it would be appropriate for the two leaders of the most successful project this business has ever delivered on budget and on time . . . to go together."

"Okay," I said uncertainly, narrowing my eyes at him. "Are you saying you're taking *me*?"

He shrugged nonchalantly. "Yeah, I 'spose I am."

With a piglet squeal, I leaped out of my chair and hugged him, accidentally pushing him over. We landed on my desk, me pinning him down, as papers flew to the ground and my laptop began to teeter precariously on the table's edge. I let out a panicked squeal, reached across a now prostrate Will, and grabbed it before it went crashing to the floor.

Pinned beneath me, Will looked up at me, and said, "Well, that's one way to thank me, but really, Dunny, what would your boyfriend say?"

I suppressed a smile as heat rose in my cheeks. Lying on top of my coworker—my firm, muscular, coworker at that—on my desk in the middle of the work day wasn't quite the image I wanted to project. A blush crept up my neck and took residence in my cheeks. I could feel Will begin to laugh below me. It was contagious. I giggled, putting my hand to my mouth.

"Are you going to get up?" he asked between chortles. "I mean, it's fine by me if you don't. I'm not the kind of guy to push a beautiful woman off me."

I laughed and slapped his arm. "I bet!"

Wait. Will thinks I'm beautiful?

Embarrassment took root. I pushed myself off the desk and straightened back up, self-consciously tucking my shirt back in and pulling my skirt back around. My blush intensified. If anyone were to walk in on us right now, they would think we were having an office fling.

I cleared my throat. "I'm sorry. I didn't mean to, you know—"

Will pushed himself up off my desk, back into his sitting position. "Throw yourself at me?" He raised his eyebrows suggestively, flashing me that cheeky grin of his. "Really, Dunny. I never knew you cared."

"It was an accident!" I insisted a little too loudly. As I smoothed out my skirt, I thought of Paige. Will was being his usual flirty self, but she would be mortified to know only seconds ago I was in the throes of full-body contact with the guy she wanted to be her One Last First Date! I squirmed uncomfortably.

Still grinning, Will waved the ticket in the air. "Still want it?"

"I—" Should I take it? Only seconds ago, going to a concert with Will Jordan and a gaggle of his adoring female fans felt harmless, a no-brainer. Now? Somehow it was different, like I'd be cheating on Parker or something. I guessed lying on top of a hot guy on your desk in the middle of the day could do that to a girl.

"Come on. We deserve this. We've worked really hard on this project. Let's go out and let our hair down."

I lifted my hand to touch my ponytail. What could it hurt? He was right, we *had* worked hard on this project, and it had turned out great. Now we'd delivered it, a fun night out could be just the thing to take my mind off Laura's impending decision on the Regional Manager's job. Even if it was with my rival.

I nodded at him. "Okay. That would be nice. I would love to go to the concert with you and your horde of adoring women."

He handed me the ticket. "Excellent choice, Dunny. We are going to have an awesome time. Drinks at my place beforehand. I'll text you the address."

* * *

The night of the concert, I arrived at the address Will had given me right on time. I looked up at the modern apartment block, located on a leafy street only a couple of suburbs away from my own. I rang the intercom and was buzzed in. I climbed a flight of stairs and found Will's front door. Number 174. I knocked.

A second later Will, dressed in jeans and a T-shirt, opened up. "Dunny!" he exclaimed, standing back for me to walk in.

"Hey, 'Poop Boy'," I replied, handing him my jacket as I surveyed the room. It was a New York loft style place, with wooden floorboards, exposed brick, and large windows. For a guy, the condo was tastefully decorated, no Playboy posters or beer pictures in sight. I whistled. "Nice place you've got here," I commented, trying to act as though it wasn't an incredibly odd experience to be at Will Jordan's home—the guy, up until recently, I had despised.

"Thanks. We like it, don't we, Killer?" He leaned down and picked up a fluffy Persian cat who virtually purred his head off at the attention.

I cocked an eyebrow. "You called that beautiful creature 'Killer'?" I reached over and patted the cat's soft fur. "Hello, Killer. What a horrible name your daddy gave you."

"It's a great name!" Will let the inappropriately named cat jump down to the floor and slink off. "Drink?" He walked into his gleaming stainless steel kitchen at the back of the room and opened the refrigerator. "I have wine, beer, juice, and your choice of soda."

I followed him, placing my purse on top of the kitchen counter. "I'll take a Coke, please."

"No problemo." He cracked open a couple of bottles and handed one to me. He raised his bottle, and we clinked. "Cheers." He took a sip. "The others will be here soon."

"Who are the others?" I took a sip. The bubbles traveled up my nose, making it tingle.

"Jacinta and Lori. A couple of old college friends. You'll like them, they're fun. They're big fans."

I raised an eyebrow. "Of you or Lada Gaga?" I suspected both.

"Ha, ha," he deadpanned. "Lady Gaga, of course."

As if by some supernatural force, the intercom buzzed on cue. "That'll be them." Will walked back to the door and answered it, buzzing his friends up. I sat down at the kitchen counter on one of his black leather barstools, looking around the walls as I sipped my drink. There were several photos of people I assumed were the grandparents who had raised him, a photo of poor Killer wearing a Blues rugby team cap and scarf, and a photo of an attractive young couple, smiling at the camera. Although I had no idea who they were, something inside me told me they must be Will's parents. A strange sensation traveled over my chest.

I stood up when Will walked back into the kitchen, accompanied by two gorgeous women who were chatting excitedly amongst themselves. They were dressed like me, in pants and strappy tops, but one of them was wearing a tiara and gloves, looking every inch the diva.

"Dunny, this is Lori and Jacinta," Will said.

"Hey!" Lori said, adjusting her tiara. "That's a weird name. What's it short for?"

I rolled my eyes. "That's just Will's nickname for me. My name is Cassie."

Her eyes got huge. "Well, then, it's great to finally meet you, Cassie!"

I narrowed my gaze. What did she mean, "finally meet me"?

"Um, yes. It's great to meet you, too." I shot an enquiring look at Will. He didn't make eye contact with me, instead offering his friends drinks as he had me.

"So, you work with Will, huh?" Lori asked as the three of us women sat down.

"Yes, I do."

"That must be so fun. He's the life and soul, I bet," Lori replied.

I glanced at Will's back as he busied himself with the girls' drinks in the kitchen. "Something like that."

"I remember when we were all doing that business admin course, remember, Jacinta?" Lori said.

"Oh, yeah. *That* was riveting." Jacinta's voice dripped with sarcasm.

Lori rolled her eyes. "I know, right? That's where we met Will, you see, Cassie. He was like the guy everyone knew, Mr. Popular, always joking around with everyone."

Sounded like the Will Jordan I knew. "I can imagine."

"But when Jacinta got mono, he would make her notes of the lectures she missed and email them to her every day. Right, Jacinta?" Lori asked.

"Yup. He's the best."

"Totally."

"That's . . . great," I said. What was this? Will Jordan's personal fan club of besotted females?

The man himself returned to the living room, drinks in hand. "Here you go." He handed his friends their bottles.

"We were just telling Cassie how awesome you are," Jacinta said as she took hers.

"Were you now?" Will sat down on the sofa next to me. "Don't listen to them, Dunny. I had them brainwashed the first week I met them."

"Sounds like it to me," I replied, taking a sip of my drink.

"Cassie and I are in the running for the same promotion at work, aren't we?"

Surprised he raised the elephant in the room so casually, I nodded, "We sure are."

Jacinta raised her eyebrows. "Well, you need to put that corporate rivalry away tonight and become Gaga's Little Monsters!"

We all laughed and clinked drinks. As the others chatted, I couldn't help but size the women up. They were gorgeous, with their long, skinny legs and pretty smiles, but they were also fun and warm—not what I'd expected. But then, I didn't know what to expect of Will anymore.

When it was time to leave to go to the concert, I collected the empty bottles and took them to the kitchen while Lori and Jacinta chatted on the sofa by one of the large picture windows.

"Thanks, Dunny," Will said, taking them from me and putting them in his recycling bin. Will Jordan, a tidy and organized man? Who'd have thought it?

"You really want the Regional Manager's job, don't you?" Will asked, his back to me.

I didn't hesitate in answering him. "Oh, yes. Almost as much as I want to marry Parker. Well, I want both of those things."

He turned to face me, nodded, and smiled. "And that would be your perfect world? Regional Manager and Mrs. Parker Whatever-His-Name-Is?"

"Hamilton. I'd be Cassie Dunhill-Hamilton." I smiled. I liked the sound of that. *Mrs. Cassandra Dunhill-Hamilton, mother to Christopher and Charlotte.*

"Well, I don't know about the whole marriage thing, but I guess we'll find out pretty soon who's got the job, now the project's done and dusted."

I nodded back, the nerves pinging right down to my fingertips. "I guess we will."

He extended his hand. "It's been a good race, the future Mrs. Cassie Dunhill-Pamblington."

I rolled my eyes. Was he doing this on purpose? "Hamilton. Ham-il-ton."

He shrugged, grinning. "Whatever. May the best man win." He extended his hand toward me.

We shook as I let out a laugh. "Thanks for thinking of me as a man."

He smiled and shook his head. "We'd better get going." He pulled his hand away. "Ladies? It's time to go."

Jacinta and Lori were up and ready to leave before you could say "Mother Monster," and we headed out the door, Will and his three lady friends.

And the concert was out of this world. The music, the costumes, Lady Gaga. We danced, we sang, we had the best time. By the end of the evening, Lori, Jacinta, and I were like old friends, laughing at one another's jokes and finishing one another's sentences. At one point, Lori called us "Will's Angels," and I was having such a good time with them all I didn't even mind.

Yes, I was seeing a different side to Will. And I liked what I saw.

CHAPTER 20

THE FOLLOWING MONDAY, BAILEY delivered our sugar-fix of choice as we sat at our usual table in the window of the Cozy Cottage Café.

"What's this big news of yours, Paige? Only, I think I might have an idea." Marissa let out a giggle as she waggled her eyebrows.

"Well," Paige began, her cheeks flushed and her eyes bright, "I decided it was about time I got on with things."

"And?" I led. By the looks of her she had "gotten on with things" and liked the way they had turned out.

"And"—she paused for effect, her eyes dancing—"I asked Will out." Her grin was so wide, it almost met her ears.

"Oh, my god!" Marissa squealed, bouncing up and down on her seat. "You did it! That's so amazing, Paige!"

"What did he say?" I knew what she was going to say before she even said it. For some reason, I had a sinking feeling in my belly. What I couldn't work out was *why*? Why would it bother me if Paige dated Will? What business was it of mine? Will and I may have become almost-friends over the last few weeks, but it wasn't like we had any romantic feelings for one another or anything.

"He said yes! We're going out on Friday night after work."

"Oh, Paige." Marissa put her hand to her heart in an uncharacteristically sentimental gesture. "You see? I told you it was you! Didn't I, Cassie? Cassie?" She nudged me with her elbow, bringing me back to earth.

"What? Oh, yes. Yes, you did."

Marissa shot me a look.

"That's great, Paige." I smiled at her, trying not to think of my own woes. *Parker doesn't love me. He dated Sara for years.*

"Bailey!" Marissa called across the café, giving me a jolt as heads turned in our direction. "You have to hear this!"

Never one to miss a juicy bit of news, Bailey finished serving a customer, apologizing for her unruly customer at the table in the window, and headed over to our table. She pulled up a chair from a spare table and sat down. "What's happening?"

Marissa stared at Paige in expectation, a grin teasing the edges of her mouth. "Paige? Care to share your news with Bailey?"

"Well," Paige began, clearly loving having the opportunity to tell someone else her news, "Will and I are going out on a date."

Bailey's eyes got huge as her jaw dropped. "He asked you out?"

"No, I asked him," Paige confirmed.

"That's so exciting! When? How?" Bailey asked eagerly.

"Yes, tell us everything," Marissa insisted.

We listened as Paige told us how she had plucked up the courage to ask Will out after weeks of fretting over it. How she'd worn her lucky dress, the one with the white cuffs and collar. How he was about to be her One Last First Date. As she spoke, her pretty face glowed with happiness. She was fulfilling the beach pact, she was always meant to be with Will. He was her "One."

"Where are you going?" Marissa asked.

"We're just going for a drink at O'Dowd's, all very casual and familiar. It was his idea. And I like it."

I thought of our usual Friday night grab-a-quick-drink-after-work spot. O'Dowd's was rowdy and fun—not exactly a romantic spot—but then I knew Will's taste. Unpretentious and fun, O'Dowd's was totally his style.

"And then we're going to go out to dinner afterwards. I know it'll be just perfect because . . . well, because he's Will." She beamed at us across the table.

"Oh, Paige." Bailey sighed. "You girls are amazing. You'll all be married off, happily living with your hunky husbands. Well, not that I've met Parker yet, but I know Will's a total hottie."

Paige turned to Bailey abruptly. "You've met Will?"

I tensed up.

"Yes, when he came in here with Cassie a while back. He is such a nice guy. You're a lucky girl."

"You brought Will here? Why didn't you tell me?" Paige asked, a hurt look on her face. Although none of us had ever said it out loud, we had an agreement that the Cozy Cottage Café was our place. You only ever brought another person here if they were really important. And so far, none of us had.

"Actually—" I began, pausing to clear my throat. "Will was the one who brought *me* here after a meeting we went to together. He used to come to get his coffee here when he worked up the road." I crossed my arms in front of me like a shield.

"Oh," was Paige's only response.

"It's no big deal," I replied, thinking of the Lady Gaga concert. *Why was I keeping these things from Paige and Marissa?*

Bailey's eyes darted from Paige to me and back again. "Did I put my foot in it?"

"No, no," Paige insisted with a toss of her hair. "It's all fine. You're right, Cassie. It's not a big deal."

I smiled at her. "It was just coffee with me. He's going on a *date* with you." I bit my lip and consciously uncrossed my arms.

"Exactly. It was just coffee," Marissa said with conviction. "I have a good feeling about you two." She rubbed Paige's arm, who broke into a fresh smile.

Bailey stood up, pushing her chair back from the table with a screech on the tiled floor. "I want to hear all about it, but I'd really better get back to work." She gave Paige's shoulder a squeeze. "I'm so happy for you."

With Bailey gone, Marissa asked, "What are you going to wear?"

As Paige rattled off her wardrobe options, I took a few deep breaths, trying my best to focus. "You should definitely go for that shirt with the hearts. You look amazing in that," I said, trying to get into the swing of the conversation. But try as I might, I couldn't get rid of that strange knot in the pit of my stomach, the one telling me something I didn't quite understand.

* * *

Back in the office later that day, Marissa grabbed a hold of my arm as I passed by on my way to the printer and dragged me into the kitchenette.

"What the—?" I began loudly, my eyes huge with astonishment at being manhandled. I tugged my arm away from her firm grip and gave it a rub.

"Shh!" she said, her finger to her lips. She poked her head out the door, and then back inside. "What's got into you?" she asked in a loud whisper.

"What's got into me?" I asked, incredulous. "You're the one dragging people around like you're one of The Cavemen!"

"Shh!" she repeated. "I don't want Paige to hear."

My shoulders slumped. In a flash, I knew exactly what she was referring to. "Oh, that."

"Yes, *that*." She looked at me with expectation.

I let out a sigh. "I don't know. I guess things aren't that great with Parker."

"They're not?" she asked, leaning in toward me as concern clouded her eyes.

I shook my head, my face downcast. In hushed tones, so the world and its dog wouldn't learn my sad love-life woes, I launched into the full spiel: how I'd accidentally told Parker I loved him in the car that day; how his mother treated me like some sort of interrogation project as his dad leered at me over the smoked salmon; how this new threat in the form of Sara, his ex-girlfriend, had seemingly materialized out of thin air.

"I may be his rebound girl, not 'The One.'"

"Oh, my god, Cassie. I had no idea," Marissa said, rubbing my arm. "Why didn't you tell us?"

I shrugged, played with the cuff of my shirt. "I don't know. I guess I had this plan and the beach pact and everything. I mean, I said I was going to marry the next guy I dated, and I guess I didn't want you to know it wasn't working out the way I thought it would."

"That is the stupidest thing I've ever heard in my life," she pronounced, her hands on her hips.

"Gee, thanks for your support," I shot back, wounded.

Marissa took me by the arms, forcing me to look directly at her. What was with this manhandling today? "Look. Just because you agreed to this One Last First Date thing doesn't mean you have to go through with it. It was just some stupid thing we did on the beach after one too many wines."

It took a moment for what Marissa was saying to sink in. *Not* be with Parker? Abandon the whole thing? Forget about the beach pact? I opened my mouth to speak. All I managed was, "But, I—" before I closed it again.

"Cassie, look at me."

I did as instructed; I didn't want to be grabbed again.

"Date Parker if that's what you want to do, but forget about any of that ridiculous beach pact stuff. None of that matters."

I nodded. Not dating Parker—the man I *knew* was my future husband, the future father of my children, fellow pet owner, and Volvo owner—was so far away from what I was sure I had wanted. I let out a long, slow breath. "No. It's good. I want to be with him. We're just having some speed wobbles, that's all."

"As long as you're sure."

"I am." I sounded about three hundred percent more convinced than I felt.

CHAPTER 21

AND THEN DISASTER STRUCK. Well, not quite disaster, more the potential to ruin my life irreparably forever. So yeah, disaster.

On Friday night, I was out on my own date, back at the club we'd had one of our first dates at all those months ago. I'd endured ninety entire minutes of incomprehensible noises coming out of the lead singer's mouth as his bandmates seemed to play whatever they felt like on their respective instruments. Cacophony didn't even begin to describe the racket. So yeah, we were at the jazz club.

When the final set was over and the band had mercifully left the stage, Parker wrapped his arm around my shoulders, beaming at me. "I'm so happy you like The Scat Cats, Cassie. They have such a great sound, don't they?"

"Yes, they're very"—I searched my brain for the right word, like a frantic mother hen looking for her lost chicks—"uniquely talented."

Parker seemed more than happy with my response. "They are, aren't they? I'm so pleased you've learned to appreciate jazz. It means a lot to me."

I shrugged, enjoying the compliment.

"You've come a long way since the 'cat' debacle," he added.

"Ah, yes. A long way." He had to go reminding me how I thought "scat" was "cat" because the people who do it sounded like cats to me, yowling and carrying on. I wouldn't say it to his face, but I stand by my mistake. The Scat Cats front man sounded like a feline in need of emergency vet treatment, if you were to ask me.

Parker reached across and took my hand in his. He looked into my eyes. "Cassie. You're amazing, you know that?"

My mouth went dry. Was this the moment? The moment I'd been waiting for?

"Thanks. You're pretty amazing, too." I smiled at him, my lips trembling, my heart hammering away like it had a couple of carpenters in there, bashing nails into floorboards.

He looked down and began to play with my fingers. "I—" he began. He cleared his throat. "That is, I wanted to say that—" he hesitated, looking up at me.

Oh, my god. This was it! This was the moment he was going to say, "I love you"!

"Yes?" I encouraged, swallowing hard. I opened my mouth, ready to respond with an equally emphatic "I love you, too." He paused.

Say it. Say it.! SAY IT!!

"Sara?"

What? *Sara?* Had the man lost his mind? Against my better judgment, I was about to correct him when, in one fell swoop, he abruptly pulled his hand away from mine, dropped his other hand from my shoulder, and stood bolt upright, his chair crashing to the floor behind him.

"H-hello," Parker stammered.

Rooted to my seat, I looked up at him, dumbfounded, my mouth gaping wide. He was about to tell me he loved me—I was *sure* of it—and now he was standing, looking like a starstruck teen, deep in shock, staring at a woman who was not me. With a superhuman effort, I pulled my eyes away from him to look at the object of his attention. What I saw stopped my heart for several beats, possibly more. *Sara.* Beautiful, elegant, slim, Sara. With her long auburn hair, chic strappy top and slim-fitting black pants, and her long string of old money pearls.

She looked like me, only better. A whole lot better. I tried to swallow down a rising lump in my throat.

"Parker." Her face lit up, rendering her even more beautiful than before. Unlike my boyfriend, who now looked like he could throw up, Sara appeared relaxed and at ease. Bumping into him had clearly not rattled her one iota. "How lovely to see you."

"Yes, ah, Sara. I should have known you'd be here tonight," Parker mumbled, not taking his eyes from her.

Action was needed. And fast. I stood up and stepped next to Parker, sending a clear message: he's mine. "Hello. I'm Cassie. It's nice to meet you, Sara." I stretched my hand out toward her. She took it and smiled at me.

"Hello, Cassie. It's lovely to meet you, too. This is Justin." Sara gestured to a man I hadn't even noticed standing next to her. He reached out and shook my hand, then shook Parker's.

We stood in uncomfortable silence for what felt like a week before I asked Sara, "Did you enjoy the band?"

"Oh, she would have," Parker answered for her, smiling at me with his eyes virtually popping out of his head. "Sara always loved The Scat Cats."

Sara lifted her long, elegant hands into the air in surrender. "Guilty as charged."

"I haven't been to one of their gigs in a couple of years. I really liked the block chords, didn't you?" Justin said.

"Yes, they were brilliant." I had no idea what block chords were—and doubted I ever would—but I wasn't about to look like a jazz ignoramus in front of Sara. "I liked all the chords, actually." I smiled at everyone, ignoring the tension emitting in waves from Parker's head.

Justin shot me a look that questioned my sanity. "Yeah, great. Anyway, I thought it had integrity, great dramatic meaning, right, Sara?"

I blinked. He'd got "great dramatic meaning" from the noise we'd all just sat through?

Sara agreed with Justin, said something about the musical progression, all the while still smiling her dazzling smile. And still being stared at by an unblinking, unmoving Parker.

I slipped my hand into his and gave it a squeeze. He turned and looked at me. Finally, he snapped out of his perfect, jazz-literate, ex-girlfriend-induced haze. "Well . . . it's been great to see you again, Sara. Hasn't it, Cassie?" He didn't wait for my response. "And it's nice to meet . . . you." He nodded and smiled at Justin— he clearly had no clue what his name was. He'd been too busy gawping at Sara. He tightened his grip on my hand until it was almost vice-like.

"You, too," Sara simpered. She leaned in and kissed Parker on the cheek. I couldn't help but breathe in her scent—an intimidating mixture of Chanel and the aroma of flawlessness—and watched with dismay as Parker stood stock still, unmoving, a hard, steely expression plastered across his face.

"Take care, Parker. It was wonderful to see you again. You're looking great." Sara turned to me. "Bye, Cassie." She smiled at us both before floating away into the dimly lit club, Justin at her side, spouting on about sharp riffs and open voicing—or something.

Still gripping my hand, Parker looked around the room, his chest heaving. His face was pale, his nostrils flared.

I'm guessing that didn't go so well.

"Ah, Parker? That kinda hurts."

He looked down at my hand. Something in him seemed to change, and suddenly *my* Parker was back. I pulled my hand away from his and tried to shake off the pain.

"Are you all right? God, I'm so sorry. Did I hurt you? Here, let me take a look."

With reluctance, I let him take my hand in his. He inspected me, and then put my palm to his mouth and kissed it. "Let's sit down. Okay?"

"Sure," I replied uncertainly.

He righted his seat, and we sat at the table together. I went to speak, but he held his finger up and drained his glass of red. After a moment, he sighed, took my injured hand in his once more, and kissed it again. "I'm sorry about that," he repeated.

"It's okay. Nothing broken."

"No, I didn't mean your hand. I meant about bumping into Sara like that. I . . . I wasn't prepared."

I shrugged. "It's hard to bump into an ex. It's only natural to get a little freaked out by it." I was trying to be the kind of mature and together person I read about in magazines, able to allow my life partner to have feelings for another woman yet still feel comfortable in our own relationship. Or some other such total bull.

"That's exactly it!" He looked like he might pop with exhilaration. "I didn't expect to see her, I wasn't prepared, she had that . . . guy with her, and that's it!"

I played with the stem of my wine glass. "Yes. And it doesn't mean you have any feelings for her or anything," I lead.

"No. Of course not." He squeezed my injured hand.

"Ow!" I squealed in pain. *What is this man trying to do to me?*

He dropped my hand to the table like a hot coal. "Sorry, sorry. God." He buried his head in his hand. "I'm really messing up here." He looked back at me, his face a study in dejection. "I'm sorry, Cassie. I really am. I'll get myself together. Don't you worry."

I nodded at him, clutching my hand to my chest. There was no way on earth I was going to offer it to him again tonight. If I was entirely honest, an infinitesimal part of me wanted to enjoy this moment, a moment in which Parker was the one feeling embarrassed instead of me. But I couldn't. Witnessing his reaction to Sara tonight, my heart sunk deep, deep down into my belly.

"You and me?" He pointed from himself to me and back again. "We're solid. We're good. Right?"

"Sure. Yes. Totally." I smiled weakly at him, even though all I wanted to do was cry. Cry until I couldn't cry anymore, until my eyes were swollen shut, my nose a blob of red, my throat raw.

He wrapped his arm around my shoulder. "Good. You're what matters to me, Cassie."

"Sure," I breathed, trying to swallow the rising lump in my throat.

A pile of heavy bricks joined my heart in the pit of my stomach. Parker was in love. And it wasn't with me.

* * *

And those bricks stayed down there all weekend. They sat, heavy and foreboding, telling me things were wrong wrong wrong. Try as I might, I couldn't get that look on Parker's face when he first saw Sara out of my head. He looked like he'd been struck by lightning. And not in a good way.

And Sara. Every time I thought of her, I cringed from my toes right out to the ends of my hair. I simply couldn't get past the fact she looked so much like me! Or rather, as I was quickly realizing, the fact *I* looked so much like *her*. Until Friday night, I had thought Parker's dad, Dickie, was just bad with names, mixing me up with Sara. Now, I could easily see how he would have confused me with her. Really, lose ten pounds, gain a few inches in height, throw on a string of Mikimoto pearls, and I could easily *be* Sara Winston-Smythe. That was her name: Sara Winston-Smythe. *Of course* it was. She was the queen of golf and tennis, jazz aficionado and art collector. And to top it all off, she was a doctor. A doctor! How could I ever have a hope of competing with her in Parker's eyes? I mean, come on! The woman was hardly playing fair.

Parker spent the rest of the weekend telling me how important I was to him, how much he loved being with me, how he could see a future with me. In a nutshell, everything except those crucial words: "I love you, not Sara." He apologized close to a gazillion times for his awkwardness in seeing her at the jazz club, saying he wasn't expecting to see her, she'd caught him off guard, next time he'd be prepared. Yada yada yada.

I tried to believe him. Oh, how I tried. But I was there, I saw how he'd looked at her, I saw how stricken he was. It was as clear as a summer day to me he wasn't over her. In my darkest moment, at three in the morning when I lay awake, staring at the ceiling, I realized the painful truth: Parker was still in love with Sara Winston-Smythe, and he'd chosen me, her look-alike, as a consolation prize.

* * *

"Come on, Cassie. You have to come," Paige pleaded with me, standing at my desk on Monday morning, looking super cute in a new princess blue dress and the biggest smile I'd seen in days. "I need to tell you about my big date!"

I sighed. "Sure. I'd love to hear about it." I forced a smile, trying to appear happy for my friend. Which was a big ask when my own love life was in the proverbial toilet, about to be flushed away by Sara-I'm-Parker's-perfect-ex-girlfriend-Winston-Smythe.

"Good." She stretched out her hand to help me out of my chair, somehow intuiting I could barely manage it myself.

"Wow. You really look like you could do with some caffeine therapy," Marissa commented as we greeted her at the elevator. "Rough night?"

I had called Marissa in floods of tears, sobbing incoherently into the phone, after Parker had finally abandoned his mission to make me believe him on Sunday. Barely able to make out a word, Marissa had jumped in her car and turned up on my doorstep with wine, two flavors of ice cream, and a large box of tissues.

Best. Friend. Ever.

In between blowing my nose like I was in the brass section of one of Parker's god-awful jazz bands, I updated her on my sorry tale: how he still hadn't said "I love you" and how I was certain he was still in love with his ex.

"Do you think he was trying to make you into her? You know, with taking you to jazz clubs, playing golf with you, and things?" Marissa had asked.

Up until that moment, I had only thought he wanted a girlfriend to *look* like Sara. Fresh tears welled in my eyes. "Now I do."

"Oh, honey." Marissa handed me a fresh wad of tissues, which I made use of as my tears flowed.

"Right. So. The way I see it, you have two choices here: either put on your big girl panties and end it with Parker . . ."

I let out a gasp. The thought of breaking up with Parker was too much. "Or?"

"Or . . ." She had looked into the distance, scrunching up her face, deep in thought. "Or nothing."

I swallowed. Hard.

"Cassie, I just don't see another way around this. Do you? If you are his rebound girl, then you're wasting your time."

"But . . . but what about the beach pact?"

She had dismissed my concern with a wave of her hand. "We've already agreed that's a load of old hooey."

"Well, *you* said it was a load of old hooey, not me," I corrected her, my voice timid, worn out.

"What are you going to do, flog a dead horse just so you make sure you marry this guy? Just so you don't go upsetting the Goddess of the Sea, or whatever it was Paige called her."

"Beach. It was the Goddess of the Beach."

"Whatever. It doesn't matter. Cassie, be realistic."

I'd looked down. It may have meant nothing to Marissa, but I believed it. And I was convinced it would work. Until now.

Marissa had placed her hand gently on my arm. "Cassie, I'm your friend, right?"

I'd nodded grimly.

"Keep your dignity. Move on. He's not worth it. And you will find the right guy someday, I'm sure of it. And he won't be in love with someone else."

At the elevator in the office, I let out a heavy sigh. "Not a whole lot of sleep last night, I guess."

Marissa wrapped her arm around my shoulders. "You need chocolate. Stat!"

Ten minutes later, we sat at our usual table in the window. Bailey took time out to sit with us as I shared my sad and woeful tale with her and Paige, Marissa nodding along, throwing in her two cents every now and then.

"She needs to move on," Marissa pronounced at the end of my spiel. "You can all see that, right?" Things were very cut and dried with Marissa on this topic. Shame I couldn't share in her decisiveness.

"Maybe," Bailey said, shrugging. My ears pricked up, a ray of hope?

"Why? What do you think?" I asked.

"Well, let's see." Bailey numbered points off on her fingers. "You've been dating for months and it's been going really well. You're really into him and he seems to be really into you, too. He introduced you to his parents, and guys don't do that unless they're pretty serious, right?"

Everyone at the table nodded.

"Plus, he apologized for the way he reacted when he saw his ex. I get it. If I ever bump into my ex, I think I'll probably have a heart attack or worse! It's only natural."

I could feel a smile try to take shape on my face as my heart began to float up to its rightful place for the first time since "The Sara Incident," as I now referred to it. Everything Bailey said was reasonable, logical. Maybe I was overreacting? "You might be right."

"He's worth it, right?" Bailey asked.

"Yes," I replied without even having to think about it. Parker was meant to be my future husband. I needed to fight for him— Sara Winston-holy-crap-Smythe or not.

"Yes, yes!" Paige added eagerly. "Oh, Cassie, it's at least worth a shot. Talk to him, give him another chance. Please." She looked at me pleadingly, like a puppy waiting for a treat.

My smile now fully formed, I agreed to talk to Parker. I needed to give him another chance. Perhaps I had been overreacting? Perhaps Sara and I were simply Parker's "type" and it was no big deal? I mean, we all had a "type," right? There was only one way to find out. Before I lost my nerve, I got up from the table and walked out onto the street to text him. I needed space to work out what to say. I stared at my screen, at all the texts I'd received from him over the last forty-eight hours. Why would he send me so many texts if he didn't care?

I began to type. I asked to meet him tonight, saying we needed to talk. I half expected him to run a mile. Didn't guys hate those four words, "we need to talk"? I got a text back within moments, thanking me, agreeing to meet me and assuring me, "You won't regret this." I swallowed. *God, I hope I don't.*

As I walked back into the café, Bailey was serving customers. I gave her the thumbs-up. She shot me a grin before turning back to her line of hungry customers.

I took my seat at the table with the girls. I smiled when I saw my café latte and a slice of flourless chocolate and raspberry cake sitting in front of me. I mouthed a "thank you" to Bailey who winked at me.

It was official; my friends rocked.

"Did you do it?" Paige asked.

I let out a puff of air. "We're meeting tonight after work at my place."

"Good," Paige said. "Right, Marissa?"

Marissa shrugged. "Sure, I just think—" She was cut off by Paige.

"Let's see what Parker has to say, okay?"

"Sure," Marissa conceded.

I needed a change of topic. "You've heard about my disastrous weekend. How was yours?"

"Mine was the usual: dateless, sad, and lonely," Marissa said with a sigh. "Paige's wasn't, though."

Paige's blush was instant. I raised my eyebrows in question. "So?" I lead. In the disaster that had become my love life, I had completely forgotten about Paige's date with Will.

She sighed one of those happy sighs people in love do. "It was wonderful. Will is such a great guy. We went for a drink at O'Dowd's, which was fun. We had a great time. He's so funny. I spent most of the night laughing."

We listened as she told us about their evening, from what he wore to what they ate and everything in between. It was clear to me she was buzzing out over Will and the prospect of a future with him.

"So that's me done and dusted. I've been on my One Last First Date." Paige grinned at us both.

"That's so great, Paige," I said, trying my best to feel happy for her. I envied her confidence. But then, I had been confident Parker was the man for me after my One Last First Date, too. And, perhaps, he still was.

Back in the office, I got the call from Brian that Laura wanted to see me in her office. With the way things were going for me, I admit, I expected the very worst. She was going to let me down gently, explain to me that Will was the better team player, had stronger leadership skills, was basically a superior human being in all conceivable ways. And right now, I'd have to agree with her.

With a heart about as heavy as an elephant with a late-night food binge habit, I trudged up the stairs to the twelfth floor. Every step I took was labored, my black court shoes clanking on the tiled surface, my hand grasping the rail just to keep some modicum of momentum to get me to the top. I was taking the death march. I knew what was coming. It was all over, and Will had won.

Brian greeted me with his usual lack of enthusiasm, and without even the chance to sit down, I was ushered into Laura's office, the door closed firmly behind me.

Laura looked up from screen, removed her reading glasses, and smiled. "Cassie. Thank you for coming."

I gave her a toothless smile—all I could muster in my final moments of contender for the job. In a matter of moments, I'd be an "also ran," having to congratulate Will on his ascension up the corporate ladder, my one opportunity turned to dust.

Laura walked around her desk and offered me a seat on one of her plush leather chairs. She sat opposite me and made small talk, asking me about my weekend.

I thought of Parker being in love with Sara. "Oh, it was great, thanks. Yours?" My eye twitched, right on cue.

"Wonderful. We took the boat to Lake Taupo. My husband's a mad fisherman, you see."

"Oh." I wasn't capable of small talk. *Just get this over with so I can go slit my wrists.*

"So, Cassie. I imagine you know why you're here."

"I do." My stomach sank. I bit my bottom lip. *Will Jordan: Regional Manager.*

She smiled her we're-letting-you-down-gently smile at me. "We've come to a decision concerning the Regional Manager's position."

"Okay." *It's Will.*

"It was a very close call between the candidates, and you both did a wonderful job delivering the project."

"That's good. Thank you." *Just say it, just say it's Will.*

"We were very impressed with you, Cassie."

But . . .

"We have decided to offer you the role of Regional Manager."

I shrugged. "Well, I'm sure he'll do a great job." I hoped I sounded magnanimous in defeat.

"Did you not hear me? We want to offer *you* the role, Cassie."

My breath hitched in my throat. "Me?" My eyes got huge.

Laura laughed, leaning back in her chair, her perfectly manicured hand against her chest. "Yes, you."

"I . . . ah . . . I don't know what to say." *Will didn't get the job?*

"We felt you were the best fit for the role." Laura stood and stretched her hand out toward me.

In a fog, I stood and took it. "Err, thank you."

"You are more than welcome. Congratulations, Cassie. I think you're going to do a wonderful job."

I got the job? I got the job?!

I swallowed. "Thank you." I couldn't believe it. I beat Will Jordan—Mr. Can-Do-No-Wrong, star salesperson, teamwork extraordinaire—to the Regional Manager's job? "I would love to be your Regional Manager. I won't let you down, I promise."

Laura let out a laugh. "I know you won't, Cassie." She looked down at our hands. "Could I—?" I was still gripping and shaking it so enthusiastically I was in fear of unhinging her shoulder.

"Oops, sorry." I dropped her hand like a hotcake. "I . . . ah, wasn't expecting this."

Laura walked toward the door, motioning our meeting had ended. "Schedule something with Brian for later in the day. We can talk about the next steps then."

"Okay. Yes. I'll talk to Brian," I confirmed as she opened the door. "And thank you."

She laughed again. "You already said that. I'm pleased to have you on board."

In a total daze, Brian and I agreed on a time for me to meet with Laura after lunch, and I floated down the stairs to the sales floor, past my team members who were totally oblivious to how my life had just changed, going about their daily business as usual. I reached my cubicle and sat down heavily in my seat.

I got the job. *Cassie Dunhill: Regional Manager.* I bit my lip as excitement bubbled up inside my belly.

I did it. I actually did it!

CHAPTER 22

I SAT IN MY seat, staring at my cubicle wall, a goofy smile splashed across my face. I could still barely believe it. After all this time, after wanting this job for so long, I finally had it. Cassie Dunhill: AGD Regional Manager.

I was so lost in thought I didn't notice Marissa arrive at my desk until she spoke. "Have you heard the news?"

I grinned at her. How did she know? Surely Laura hadn't announced it yet? "Well, of course. I'm pretty excited about it."

She scrunched up her face. "You are?"

"Yeah! It's awesome." *What is she, insane?* "It's what I've wanted for so long."

"Jeez, Cassie. I know you don't like the guy, but that's kind of mean."

"Mean? Look, as Will said, may the best person win. Well, actually, he said may the best *man* win, but I figured he was just being sexist, so . . ."

She gawped at me.

I stopped talking. "What?"

"Will's quit. He's leaving."

"What? Why?" Then, the penny dropped. "Oh. I get it. It's because he didn't get the job."

Marissa looked confused. "Is that why?" She narrowed her eyes. "Hang on, does that mean you did?"

I beamed at her, nodding. "Mm-hmm."

She grabbed my hands and pulled me up, jumping up and down

on the spot. "Oh, my god! Cassie, that's awesome!"

I swelled with pride. "Thanks. It kinda is, isn't it?"

"Yes!" She stopped abruptly. "Not for Will, though."

I peered over the top of my cubicle at his office. The door was ajar, and the room empty but for the furniture, cabinets, and a picture of Auckland's harbor on the wall. *He's gone already?* "I guess not. But why would he leave?"

"He probably didn't want to have to report to you. You know, male ego and all that. It's a total cop-out, if you ask me."

I furrowed my brow. Marissa was right, this was sour grapes, pure and simple. He lost. He didn't want to see me become his manager, to have to report to me, to have me in charge.

"I'll be back in a minute," I said.

"Where are you going?" she asked as I walked out of my cubicle and headed to Will's office. One sweep confirmed he'd packed up all his belongings and gone. With my jaw clenched, I scanned the sales room. No sign of him. I walked over to Big Jake's desk.

"Have you seen Will?" I asked, my tone curt.

"Haven't you heard? He's gone." His expression was pinched.

"Yes, yes," I replied impatiently. "But is he still *here*, in the office?"

"He might be. He was in the kitchenette a few minutes ago, saying goodbye to some people."

Without a backward glance, I headed straight for the kitchenette, only to find it empty but for Bobby, one of our tech support guys, rummaging through the refrigerator. I slapped the doorframe in annoyance, making Bobby jump and turn to me, a guilty expression on his face. *Stealing other people's food, are you, Bobby?*

"Seen Will?" I asked.

"What? No, nothing," he replied, trying to hide a fruit yogurt behind his back.

I rolled my eyes and turned on my heel, scanning the room. I had no time to deal with petty thievery right now. I had a bone to pick with Will the size of a T. rex's hind leg. The gall of the man to quit because I beat him to the job! I turned the corner and caught a glimpse of him entering the elevator, a box held in his arms with a plant poking out the top, looking every inch the cliché of an employee on his way out.

"Hey!" I yelled, picking up my pace. "Will!" I reached the elevator as he placed his foot by the door, halting its closure.

"Cassie, hey," he said, as though he hadn't just quit because I got the job and he didn't or that he wasn't a spineless piece of crap. Not that I knew how that should look exactly.

I shook my head at him. "Why are you doing this?"

"Well, I'd prefer to take the elevator rather than the stairs." He brandished his box at me. "We're eleven stories up here, you know, Dunny. This box is heavy."

I narrowed my eyes at him, my hands on my hips. He was making a *joke*? "You know what I mean. Don't be a jerk."

He paused for a beat, two. He looked at me, his smile gone. "It's for the best."

"Whose best? Yours or mine?"

He shrugged, his jaw locked. "Mine."

We stood looking at one another—me glaring, my anger bubbling, and Will with an expression on his face I found hard to read. Will must have removed his foot because the doors began to close. I didn't know why, but I did not want him to leave. Not the company. Not now.

I thrust my own foot out and halted the doors' progress. "You shouldn't be doing this."

"Look, Dunny—" he began. He let out a breath. His expression changed. "You know what? It's all good. In fact, I've got another job."

I gawped at him. "You do?"

"Yup. Now, if you wouldn't mind removing that foot of yours, I need to get going."

I looked down at my foot and back up at Will. Defeated, I pulled it back and waited. What for, I didn't know.

"Thanks. Hey, come to my leaving drinks. O'Dowd's at five."

"Sure," I muttered as the doors closed. I stood for a moment, deep in thought. I chewed on my lip. Will had another job? That was fast work indeed. Maybe he knew I was going to get the job and went looking a while ago. Maybe he just made it up to stop me being angry with him. Well, it didn't work. No siree bob. Will Jordan was a spineless coward, and I was lucky he was gone. The kind of person who simply bailed out when the going got tough wasn't the kind of person I needed in my team.

* * *

After hours of company gossip about Will's sudden departure, Laura called a full sales team meeting in the boardroom to announce my promotion. Amid the congratulations, I could detect pennies dropping all over the place as people put two and two together and realized why Will was gone.

As I packed up my desk and slipped on my jacket at the end of the day, Paige and Marissa arrived at my cubicle.

"Coming for a drink to say goodbye to Will?" Marissa asked.

I busied myself with arranging my desk, straightening my pens in their tray and stacking my different-colored Post-it note pads in order of size. You know, life changing, important stuff. "I don't know. Probably not."

"Come on, Cassie. Everyone will be there. You're the new boss. You need to show you're fine with this," Marissa reasoned. "We're both going, aren't we, Paige?"

"Well, he is my future you-know-what, so of course *I* am," Paige replied.

"Sure. Why not," I conceded with a shrug, my lack of enthusiasm obvious to just about anyone. I knew they were right; I did need to appear as though Will quitting was no big deal. Which it wasn't, of course. Just a minor speed bump in my ascension up the corporate ladder.

We arrived at O'Dowd's five minutes later. Most of the sales team, half the marketing team, and even a couple of the executives were gathered together in a large, rowdy group with Will at the center, laughing and joking. Paige caught Will's eye and waived, blushing so much we could toast s'mores on her face. *Oh, yeah, she's got it bad.*

We went to the bar and ordered our drinks. When we joined the group, it was clear Will had been there for some time enjoying the beer on tap with The Cavemen.

"Ladies!" he said, grinning at us. "How wonderful you joined us."

Paige sidled up to him. "Hi, Will," she purred, still the color of a Hawaiian sunset.

He wrapped his arm around her shoulder. "Millsey!"

I turned away, unable to stomach their mutual affection. What Paige saw in that gutless wonder was beyond me.

As I chatted to one of the team, I caught Will's eye and he grinned at me, raising his glass. I smiled back and looked away. I had no idea what to say to the guy anymore. The sooner I got out of here and back to Parker—*Oh, my god*! In all the excitement of the day's events, I had completely forgotten to meet up with him. I glanced at my watch, five forty-three. I had precisely seventeen minutes to get back to my car, drive through the busy Auckland streets, and get to my place.

I squeezed through the throngs to explain to Marissa why I was leaving.

"Good luck," she said, giving me a hug, although her expression suggested she thought I'd need significantly more than mere luck.

I turned and scanned the bar for Will. It was the right thing to do to say goodbye to him. I would probably never see him again, and although I didn't think a whole lot of him now, I owed him that.

As I made my way through the crowd, one of the executive team, Malcolm, a short, bespectacled man with wiry hair and a penchant for cravats, quietly congratulated me on my new job. "It'd be in poor taste at this event to mention it publicly, but I did want to congratulate you on your promotion, Cassie."

I smiled at him. This man was now my peer. It felt strange—in a good way. "Thank you, Malcolm. I'm looking forward to the challenge."

"I'm sure you'll do a fantastic job. And with Will pulling himself out of the race, you were the logical choice."

Stop the bus. *What*? "I'm sorry?" I questioned, trying to keep my tone light. "When, exactly, did Will pull out of the race?"

"I think Laura mentioned he did it over the weekend." Malcolm picked up on my shocked expression. "Look, I don't want you to take this the wrong way. From what I understand, you were a strong candidate for the role all along."

I swallowed. "So, he should have got the job?" There was a definite tremor to my voice I hope he didn't pick up on.

Malcom put his hands up in surrender. "I shouldn't have said anything. I'm sorry."

"No, no. It's . . . f-fine," I mumbled. I looked over at Will. He was standing in a group of people, laughing at something someone had said. Paige was standing next to him, laughing along with him.

I made my way through the crowd to him. I needed to talk to him, to find out why he had done what he'd done.

"Hey, Will. Can I have a word?" I asked, trying to appear calm and relaxed.

By the look on his face, I had failed. "Sure. Get some air?"

I nodded and followed him to the front of the bar and out onto the street. Several smokers were chatting, leaning up against the wall.

"Let's go upwind," Will suggested.

A moment later, we stood facing one another as a truck drove past, revving its engine loudly. Suddenly nervous, I looked down at my feet. "Why did you do it?" I looked up into his eyes.

"Do what?" he bluffed. He gave up the pretense within two seconds flat. "You wanted it more than anything. You told me." He shrugged, as though throwing his career away for me was a perfectly sane thing to do.

My breath hitched in my throat as my heart slammed against my ribcage. "You did it for me? Why?"

"Cassie, I—" He pursed his lips and looked up the street at a passing car. He turned back to face me and shook his head. "Never mind why. The job's yours. You being happy is . . . well, I want you to be happy, let's just say that."

I looked down at my hands, clutched in front of my belly. Will left the company so I could become Regional Manager. He gave up a huge opportunity—for me. My heart was still banging in my chest. My mouth went dry. As I looked at him, his Poldark-handsome face, nothing else mattered. Not the job, not our rivalry, not even Parker and his "is-he-slash-isn't-he-still-in-love-with-Sara" drama.

In that moment, all that mattered was that Will cared enough for me to step aside and allow me to win.

"Can you answer me one thing?" he asked.

I nodded, not trusting myself to speak.

"Are you—" he began only to pause, pressing his lips together.

"Am I what?" I asked. My voice breathless, barely audible

above the thudding of my heart.

"Look, don't take this the wrong way. And I don't want to pry into your private life or anything. But . . . do you think Parker is the right guy for you?"

I shook my head. Parker? He wanted to know about Parker? "Err, yes." Other than the fact he's in love with someone else, that is.

He looked crestfallen. "Oh."

"Why?" My voice trembled.

"It's just." He stepped closer to me. My whole body tingled. "I wanted to know, that's all."

He was now so close to me, I could feel his warm breath on my face. Completely against my better judgment, I made the mammoth mistake of looking up into his rich brown eyes. I had long since known they were the kind of eyes a girl could get lost in.

Looking into them now, I knew it was game over.

In a moment that should have had its own romantic soundtrack, not the muffled *thud thud* of the music from inside the bar, without even knowing why I was doing it, I pulled his face down to mine with both hands and pressed my lips against his. I could feel him surrender as he kissed me back, pulling me into him until I was pressed up against him, his arms sliding around my waist. I inhaled his aroma and melted into him. Our kiss was warm and soft, it was . . . perfection.

He ran one of his hands up my back, slipping his fingers into my hair as our kiss intensified. My sudden need for him was overpowering. I tugged at his shirt, reaching my hand inside to feel his taut belly. A shot of desire ran through me, settling deep down, rendering me breathless, my legs suddenly unsteady.

Almost inaudible at first, a little voice inside me got louder and louder, telling me this was wrong. So, so wrong. It might have been an incredible kiss—quite possibly the best I'd ever had—but that didn't make it right.

A moment or an hour later—I wouldn't be able to tell you if my life depended on it—I finally came to my senses. With a strength Superman himself would be impressed with, I pulled away from him, utterly appalled with myself. And the way he'd made me feel.

I put my hand to my mouth, trying to wipe away our kiss. It was pointless, of course. What was done was done. I couldn't un-kiss Will any more than I could make Parker love me.

"We shouldn't be doing this, Will. It's not right."

He shook his head, his face full of desire—for me. "It's not, Cassie. Can't you see?"

I took another step back. "No." I shook my head. "No."

He reached for me, his eyes on fire, his lips parted. He took my hand in his. "You feel it, too. I know you do."

My breathing was rapid, shallow. He was wrong. I couldn't feel anything for him.

I swallowed, trying to control my breathing. "But . . . what about Paige?"

"What about her?"

"What do you mean? You're dating her."

He chortled. "No, I'm not."

I gave him a sideways glance. "Yeah, you are."

"Dunny, I think I'd know if I was dating someone."

It was a good point. "Well, she thinks you're dating."

He let out a sardonic laugh. "Good for her. We're not." He slipped his hand around my waist once more. He leaned down and brushed his lips against mine. I lingered, relishing the way he felt, his scent, his hard body pressed against mine.

No. This had to stop.

I stepped out of his embrace, resolved. "Paige or not, you're only kissing me because you're emotional leaving the company, or something. And I'm"—I wracked my brain for an excuse for my shocking behavior—"I'm drunk." I'd had half a glass of wine. I wasn't a huge drinker by any stretch of the imagination, but not even I could get drunk on that tiny amount of alcohol.

He shook his head. "If anyone's had too much to drink, it's me. I promised myself I wasn't going to say anything. Do anything. But to hell with it." He put his hands on my shoulders, forcing me to look into his eyes. "Cassie." His voice turned breathless, his dark brown eyes boring into me. "This is real. You have to know I'm in love with you."

I shrunk back from him, my eyes huge. "You're . . . in *love* with me?" I could join the Chip 'n Dale line up, my voice was so unnaturally high.

Was this some kind of a joke?

He nodded, smiling, as though this was the best news in the world. "I love you."

I took another step away from him, wanting to put as much safe air between us as possible. He watched me, still with those eyes I could get lost in, still with that look of desire for me written all over his face.

"No. No. We can't do this, Will."

Pain flickered in his eyes. "Why not? I *know* you have feelings for me. Cassie, we're so right together."

I smoothed down my skirt self-consciously, looking around me. A couple of the bar patrons smoking their cigarettes were watching us. I smiled weakly at them, and they turned away, talking quietly among themselves. We'd put on quite the show for them tonight.

Resolved, I shook my head, my lips locked together. I cast my eyes down to avoid his. I'd made that mistake once tonight: I wasn't making it again. "I'm . . . I'm in love with Parker. I'm going to marry Parker. That's just the way it is." Forget the fact he was probably in love with another woman. "I . . . I have to go."

"Cassie, don't do this."

Without looking at him, I turned away and headed briskly down the street, away from the bar and Will, as fast as my heels would take me.

I knew I was running away, I knew I was being as spineless as I had thought Will was being over leaving AGD. I had to get out of there. I had to get far away from Will. Will who loved me. Will who I had, only moments ago, kissed like my life depended on it. Amazing, incredible, confusing Will.

A block away and I began to breathe again. I was almost safe. It was then I noticed someone calling my name. It was a woman's voice. I turned to see Marissa, rushing down the street toward me. "Cassie!"

I had to decide in a split second whether to stop and plaster on a fake smile for her, as though I'd been running for fun and not to get away from Will, or to simply keep on running.

I'm not proud. I chose to run.

CHAPTER 23

I REACHED MY CAR in the AGD building basement, threw my purse on the passenger's seat, and sat down heavily at the wheel, slamming the door behind me. My mind was racing faster than a supersonic jet, trying to make sense of what had happened. In the same few short days, I had probably lost Parker to another woman, gained the job of my dreams, and had Will declare his love for me. Will!

I let out a bitter laugh. I had finally heard those magic three little words I had wanted to hear for so long. Only they weren't from Parker. They were from Will.

I banged my head against the steering wheel, hoping to bash some sense into my deeply jumbled brain. *Will loves me.* It was bizarre. No, it was beyond bizarre; it was *surreal.* I'd stumbled into *The Twilight Zone.* I half expected Forest Whitaker to jump out from behind a tree, shouting, "Surprise!"

How did this happen? One minute, Will and I were work colleagues, vying for the same job, and somehow, through it all, becoming friends. Next, he was leaving the company so I could get the job we both wanted, making declarations of love for me!

I turned the ignition over and pulled out of my parking space. I pushed Will from my mind. I could work it all out some other time. It had to wait. *Parker.* I needed to get to him. I had a relationship with the man I was meant to marry to save. I didn't have time for handsome men, telling me they loved me outside rowdy Irish bars.

Twenty-minutes of pushing the day's events from my mind at least three hundred thirty-seven times, I noticed Parker leaning against his car as I pulled into my driveway. I took a moment to collect myself before I pushed my door open and stepped out of my car.

Parker was by my side immediately. "Cassie. Where were you? I was worried."

I smiled up at him, tears threatening my eyes. "Sorry, I got tied up. Let's go in." I opened my front door, flicked on the lights, dropped my purse and keys on the side table, and plunked myself down on the sofa. Parker followed, facing me as he perched on the edge.

Without preamble, he launched with, "I went to see Sara." He looked at me through hooded eyes.

"Oh." I had no clue what he was going to say next. He could be about to break up with me for good, for all I knew. He could be about to tell me she was an Amazonian alien, here to take over the world, for all I knew. Today had been a very weird day, anything was possible.

"We had a good long talk. About her and me, about everything."

My belly twisted up in a reef knot. "Are you back together?"

He shook his head, and I let out a rush of air in utter relief. "She's moved on."

"Have you?" I whispered, not sure I wanted to hear the reply.

He clasped his hands together on his lap. "I'm going to be honest with you, Cassie."

I gulped. Telling someone you're going to be honest with them is usually the preamble for telling them something they do not want to hear.

"I thought I was still in love with her. I thought she was my perfect woman. I was . . . thrown when I saw her at the club on Friday."

You can say that again.

"I went to see her to ask her if she'd consider coming back to me."

Tears welled in my eyes. I tried to blink them away, instead they rolled down my cheeks. That was that, then. We were over. Dead.

"The thing is I realized after I saw her that yes, I have moved on. Seeing her made me face up to a few things. It forced me to get closure." He took my hands in his. "It made me realize how I feel about you, Cassie."

My heart stopped. "It did?"

He nodded, smiling, his green eyes soft. He took my hands in his, forcing me to look at him. "I love you, Cassie."

My jaw dropped. I blinked at his happy, shining face. *He loves me*? I had to work hard to shake myself out of my disbelief. "Are you sure?"

I kissed another man only thirty minutes ago, felt things I never thought I would feel for him, and now Parker was telling me he loved me?

He slid across the sofa, leaned in, and kissed me. Knowing where my lips had just been, it was uncomfortable, to say the least. I had to cut it short.

"Cassie?" he questioned, looking wounded as I moved away.

"Sorry, I—" I casted around for an excuse. I didn't think telling him I'd been in an adulterous lip-lock was the right thing to say following his love declaration—the declaration I'd been waiting for so long to hear. "I'm surprised, that's all. I thought you were going to say something else. Are you sure?"

He laughed, his eyes sparkling. "Yes, I'm sure. It's you, Cassie." He smiled the smile of a man happy with the world and his place in it, a man who knows he's in love—and loved back.

I, on the other hand, felt like I'd been put through a concrete mixer and tossed out the other side of reality.

"Can we make this work? You and me?"

I wiped my tears away and took a deep breath. "Yes," I said. "I would love to."

* * *

How did this *ever* happen? Two men professed their love for me on the same night—no, within the same hour! It was ridiculous, laughable even. The sort of stuff madcap Hollywood movies from the fifties were about. Only it was very, very real.

I guessed it was true what they said about men being like buses: you waited around for one to come for what felt like a lifetime, and then suddenly, two arrive at once.

Parker and I had spent hours talking that night after his big announcement. He came clean about wanting me to be like Sara—the golf, the jazz club, even the way he liked me to wear my hair—and apologized profusely for it. And I forgave him. Sure, I didn't like it, and it was more than a little bit creepy, but I believed him when he said he loved me and wanted to be with me. And it felt good.

Especially if I didn't think about Will Jordan.

The following day, he suggested we go out to lunch at Alessandro's. With a start, I realized I had never taken him to the Cozy Cottage.

"Let's go to my café for a change, okay?"

"Sure. I'd love to." He smiled at me as he took my hand in his.

When we walked through the door, Bailey was at the counter, chatting with a good-looking guy. She was blushing and clearly flirting. "Good for you," I thought.

"Where do you want to sit?" Parker asked.

"Oh, we always—" I gestured at my usual table in the window and noticed there was a couple sitting there with their young son. "Oh. It's being used. Oh well, let's sit somewhere else."

We found on a table on the other side of the room. While Parker settled in, I went to the register to see Bailey, now hot guy free. "Hey, you. Who was that?"

"Oh, the guy I was just talking to?" she replied, trying to play it cool. "He's just a regular. Comes in here most Saturdays."

I raised my eyebrows. "He's cute."

"Really? I hadn't noticed." She flashed an embarrassed grin. "Anyway," she began, clearly changing the subject, "what are you doing here on a weekend? You're a strictly weekday girl around these parts."

I nodded toward Parker, who had picked up a magazine and was leafing through it, looking at ease with the world. "I'm here with my boyfriend."

Her face broke into a grin. "You're back together?"

I nodded, happiness bubbling up inside.

"See? I told you it was worth talking to him. And now you're going to fulfill the beach pact."

"I am."

Parker and I ate a delicious lunch together, luxuriating in our little love bubble. Once we'd drunk our coffee and were ready to go, Parker declared the Cozy Cottage as his second favorite café in all of Auckland. This was progress, although I clearly still had work to do convincing him of the error of his ways. After we said goodbye to Bailey and she gave me one final thumbs-up, we strolled hand in hand along the street, soaking up the warm spring air. We peered in shop windows and strolled through the Domain, a beautiful patch of greenery amidst the urban jungle.

Life felt good; it felt right. Just as long as I didn't think about Will.

Only, I couldn't stop him from popping into my thoughts. I found my mind wandering to what it would feel like to be with Will. I looked out the window of my house at the trees being buffeted around by a storm raging outside. I let out a long sigh. Will was messy. He wasn't in the plan. It was so much easier to be with Parker. We were destined; we were right. Sure, we'd had some hurdles to leap over, but we'd done it and things were now great between us. Parker was my One Last First Date. He was it for me. Neat, orderly, organized. Just the way I liked it. It *had* to work out.

The following day, guilt-ridden and in serious need of distraction, I accepted Paige's invitation to the Cozy Cottage Café. Although the very thought of seeing Paige had me twisted up in a series of tight knots, I told myself I needed to act as though nothing had happened with Will. Which of course it hadn't—just an ill-advised kiss and some drunk talk he didn't mean. No, Will wasn't in his right mind when he said he loved me. He would have realized when he woke up the next day and probably felt thoroughly embarrassed about the whole thing.

Nevertheless, it was with trembling hands I pushed the door open to the café, just before ten in the morning. I sat down in our reserved spot and texted Paige, letting her know I was already here. I had given Bailey a brief wave on my arrival, ignoring her signal to come over and talk with her.

My phone beeped, giving me a surprise. I picked it up and smiled as I read a text from Parker, telling me he loved me and he'd see me for dinner tonight. I fired off a quick text and placed my phone back on the table.

"*You* have some explaining to do," Marissa said, standing over me menacingly, her arms crossed.

"Marissa! I . . . did Paige invite you?" Suddenly seeing Paige felt like a pleasure cruise in comparison to having to answer Marissa's inevitable questions.

She pulled out a chair and sat down opposite me. Her face was hard and uncompromising. I half expected her to pull a flashlight out of her purse and shine it in my face to begin her interrogation. Possibly throw in a thumbscrew, too. I knew I was in for a rough ride.

"I set this up. Paige is out of the office today on some Marketing thing. You haven't been returning any of my messages or calls, so this was the best way. You need to give me answers."

I studied my hands, the knots in my belly tightening. It was true: I'd been avoiding Marissa like she was the Black Death. Even though I didn't know for sure, I suspected she'd seen me with Will that night we kissed. The fact she was now sitting opposite me, looking like a severe school teacher about to give me a hiding, confirmed my fears. "You mean about Will, right?"

"*Of course* I mean about Will," she scoffed.

My heart skipped a beat at the mention of his name.

"And before you go denying anything, you should know I saw everything."

I swallowed. "Oh."

She crossed her arms and nodded, her lips pursed. "Talk."

My chest tightened. "I don't know why I did it. It was wrong, and I regret it. It didn't mean a thing." My annoying eye twitch made an appearance.

"Then why did you do it? You know how Paige feels about him."

Guilt whacked me in the guts. I hung my head. "I know. I feel terrible." I looked up at her. "You haven't told her, have you?"

She shook her head. "I figured I'd give you a chance to explain yourself first."

I tried to smile at her. "Thanks."

Her gaze was ice cold. "I didn't do it for you."

"Okay."

"So? What's going on? Is he two-timing Paige? Are you two having an affair or something?" She raised her eyebrows in expectation.

I guffawed. "No!" I shook my head. "God, no. To be honest, I don't really know how it happened. And believe me, I know that sounds like a total cop-out." I thought of Will, and my tummy did a flip. I explained to Marissa how I'd found out he had resigned so I would get the job, how he'd told me all he cared about was my happiness.

"Why? Is he in love with you?" she half joked.

To my surprise, tears welled up in my eyes. I wiped them away.

"Oh, my god! He is, isn't he?" She leaned back in her seat. "You're the one."

I nodded, grim. Will was in love with me. Paige would never talk to me again.

"Oh, poor Paige. We were convinced it was her, weren't we? She's going to be devastated."

"I know." I hung my head. The last thing I ever wanted to do was hurt Paige. She was the sweetest, kindest person I knew.

"Tell me exactly what he said."

And so I did. I told her about how nice he'd been to me, about how I'd judged him without even knowing him. I told her about how we'd gone out for meals after golf, how he'd taken me to the Lady Gaga concert. As I talked, I felt an inexplicable sense of calm pervade my once knotted belly, a smile warming me in a way I hadn't felt for some time.

Eventually, once I'd told her the whole sorry tale, she put her hand on mine. "You're in love with him, aren't you?" she asked softly.

I stared at her, wide eyed. *I* was in love with *Will*? Was she out of her *mind*? "No!" I exclaimed with such force I shocked even myself. People at the table next to us stopped and stared. I tried desperately to swallow down a rising lump in my throat. "I love Parker," I said in a quieter voice.

She arched one of her eyebrows. "Do you?"

I nodded as tears pricked my eyes. Of course I loved Parker! And he loved me back. Parker was the one I was meant to be with. He was right for me. Not Will. A tear rolled down my cheek. I wiped it away.

"Cassie," Marissa said with such kindness I hung my head, my tears flowing, unable to stop them as they splashed onto the table.

"Oh, honey. Here." She handed me a napkin.

Was I in love with Parker? Suddenly, I wasn't so sure. Me, the girl who had her life mapped out so thoroughly, knew exactly when relationship milestones needed to be met, had clear, achievable goals in life. Me, the woman who had decided, even before our first date, Parker R. W. Hamilton was the man I was going to marry. All that effort, all that planning, everything. How could I not be sure?

I wrung my hands, my mind whirring. I'd been so desperate to push Will from my mind, my feelings had become completely scrambled in my head. I wiped my tears away and raised my chin, defiant. "It's Parker I love." It is. It *has* to be. I didn't research Will. I didn't spend hours ensuring he was the right guy for me. And he's not Mr. Great-On-Paper the way Parker is: he doesn't even come close. He's arrogant and loud and rude. He calls me Dunny, for God's sake. He's not the man I could ever be with. Parker is. It's Parker.

Marissa narrowed her eyes at me. "As long as you're sure."

I squared my shoulders, resolved. "I am."

CHAPTER 24

AFTER "THE DAY THAT WAS", as I began to refer to that Friday—you know the one, in which two men told me they loved me and I got the job of my dreams? Yeah, *that* one—I threw myself into my new job with such vim and vigor, it was like I was on a combined sugar-caffeine high one hundred percent of the time. I moved into my new office, claiming it as my space by hanging pictures on the walls and adding a few girly scatter cushions to the sofa. And I *loved* my new job. The responsibility of delivering sales targets within budget, of managing staff, of being a part of the decision-making executive team, did not faze me in the least. No, I relished it. I was the last to leave the office at night, and one of the first there in the morning.

In fact, I was so busy and focused on my new job I had to forgo my daily Cozy Cottage Café ritual with the girls. But I knew they'd understand. I was the boss now; I had big responsibilities. People to see, places to go. That and the fact I could barely look Paige in the eye after that kiss with Will.

And what he'd said to me.

She was still totally smitten with him, and I tried to be happy for her, knowing the truth about where his affections lay. Part of me wanted to tell her she was beating the wrong bush, barking up the wrong tree, and other horticultural slash canine metaphors. But why would she believe me? Unless I told her about that night, she'd dismiss my objections as me simply not liking him—because that's what the world thought. And how could I ever break her heart that way? Telling Paige what had transpired between Will and me that evening could never have a good outcome. All I could do was hope Will would fall for her in time. And I could get out of jail for free.

But it was so hard to keep Will from my mind. Like some kind of hot guy ninja, he kept creeping up on my thoughts—his smiling face, his wry sense of humor, that incredible kiss.

On the plus side, Parker and I had entered a new phase in our relationship. With the whole Sara thing put to rest, it was like he was a new man: more attentive and more relaxed. Plus, I didn't have to play golf or go to jazz clubs anymore, which was a huge relief. I could be me, and Parker loved me just the way I was.

I was on my way back from a meeting downtown when I had a sudden hankering for a slice of Bailey's amazing flourless chocolate and raspberry cake. I may be the boss, but I'm still human. As luck would have it, I found a parking spot right outside the Cozy Cottage Café. It was a sign.

Walking in, I breathed in the aroma of coffee, treats, and that special, familiar Cozy Cottage Café scent I knew and loved so well. I waited in line to order, responding to the emails that had piled up while I was with a client. I tell you, people were constant communicators these days. One hour off-line and I had thirty-five emails requiring action. Thirty-five! Ridiculous.

"Hello, beautiful! Long time no see."

I looked up to see Bailey, smiling at me from behind the counter, dressed in her usual red polka dot apron with a girly frill.

"I know. It's so good to come here! I've totally missed you and this place." I leaned across the counter and gave my friend a quick hug.

"Well, you look amazing," she said, eyeing my new navy suit. "Management clearly suits you, Cassie Dunhill."

I grinned at her. "Thanks. Yup, it's pretty good being the boss."

She let out an easy laugh. "You just missed Paige and Marissa, but Will's here."

I swear my heart completely stopped at the mention of his name. Bailey continued to chat about Marissa's new hairstyle and other things, but all I could do was concentrate on breathing. *In out, in out.* Will was here? Now? Every part of my body tingled, and I could almost feel his eyes boring into my head, my soul.

I turned around and saw him, sitting at a table by the window, tanned and oh-so-handsome, his hair a little longer, dressed in a T-shirt and pair of shorts. Watching me.

He stood up. Without preamble, I took a step toward him, as though he had some kind of tracker-beam pulling me into him. As clichéd as I knew it was, I was powerless to resist. He took a few steps toward me, and within seconds, we were face-to-face, close enough to touch.

"Cassie."

I swallowed, trying to steady my breathing, light-headed and dazed. "I—" I couldn't think of a single word to say to him. Instead, I simply stood there, gawping at him, my head clouded by the very sight of him.

He reached out and took me by the hand. "It's good to see you. How are you?" he asked.

I nodded, not trusting my voice to work.

He smiled. "Look, do you want to sit down and talk?"

I shook my head. In that moment, I knew what sitting down to talk would mean. It would mean letting him in. And I didn't want to do that. No way. That was the very last thing I wanted to do.

My life was perfect. I had my dream job and Parker, my dream guy. We were in love, heading down the aisle in the not-so-distant future, I was certain of it. Parker had been my One Last First Date. Why would I want to sit down and talk with *Will*?

Abruptly, the sound of people talking, the smell of the food and coffee, the closeness of the café atmosphere, became too much for me. I needed to get out. *Now.* Without saying a single word to him, I turned on my heel and blindly headed to the door. I needed fresh air. And I needed to be far, far away from Will Jordan.

I took a step and pushed past a middle-aged woman, muttering an apology. I stumbled into a chair that hadn't been pushed under a table fully. I rounded another table, the door mercifully in sight.

I can't breathe, I can't breathe, I can't breathe.

Seemingly out of nowhere, Bailey materialized in front of me, concern etched on her face. "Cassie? Are you okay?"

I nodded, knowing I looked anything but. "Gotta go."

"Sure." She stepped aside for me, and I staggered past, through the door and out into the fresh summer morning air. I took large gulps of it, as though I'd been holding my breath in there. Which, perhaps, I had.

I reached the tree a few feet from the café door and leaned up against it, feeling the rough bark with my fingertips, desperately trying to bring myself back to earth.

Oh, god oh, god oh, god.

Just as I began to gain my equilibrium, Will arrived at my side, gently taking my hand in his. "Cassie," is all he said. Until that moment, I had never known so much could be embodied in one, single word. A world of hurt, of pain. Of love.

I could almost smell the smoke from the funeral pyre of my life as we stood in silence. Against my better judgment, I looked up into his rich, brown eyes. Why I did that, I will never know. Some part of me knew it would spell d-i-s-a-s-t-e-r with a capital *D*. But I did it anyway. He held my gaze and smiled at me. He didn't say a word.

He didn't need to.

You know how people who've had near-death experiences say they see their lives flashing before their eyes? Well, that's what happened to me, standing under that big old tree, the two of us looking at one another, holding hands, not speaking. Not doing a thing.

I thought about the pact on the beach and how much it meant to me; of Parker and how I had wanted so badly for him to be The One; of Paige, poor, sweet Paige, who would be devastated by all this. And of Will.

In a beat, my mind went from a chaotic jumble to utterly calm, my belly unknotting itself. For the first time in a long time, I was clear.

It's Will.

I bit my lip, my eyes still holding his gaze. A smile began at the edges of my mouth, growing until my face was aglow with happiness—and with love.

Why had I been fighting this? This was officially The. Best. Feeling. In. The. World—better even than Bailey's flourless raspberry and chocolate cake. And if you'd ever had a slice, you'd know how good that was.

I nodded at him, still smiling like a love-struck idiot. "Okay."

He grinned back. "Okay." He reached his hand up and stroked my cheek.

"Give me some time to work things out?"

"Of course."

With enormous reluctance, I let his hand fall to his side. "'Bye. For now."

"See ya, Dunny." His grin was atomic.

I let out a giddy laugh, so happy I could float away on a cloud. "See ya, 'Poop Boy'."

CHAPTER 25

I SPENT HALF MY time in the office the following day trying to work out what to say to Paige. Even though I knew she and Will weren't dating, she still had major feelings for him, and the guilt was almost killing me. I kept telling myself I didn't plan on falling in love with Will, but it didn't make me feel any better about the situation.

Eventually, after chickening out so often I was in fear of being made into nuggets, I approached Paige's desk. She was in the middle of a call. She looked up at me, standing in front of her, wringing my hands, and greeted me with a warm smile, her finger in the air to indicate she needed a moment.

I nodded at her and turned around, feigning interest in a photo of her with her team at a conference last year I'd seen many times before.

She finished her call. "Hey, Cassie. This is a nice surprise. We don't get to see busy Ms. Regional Manager much these days."

"Oh, I was just . . . in the neighborhood. You know." I played with a pen sticking out of a mug on her desk. "Have you got a moment?"

She glanced at her watch. "Sure. Got a meeting at two thirty, though. What's up?"

"It's a gorgeous day. How about we take a walk?" I didn't want to break her heart—and probably end our friendship forever—in the office.

A few moments of nervous small talk on my behalf in the

elevator later, we walked through the revolving door, out into the morning sun. There was a small patch of green over the street, with a couple of unoccupied park benches, so I suggested we stroll over there and take a seat.

". . . and it's so annoying because I'd actually already provided a report on that last week! Portia is impossible," Paige complained as we took a seat on one of the benches.

"Oh, that's no good," I cooed, having no earthly idea what she was talking about, my nerves threatening to swallow me up.

"Hey, Paige?"

She raised her eyebrows. "What's up?"

"I . . . err—" My mouth went dry. I had practiced what to say to her so many times in my bathroom mirror at home, but now that it came down to doing it, I had no clue where to begin. I forced a smile as I clenched my fists by my side. It was time to pull my big girl panties up. "I have a question. You know the beach pact? Well, I have a question. What happens if someone, I don't know, breaks the pact or something?"

"Breaks the pact?" she shrieks as though I've suggested we murder someone or start farming babies or something.

I look around the park. No one was looking at us. Nevertheless, I lowered my voice in the hopes Paige will follow suit. "Sort of. It's just . . . I was thinking . . . maybe just a little?"

"Cassie. You either break the pact or you don't. There's no such thing as breaking it 'a little.'"

I nodded at her like one of those bobblehead figures you see in the backs of people's cars. "Okay. Got it."

She gave me a sideways glance. "Are you asking because *you're* thinking of breaking our pact? Has something happened with Parker?"

My tummy clenched at the mention of his name. Parker was my *next* conversation.

"It's a hypothetical question, that's all. I'm interested in knowing what could happen if say . . . Marissa decided she was going to break our pact." *Wimping out much, Cassie?*

Her eyes widened. "Marissa's going to break our pact? Why? She's never said anything. I thought she was still looking for the perfect guy."

Wow. This is much harder than I thought it would be. "I don't think she is, but what if she was? What would happen?"

Paige leaned back in her seat, letting out a puff of air, her face serious. She sat like that for an uncomfortably long time. "Breaking the pact is a serious crime, Cassie. A serious crime."

Despite my climbing anxiety, I scoffed. "It's hardly a *crime*, is it?"

"Well, she's not going to go to prison for it, but there will be consequences."

"Such as . . . ?" I lead.

She leaned in toward me. "Probably one of two things. Either the Goddess of the Beach will intervene and what was meant to be will be."

Well, that's not so bad. I could live with that.

"Or Marissa will never be happy and die a lonely, old woman."

Ah.

I swallowed. "Okay. Good to know."

She narrowed her eyes at me. "You know what? I didn't come down in the last rain cloud, you know. Something's up, isn't it?"

A pang of guilt hit me, *smack*, right between the eyes. Paige was going to be devastated—either that or she'd turn into a homicidal revenge queen. Either way, this was not going to be pretty.

I looked down at my hands. "Yeah, kinda."

She moved to the edge of her seat. "You've broken up with Parker?"

I curled my toes. "No. I'm going to, though."

She recoiled from me. "Why? After all you've been through? And he only just told you he was in love with you!"

She was right, it was totally illogical. But then, love wasn't exactly famed for being rational, was it?

"I . . . err . . . I fell in love. With someone else." I looked up at her, my chest tight.

Her face was incredulous. "You did? Who?"

"Well, that's the thing. It's . . . well, let me just say I didn't plan it this way."

"Okay," she said slowly. "Who is it?"

I clasped my hands together, almost twisting a couple of digits off.

When I didn't reply, she said, "Cassie, tell me." Her voice was low, devoid of warmth.

I swallowed. Hard. "Paige, I'm so sorry. I didn't mean for it to happen. I never planned it this way." In my desperation, I pulled out the biggest cliché of all time. "It just kind of . . . happened."

Her face hardened, her lips forming a thin line. "You still haven't told me his name."

Once again, tears stung my eyes. This was becoming a habit for me. I needed to invest in some waterproof mascara. I bit my lip as I tried to blink my tears away. "It's Will." I hung my head, expecting the worst.

And I got it.

Paige leaped up from her seat, her hands on her hips. "Will?" she screeched. "Will?! Are you freaking kidding me?!"

Any hope I had held that people wouldn't stop and stare at us went down the toilet—right along with Paige's and my friendship. I jumped up out of my seat. "Look, Paige. I'm sorry. I think I'd wanted Parker to be my Mr. Forever so much I lost sight of the fact he's not right for me. But Will is. I don't want him to be, but he is. I'm so, so sorry."

She crossed her arms, tapping her foot in agitation. "And how does he feel about you?"

I looked down at my lap. "He . . . ah . . ."

I heard her sharp intake of breath. "Oh, my god." Her hand flew to her mouth as tears streamed down her face.

I stood up and put my hand on her shoulder. "Paige, I—"

She recoiled from me, as though I was poison. "No. Don't touch me. You—" She shook her head at me as she backed away, her face a study in outrage.

"I'm sorry, Paige. If I could change it, I would. You have to believe me."

She turned her back on me and walked away. I didn't follow her. She'd made it pretty clear she didn't want to see me right now. I slumped back on the park bench. *Well, that went well.* I pressed my eyes shut. She was angry and hurt. I knew she would be. And I totally got it. She'd been in love with Will from afar for so long. Him falling for me must have felt like a major slap in the face.

My only hope was she would understand—eventually. The last thing I wanted was to lose my friend.

* * *

Paige avoided me for the rest of the day, not returning my calls, throwing the flowers I gave her in the trash, walking the other way when she saw me in the corridor. I called Will to tell him how it'd gone.

"I know you're going to say I'm a dumb guy who has no clue. And you're probably right. I had no idea she felt that way about me."

"You're right, you have no clue," I ribbed. I let out a sigh. "She hates me."

"She'll get over it. You two are best friends."

I bit my lip. "You should have seen the way she looked at me. It was like pure hatred."

"Look, Paige is a great person. She'll forgive you some day. It might take a while, though."

I hoped so. Losing my friendship with Paige was the last thing I wanted—now, or ever.

* * *

Knowing how badly it had gone with Paige, when I met Parker later that evening, I was expecting the very worst. I knew I had to tell him the truth. I owed it to him, after all we'd been through: the good, the bad, and the Sara Winston-Smythe.

For some inexplicable reason, I wasn't as nervous telling him. Perhaps it was because I'd already done it once that day and the sting had been taken out of it. Or perhaps, I realized with a start, I cared more about Paige than I did about the man I'd hoped for so long would be my husband.

I met him outside the restaurant in Parnell, a chic suburb close to the city. He greeted me with a kiss on the cheek, and I tried not to stiffen at his touch.

"Shall we go in?" he asked, oblivious to my reaction.

"Is it okay if we walk a bit?" I asked.

He shot me a questioning look. "But our reservation is for seven thirty."

"Just a short walk? There's something I need to talk with you about."

"Sure." He took my arm in his, and we began to walk down the street.

I launched right into my spiel, wanting this over as quickly as possible. "I was wondering if . . . if the Universe, or whatever, is trying to tell us something?"

He chuckled. "What do you mean?"

"You know, with all the things that have happened on our dates for starters. The jazz 'cat' mistake, the golf? Oh, and the best one of all, the date where I punched myself in the face, busting up my nose."

He laughed. "Yes, that wasn't the best first date, was it?"

"Ah, no. Can all of those things have happened to try and stop us being together? I mean, there have been a lot of date disasters."

He nodded, taking in what I was saying. "There have been a few." He stopped and looked at me. "But no, of course I don't think that."

I chewed the inside of my lip. "I need to tell you something."

His face turned serious. "Actually, Cassie, before you do, I have something I need to tell you. I was going to talk to you after dinner, but now is as good a time as any."

Happy to put my breakup speech off for a while, I replied, "Sure. What is it?"

"Well," he began. He looked suddenly nervous. "I feel terrible doing this to you, but . . . well, here's the thing." He swallowed.

I narrowed my eyes at him. "What is it, Parker?" *Is he going to break up with me?*

He began to pace, walking straight in front of a passerby.

"Watch it, man!" he yelled.

"Sorry, sorry," Parker replied, his hand in the air in surrender.

I took hold of his hand and pulled him over to the side of the footpath, up against an illuminated shop window. I raised my eyebrows in expectation.

"Okay. Here it is. You know how I told you I was over Sara? That it was you I wanted to be with? Well, I was wrong." He looked at me through scrunched up eyes, clearly expecting me to launch into some kind of tearful, angry display.

I blinked at him. "You're breaking up with me . . . to be with Sara?"

He nodded. "I'm so sorry, Cassie. I tried, really I did. But when she came to see me last night, we were finally honest with each other. No more games, no more lies."

"You're breaking up with me to be with Sara," I repeated, as though on automatic pilot.

"Yes, that's what I'm trying to tell you." He looked at me as though I was some sort of low-IQ moron. "We've decided to give it another try. I'm really sorry, Cassie."

I was faced with a choice. I could either come clean with him about my feelings for Will or—a much more appealing prospect— I could act hurt but accepting. "I see."

I watched as he fumbled around how sorry he was and how he hadn't planned this—all the things I'd said to Paige a mere handful of hours ago. In the end, I even started to feel sorry for him. Parker was a great guy. He was smart and cultured, good-looking, and a real gentleman. In many respects, he *was* Mr. Perfect. But he wasn't *my* Mr. Perfect. Sara was lucky to have him.

When he looked like he was going to prostrate himself on the ground to ask for my forgiveness, I put my hand on his arm. This had gone on long enough. "Parker, it's all right."

He looked at me with such hope in his eyes, my heart softened. "It is? Oh, Cassie, thank you, thank you." He clutched my hand to his chest, his eyes wet.

I decided to come clean. I told him about Will, about how I had only grasped I was in love with him recently, about how I was happy to let him go to be with his true love.

How I knew more than anything I was with my own.

We parted as friends, agreeing we would stay in touch and we would always be special to one another. He was my One Last First Date, that had to count for something, right?

Standing beside my car, I turned to face him. "One last question."

He looked at me in expectation.

"Did you see what was written on my panties on our first date, that night my dress got caught on the stool?" The memory of my "Bite Me" panties flash still stung.

"No, I didn't."

I nodded. "So the whole crab 'bite me, bite me' thing was just a coincidence?"

He smiled. "I apologize, Cassie, but what are you talking

about?"

I smiled back. "It's nothing. Bye, Parker. And . . . good luck."

"You, too."

KATE O'KEEFFE

CHAPTER 26

AFTER MONTHS AND MONTHS of dating the man I had
expected to marry, I had watched him go back to his ex, fallen in
love with another, and lost one of my best friends. So, it was a
surprise when I received an email from Paige, instructing me to
meet her and Marissa on the beach at ten that night. No
explanation, nothing. Just the location and a "See you there." It
was an olive branch, and I was going to grab it with both hands.

I arrived, on time that evening, ready to have strips ripped off
me. And I knew I deserved it. I knew acting on my feelings for
Will had hurt Paige deeply. I hadn't yet given up hope she would
forgive me one day, although I didn't expect it to happen any time
soon.

Will gave me a hug beside the car. "Are you sure you want to
do this?"

"I do. She's really important to me."

"I'll be here, waiting. Okay?"

I smiled at him. Will, the man I loved. We'd been dating for
three weeks and five days and it was wonderful. Unlike dating
Parker, I didn't feel like I needed to behave in a certain way or
cultivate interests I didn't have. I could just be me. And Will loved
me.

I gave him a quick kiss, flicked on my flashlight, and turned
around, walking over the sandy ground to find Paige before my
nerve ran off into the night. I climbed up and over a sand dune and
over another before I reached the beach. I could hear the waves

rolling and crashing on the shore, a light breeze blowing my long hair in my face. I scooped it up into a high ponytail with a band from my wrist—always be prepared—and spotted a bonfire with a couple of figures about a hundred yards away.

I approached it and saw Paige and Marissa, standing, watching the flames in silence.

"Hi, girls."

They both turned to face me. "Hey," Marissa said.

Although angry with me at the time, Marissa had forgiven me, telling me you couldn't choose who you fell in love with, and if Will was the man I loved, then she was happy for me. I had pointed out it was your *family* you couldn't choose, she'd told me not to be a pain, and we'd hugged it out and returned to being the great friends we were.

Paige, on the other hand, had avoided me like I had a combination of leprosy, The Black Plague, and chicken pox, all wrapped up into one. I was hopeful her asking me to be here tonight was a good sign. Now that I saw the bonfire, I wasn't so sure.

I smiled, anxious. "It's good to see you, Paige."

She gave me a curt nod in response.

"What are we doing here?" I asked, the heat from the bonfire on my skin as it crackled and glowed.

Paige stepped forward. Without preamble, she launched in with, "Cassandra Clementine Dunhill, as penance, you have returned here to the beach from whence you came."

So that's what this was about: a Beach Goddess thing. I couldn't suppress a smile. "From whence?" I glanced at Marissa.

Paige ignored my tease. "Yes. You are here tonight, precisely one year from the date of The Pact, to make your peace with the Goddess of the Beach."

I looked from Paige to Marissa. She shrugged, shaking her head. I looked back at Paige.

"Okay. I will make peace with her." Anything to get Paige back as my friend.

"Good." She put her hand out in front of her, and immediately Marissa added hers. I followed suit. Unlike the first time we stood on this beach, hands piled high, there was no storm brewing. Tonight was warm and calm, the sun having just set below the horizon, casting a faint orange glow on us all. It was quite enchanting.

We stood in a small circle as Paige began. "We, the maidens of the beach, are here to ask for your forgiveness. One of us"—she nodded at me to ensure the Goddess knew exactly which one— "has made a different choice. We ask that you allow her to follow her heart."

The hope Paige was prepared to forgive me rose inside. "Really, Paige?"

She gave a short, perfunctory nod. "You deserve to be happy."

Tears stung my eyes. Paige had forgiven me? Paige was happy for me?

"Tell us what price she must pay, oh Goddess," she continued.

Wait a minute. *Price?*

I watched, openmouthed, as Paige turned her face skyward. Marissa rolled her eyes, buying into this whole Goddess business as much as she did the first time around. And just like the first time, my arm began to get sore from holding it in place so long.

Eventually, Paige turned her gaze on me. "You must dip in the waters to cleanse yourself. When you emerge, you will be free to follow your heart."

"Hold on. You want me to go for a swim? Now?" I looked out at the dark ocean.

She nodded. "It is the wish of the Goddess. You must follow her instructions or . . . or she won't be happy."

I looked uncertainly at the water. It was ominously pitch black. I swallowed. "Well, if you're sure."

I began to slip my jean jacket off when Paige put her hand on my arm. "Fully clothed."

"Paige!"

She glared at me.

"All right. But then it's done, right? The Goddess or whatever will forgive me for not marrying my One Last First Date, and you . . . you'll forgive me, too, Paige?"

She chewed her lip. After a beat, she gave a stiff nod.

My face broke into a broad smile. "Well, then. What am I waiting for?" And, without a backward glance, I ran down to the water's edge, my dress flapping in the breeze. I didn't stop to test the waters: I went straight in, running through the waves, thankfully now only lapping against the shore. I ran until the water was knee deep, slowing my progress. I struggled through, the water reaching my thighs. And it was cold. For such a warm summer night, it was quite a shock to the system. I glanced back at the darkened figures on the beach, turned back, and dived under the water.

As I popped back up, I heard Marissa yell, "Go, Cassie! Woo!"

I felt something slimy brush up against my bare leg. I let out a cry. Without wasting another second, I swam to shore, my clothes heavy, my sneakers loosening with each kick. Dripping wet and freezing, with salt and sand in places I didn't want to think about, I strode up the beach, back to the bonfire and my friends.

Marissa grinned at me. "That was awesome!"

I looked at Paige. "I didn't mean to fall in love with him. I'm so sorry."

She nodded, her eyes downcast. "I know. Thanks for doing that." Her face broke into a grin. "You look like a drowned rat."

I shrugged. "Well, I had to do what the Goddess wanted me to do, right?"

Paige scrunched her face. "About that . . . it was kind of my idea."

"What?" I shrieked.

She smiled at me and my heart melted. "That's okay. I get it."

Paige handed me a towel. "Thanks." I rubbed myself down, wringing my hair out. I took a step over toward her and gave her a hug. "I've missed you, Paige."

She sniffled in my ear. "Yeah, me, too."

"Good. It's about time you two made up," Marissa pronounced. "And about time we had one of these." She reached into a picnic box I hadn't noticed earlier and pulled out glasses and a bottle of champagne—the real deal, none of this sparkling wine rip-off stuff.

I watched as she placed the champagne flutes on top of the basket, warm inside, despite the fact I was shivering in my wet clothes. "Hey, why do you have five glasses? There are only the three of us."

By way of reply, Marissa stuck her fingers in her mouth and gave her farm-girl whistle. Within seconds, two figures appeared from behind the dunes. The figures—a man and a woman—walked over the beach toward us. As they got closer, I recognized their faces immediately, illuminated by the fire.

"What the—?"

"Hey, Dunny," Will said with a grin as he wrapped a second towel around me, kissing my cold cheek. "I thought you may need a change of clothes." He indicated a bag in his other hand.

My eyes were on stalks. "You *knew* about this?" I looked from him to a smiling Bailey. "And you, too?"

They both nodded, Bailey laughing. "Although it was Paige's idea, we all thought it'd be a fitting end."

"No harm, no foul?" Will asked with the cheeky grin I was once misguided enough to think was smarmy.

I smiled at him, my heart filled with love. "No harm, no foul."

There was a loud *pop* as the champagne cork went flying out of the bottle and into the fire. Sparks flew, and we all took a step back. Marissa poured the first glass of champagne until it overflowed. "Oops. Champagne wastage alert."

"Perhaps that can be another offering to the Goddess of the Beach?" I suggested, a playful twinkle in my eye. "Maybe the three of *you* need to go on your One Last First Dates now."

Marissa handed me a glass of champagne and proceeded to pour the other four. "Well, that bottle's done and dusted."

Bailey, Paige, and Marissa looked at one another. "I guess so," Marissa said. "You in, Bailey?"

She glanced around the group, a smile spreading across her face. "I'm in."

"Umm, not wanting to bring this up at a time like this, but I kinda already went on my One Last First Date." Paige glanced at Will, and then down at the ground.

"In that case, I would like to make a new pact. Raise your glasses, everyone," I instructed.

We all raised our respective glasses in the air, clinking them between us in one champagne flute huddle.

"In the presence of the Goddess of the Beach, I now declare Paige's One Last First Date as null and void. The slate is now clean."

Paige smiled, nodding.

I continued, "May the next date you go on, Paige, Marissa, and Bailey, be your last." I nodded at each of my friends.

"To One Last First Dates!"

"One Last First Dates," everyone repeated, clinking their glasses together and then taking a sip.

Will took my glass and placed it on the top of the box with his. He wrapped his arms around me and pulled me in close. "I may not have been your One Last First Date, Dunny, but I'm kinda hoping you're mine."

I grinned at him, my boyfriend, my love. "You know what, 'Poop Boy'? I have a feeling I am."

THE END

ALSO BY KATE O'KEEFFE

Cozy Cottage Café Series:
One Last First Date
Two Last First Dates
Three Last First Dates
Four Last First Date

High Tea Series:
No More Bad Dates
No More Terrible Dates
No More Horrible Dates

Wellywood Romantic Comedy Series:
Wedding Bubbles (short story)
Styling Wellywood
Miss Perfect Meets Her Match
Falling For Grace

Stand-alone novella:
I'm Scheming of a White Christmas
One Way Ticket
Manhattan Cinderella
The Right Guy

ACKNOWLEDGMENTS

You know the expression "it takes a village"? Well, it certainly does take a village to get a novel ready to be released like a duckling into the world, so I have a few people to thank. First up, thank you to my fabulous editor, Chrissy Wolfe at The Every Chance Reader. Being a New Zealander, I thought it would be enough to watch re-runs of *Friends* to write in American English for the first time. It wasn't. Thank you for your great work pulling this story together, Chrissy, and catching all those subconscious Kiwi-isms of mine.

Thanks to my small but dedicated team of fantastic beta readers, who always do a great job of providing feedback on my first drafts: Julie Crengle, Leanne Mackay, and Nicky Willis. Ladies, you rock and the next book will be on its way to you shortly!

Thank you to the incredibly supportive writers' groups I belong to, specifically Chick Lit Chat HQ and the Hawke's Bay chapter of the Romance Writers of New Zealand. Your support is utterly invaluable in this wild world of writing.

I would also like to thank my friends and family who support me in my sometimes (nearly always) crazy quest to be an author. You put up with hearing all about things you never thought you'd hear about from me, you listen to my rants, and you support me when I need it most. Thank you. I couldn't do this without you, especially Blair and Jack, my two favorite guys in the world.

And finally, thanks to my readers. Without you, I couldn't do this. And I love to do this, so please keep reading!

ABOUT THE AUTHOR

Kate O'Keeffe is a bestselling author of fun, feel-good romantic comedies. She lives and loves in beautiful Hawke's Bay, New Zealand with her family, two scruffy dogs, and a cat who thinks he's a scruffy dog too. He's not: he's a cat.

When she's not penning her latest story, Kate can be found hiking up hills (slowly), traveling to different countries, and eating chocolate. A lot of it.

Sign up for Kate's newsletter at kateokeeffe.com.

Printed in Great Britain
by Amazon

43736066R00142